LOVE STORY

This Large Print Book carries the
Seal of Approval of N.A.V.H.

THE BAXTER FAMILY

LOVE STORY

KAREN KINGSBURY

LARGE PRINT PRESS
A part of Gale, a Cengage Company

GALE
A Cengage Company

Farmington Hills, Mich • San Francisco • New York • Waterville, Maine
Meriden, Conn • Mason, Ohio • Chicago

The text of this Large Print edition is unabridged.
Other aspects of the book may vary from the original edition.
Set in 16 pt. Plantin.

LIBRARY OF CONGRESS CATALOGING-IN-PUBLICATION DATA

Names: Kingsbury, Karen, author.
Title: Love story : the Baxter Family / by Karen Kingsbury.
Description: Large print edition. | Waterville, Maine : Wheeler Publishing, a part of Gale, Cengage Learning, 2017. | Series: The Baxter Family ; 1 | Series: Wheeler Publishing large print hardcover
Identifiers: LCCN 2017016338| ISBN 9781432838850 (hardcover) | ISBN 1432838857 (hardcover)
Subjects: LCSH: Domestic fiction. | Large type books. | BISAC: FICTION / Christian / Romance. | FICTION / Christian / General. | FICTION / Religious. | GSAFD: Christian fiction.
Classification: LCC PS3561.I4873 L67 2017b | DDC 813/.54—dc23
LC record available at https://lccn.loc.gov/2017016338

ISBN 13: 978-1-4328-3886-7 (pbk.)
ISBN 10: 1-4328-3886-5 (pbk.)

Published in 2018 by arrangement with Howard Books, an imprint of Simon & Schuster, Inc.

Printed in Mexico
1 2 3 4 5 6 7 22 21 20 19 18

To Donald:

Well . . . we are nearing the end of a whole year as empty nesters. I never liked that term. And I can tell you now with all my heart that there's been nothing empty about the last year. It's been full of beautiful walks and meaningful talks, nights when we randomly jumped into the car and spent an evening with Kelsey and Kyle and little Hudson. We played tennis and Ping-Pong and hung out with friends. And yes, we miss having our family all together every day. But when they come home the celebrating never ends. What I mean is, I've loved raising our kids with you, and now I love this season, too. God has brought us through so many pages in our story. The Baxter family came to life while we were raising our kids. When they told stories around the family dinner table, we were doing the same. And when their kids auditioned for Christian theater, our kids were singing the same songs. Our family is — and always will be — inexorably linked with the Baxter family. So thank you for creating a world where our love and life and family and faith were so beautiful I could do nothing but write about it. So that some far-off day when we're old and the voices of our many grandchildren fill the house, we can pull out books like this one and remember. Every single beautiful moment. I love you.

To Kyle:

You will always be the young man we prayed for, the one we believed God for when it came to our precious only daughter. You love Kelsey so well, Kyle. And you are such a great daddy to Hudson. Thank you for bringing us joy every day. We pray that all the world will one day be changed for the better because of your music, your love and your life.

To Kelsey:

What an amazing season this has been, watching as you became the best mommy ever through all the early firsts of Hudson's life. Little Hudson is such a happy baby, such a miracle boy. His laughter rings in my heart always. What a beautiful time for all of us! Hudson is strong and kind and joyful, with a depth that tells all of us that some way, somehow, God is going to use him. I believe God will continue to use you, also, Kelsey. You and Kyle and Hudson — and whatever other kids God might bring your way. Your family is a very bright light . . . and I know that one day all the world will look to you as an example of how to love well. Love you with all my heart, honey.

To Tyler:

Watching you take wing this past year has been another of life's great joys. Long ago when I imagined you graduating from college and moving out on your own, I thought it would be with tears and sadness. The quiet in the front room where once the sound of you playing the piano filled our nights. The empty space where you once made your bedroom. But this year caught me by surprise. I was simply too happy for you to find time to be sad. You are shining so brightly for Jesus — your songwriting, your singing, your screenwriting. God has great things ahead, and as always I am most thankful for this front-row seat. Oh, and the occasional

night when you stop by for dinner and finish the night playing the piano. You are a
very great blessing, Ty. Love you always.

To Sean:

I'm so glad you're back at Liberty University, working on your degree and growing
in your faith and strength as a man. You
have grown so much, Sean. And your dad
and I are so proud of you! From the first
day we held you, we knew your spirit was
bright. You love God and people with a
passion and joy that defied your first five
years. Yet we agreed with you that it was
time to take your faith to another level. I
am convinced God has amazing plans
ahead for you, Son. I love you forever.

To Josh:

This was a year of discovery for you, and
for that I'm so grateful. You are walking
into a future where being a spokesperson
for Jesus can look a lot of different ways.
He has gifted you with special skills that
will cause you to be in demand in this
world. People will always need your help,
and along the way, I pray that you always
give them more than they expect. Because
people will always need a kind word, a
gentle smile, a prayer and an invitation to

church more than they will need any skills we can offer. I'm so glad you're my son, Josh. Love you so much!

To EJ:

What a tremendous time this is for you, EJ. You are doing so well at Liberty University, so excited about the career in film-making you have chosen. Isn't it something how God knew — even all those years ago when you first entered our family — that you would need to be with people who loved God and loved each other . . . but also people who loved the power of storytelling. I'm so excited about the future, and the ways God will use your gifts to intersect with the gifts of so many others in our family. Maybe we should start our own studio — making movies that will change the world for God. I love it! And I love you — always.

To Austin:

A very long time ago I scribbled out the years to come. 2001, 2002, 2003, etc. Under each year, I wrote the ages and grades our kids would be in — so I would get a quick glance at how fast the time would go. I remember writing out the number 2016. Because that was the year you — our youngest — would graduate from high school and move away to college. And now . . . here we are. I'm so grateful I can see you when I travel to Liberty University to teach. We will have many happy times together as you follow the path God has for you. Many breaks and special family times. But I miss you in the everydayness, Austin. You have been such a light in our home, our miracle boy. Our overcomer. You are my youngest, and no question the hardest one to let go. The quiet here is so . . . quiet. Even with your dad's jokes and little Hudson's visits. So . . . while you're at Liberty, on quiet nights when you lie awake in your dorm, just know that we have cherished every moment of raising you. And we are still here. We always will be. Love you forever, Aus.

And to God Almighty,
the Author of Life,
who has — for now — blessed me with these.

THE BAXTER FAMILY: YESTERDAY AND TODAY

For some of you, this is your first time with the Baxter family. Yes, you could go back and read more than twenty books on these most-loved characters. The list of Baxter titles — in order — is available at my website (www.karenkingsbury.com/baxters). But you don't have to read those to read this one. In fact, there will be other Baxter books coming in the next few years. If you wish, you can begin right here.

Whether you've known the Baxters for years or are just meeting them now, here's a quick summary of the family, their kids and their ages. Also, because these characters are fictional, I've taken some liberty with their ages. Let's just assume this is how old everyone is today.

Now, let me introduce you to — or remind you of — the Baxter family.

The Baxters began in Bloomington, Indiana, and most of the family still lives there today.

The Baxter house is on ten acres outside of town, with a winding creek that runs through the backyard. It has a wraparound porch and a pretty view and the memories of a lifetime. The house was built by John and Elizabeth Baxter. They raised their children here. Today it is owned by one of their daughters — Ashley — and her husband, Landon Blake. It is still the place where the extended Baxter family gathers for special celebrations.

John Baxter: John is the patriarch of the Baxter family. Formerly an emergency room doctor and professor of medicine at Indiana University, he's now retired. John's first wife, Elizabeth, died ten years ago from a recurrence of cancer. Years later, John married Elaine, and the two live in Bloomington.

Dayne Matthews, 42: Dayne is the oldest son of John and Elizabeth. Dayne was born out of wedlock and given up for adoption at birth. His adoptive parents died in a small plane crash when he was 18. Years later, Dayne became a very visible and popular movie star. At age 30, he hired an attorney to find his birth parents — John and Elizabeth Baxter. He had a moment with Elizabeth in the hospital before she died, and years later he connected with the rest of his biological family. Dayne is married to Katy, 40. The couple has three children: Sophie, 7; Egan, 5; and Blaise, 3. They are very much part of the Baxter family, and they split time between Los Angeles and Bloomington.

Brooke Baxter West, 40: Brooke is a pediatrician in Bloomington, married to Peter West, 40, also a doctor. The couple has two daughters: Maddie, 19, and Hayley, 16. The family experienced a tragedy when Hayley suffered a drowning accident at age 3. She recovered miraculously, but still has disabilities caused by the incident.

Kari Baxter Taylor, 38: Kari is a designer, married to Ryan Taylor, 40, football coach at Clear Creek High School. The couple has three children: Jessie, 16; RJ, 10; and Annie, 7. Kari had a crush on Ryan when the two were in middle school. They dated through college, and then broke up over a misunderstanding. Kari married a man she met in college, Tim Jacobs, but some years into their marriage he had an affair. The infidelity resulted in his murder at the hands of a stalker. The tragedy devastated Kari, who was pregnant at the time with their first child (Jessie). Ryan came back into her life

13

around the same time, and years later he and Kari married. They live in Bloomington.

Ashley Baxter Blake, 36: Ashley is the former black sheep of the Baxter family, married to Landon Blake, 36, who works for the Bloomington Fire Department. The couple has four children: Cole, 16; Amy, 11; Devin, 9; and Janessa, 5. As a young single mom, Ashley was jaded against God and her family, when she reconnected with her firefighter friend Landon, who had secretly always loved her. Eventually Ashley and Landon married and Landon adopted Cole. Together, the couple had two children — Devin and Janessa. Between those children, they lost a baby girl, Sarah Marie, at birth to anencephaly. Amy, Ashley's niece, came to live with them a few years ago after Amy's parents, Erin Baxter Hogan and Sam Hogan, and Amy's three sisters were killed in a horrific car accident. Amy was the only survivor. Ashley and Landon and their family live in Bloomington, in the old Baxter house, where Ashley and her siblings were raised. Ashley still paints and is successful in selling her work in local boutiques.

Luke Baxter, 34: Luke is a lawyer, married to Reagan Baxter, 34, a blogger. The couple has three children: Tommy, 14; Malin, 9; and Johnny, 5. Luke met Reagan in college. They experienced a major separation early on, after having Tommy out of wedlock. Eventually the two married, though they could not have more children. Malin and Johnny are both adopted.

In addition to the Baxters, this book will revisit the Flanigan family. The Flanigans have been friends with the Baxters for many years. So much so that I previously wrote five books about their oldest daughter — Bailey Flanigan. For the purposes of this book and those that might follow, here are the names and ages of the Flanigans:

Jim and Jenny Flanigan, both 45. Jim is a football coach for the Indianapolis Colts, and Jenny is a freelance writer who works from home. Bailey, 23, is married to Brandon Paul, 26. Bailey and Brandon were once actors in Hollywood — Brandon, very well known. Today they run the Christian Kids Theater in downtown Bloomington. Bailey's brothers are Connor, 20 — a student at Liberty University; Shawn and Justin — both age 17 and juniors at Clear Creek High; BJ, 16, a sophomore; and Ricky, 14, an eighth grader.

Dearest John,

I can't believe this is happening.

Every morning, every day all I think about is you. Where you are and what you're doing a million miles away from me. I remember what it felt like having your hand in mine, your embrace keeping me safe.

But now . . . now I wonder if I'll ever see you again. I have to believe this will get to you. When I take a breath, I breathe you in. I go to sleep and there you are, in my dreams. I'm here for you. Waiting.

I love you always.

Elizabeth

My Dearest Elizabeth,

I've heard nothing from you. No phone call or letter. Nothing to tell me where you are, or how you are, or whether you're surviving this terrible situation. I'm sick about it. I miss you more with every sunrise, every sunset.

I know you. You're still thinking about us. I have to believe that or I wouldn't find the strength to keep breathing. Please know that I'm trying. I want to find my way to you, and somehow I will. No matter how much time passes, I'm coming for you, Elizabeth.

I love you more than life.

John.

1

Cody Coleman took the football field alone, the way he did most things these days. The Southern California sunshine landed on his shoulders and worked its way through the winter in his heart. It was the first day of spring training for his Oaks Christian High School team and Cody was ready.

Ready for something new.

Even if it was only another season on the gridiron.

He adjusted his baseball cap, slung the bag of footballs over his shoulder, and walked to the coaches' bench. Along the way he lifted his face to the sun. *What's next for me, God? Is this really where You want me?*

Cody waited. Sometimes when he talked to God, he heard an answer. Or felt one. Words would appear on the screen of his soul and he would know deeply, intimately, that he had received an actual response from God.

Not this time.

Cody sighed and dropped the bag to the ground. He grabbed a stack of orange cones and walked toward the twenty-yard line. His football coaching days had been extraordinarily successful. God had blessed his professional endeavors at every turn. His time at Lyle High School, an hour outside of Indianapolis, had seen him take a losing team and turn it into a winning program.

Sports Illustrated had even covered the story and for a short time everyone knew Cody Coleman. They called him America's favorite high school football coach. But then he felt God calling him away from Lyle. He took the job here at Oaks Christian for a lot of reasons. But the one that was most compelling was a blue-eyed girl with long blond hair and a laugh that stayed with him still.

Andi Ellison.

He pictured her, months ago, standing in front of him saying goodbye. He could hear her voice and feel the way he had been lost in her eyes. Cody straightened and drew a slow breath. He couldn't think about her here. Not Andi.

Not today.

Four cones along the twenty-yard line,

four more at the thirty. Cody made his way up the field. His assistant coaches would be here in an hour. The players, an hour after that. Spring training lasted just five weeks — right up till the end of the school year. He had to take every minute seriously. Otherwise the team would pay come fall. After spring training, they'd take a month off and in July they'd start summer two-a-days. Just like last year and the year before.

The difference between Lyle and Oaks Christian was something Cody had figured out this past weekend. The thing that set them apart was purpose. The Lyle High football team had needed him. Before he showed up no one wanted to work with those kids. And Cody had seen a little of himself in the Lyle players.

A potential that took some work to find.

Whatever the reason, Cody felt like he was walking in the center of God's will at Lyle High. Here, though, he was starting to have a sense that the Oaks Christian football team didn't really need him. They were a powerhouse in the Santa Clarita Valley before he took the job, and they would remain a powerhouse long after he left.

Which might be soon.

He finished placing the cones, returned to the bench and opened the gear bag. His clipboard was at the bottom of the bag of footballs. He grabbed it, sat down and studied the list of names. Blake Miller, Hawk Austin, Sam Knell, John Vaught. The seniors had come a long way playing for him, no doubt.

Ten of the players met every Monday night for Bible study with Cody, a time where the focus was on faith in God and friendship off the field. That had been his prayer from the beginning. He smiled. Okay, so maybe he had made a difference. Even still, most of the students wanted for nothing. If he moved on, someone else would fill his shoes. A coach or a parent. Oaks Christian had dozens of mentors.

Cody peered across the field. Yes, he definitely needed a change of pace. Another state, another school. A different challenge.

Or maybe he was only missing Andi.

He never imagined living in Southern California without her. But two broken engagements were too much. For both of them. Somehow like every other relationship Cody had been a part of, his love story with Andi had fallen apart. Crashed and burned. And some days his broken heart felt like it would never mend. Not ever.

She had moved away after the last breakup. These days she worked for a Christian aid organization that helped people in the midst of national tragedies. Andi was on the disaster relief team. Ironic, since she hadn't done anything about the very personal disaster between the two of them.

Something moved near the fieldhouse. Cody lowered his cap and squinted. Aaron Baylor, junior wide receiver, was walking toward him. Cody watched the boy. Skinniest kid on the team. Baylor was still wearing his school uniform, khaki pants and a white button-down shirt. His hands were sunk deep in his pockets, his shoulders stooped.

The player looked the way Cody felt.

A minute later he reached Cody and took the seat beside him. "Coach."

"Baylor." Cody leaned over his knees and looked at the kid. "You all right?"

"Kind of." Baylor ran his hand through his red hair. "Okay, not really. Not okay."

This was easily Cody's favorite part of the job. Being here for the guys. "You wanna talk?"

"If that's okay." Baylor's eyes looked nervous.

"Of course." Cody sat up and shifted so he could see the boy better. "What's on your mind?"

"Prom." Baylor winced, as if the word had stung his lips on the way out. "People are starting to ask." He stood and raised his hands, then he exhaled hard and let his arms fall back to his sides. "I wanna ask Macy Withers. You know Macy Withers, Coach?"

Everyone knew Macy. Cody smiled. "You think you aren't the only one who wants to ask her."

"Are you kidding?" He laughed, but his voice cracked in a way that sounded pinched and anxious. This was really stressing the boy out. "Like . . . I don't know, six guys on the football team wanna ask her."

"Okay, so you be first." The conversation was pushing Andi back to the bottom of his heart. Where Cody liked to keep her. "You're a good guy, Baylor. She'll say yes."

"No she won't." The kid paced ten yards out onto the field and spun around. "Have you seen my face? Every time I work out, I get another zit. And then there's this . . ." He grabbed a handful of his hair. "This carrot top." He shook his head, his words tumbling out faster now. "I'm the biggest nerd on the team, Coach, and I can't bulk up to save my life. My dad jokes that if I turn sideways I disappear. No matter how many times I think it through, the facts are the same. Macy Withers will never say yes, even if I ask her first. Even if I dye my hair or my face clears up or —"

"Baylor." Cody patted the bench beside him.

The boy stopped. He was breathing hard from the rant. "Yes, Coach?"

"Come sit down." Cody waited.

After a few seconds the fight left Baylor. His shoulders slumped and he did as Cody asked. "It's impossible, Coach."

Advice rushed at Cody, but he took his time. He wanted to say the right thing. "I remember when I was your age. I knew exactly who I wanted to ask to prom." Cody leaned back on the bench and pictured himself, a football player with a crush on one particular girl. The coach's daughter.

Bailey Flanigan.

"Yeah, well, look at you, Coach." Baylor slumped a little. "No girl would ever say no to you."

"Except this one girl." Cody looked at Baylor. "I always thought she was better than me. She seemed perfect. And me . . . I was just some mess-up football player."

For the first time the kid seemed to really listen. "You were a mess-up?"

"Definitely. Really bad." He let that sink in. "That was before I decided to follow Jesus. I'm a different guy now."

"Got it." Baylor nodded slowly. "So the

25

girl? Did she talk to you . . . even though you were such a mess-up?"

"She did." A lifetime of Bailey memories circled him, demanding to be recognized. He tried to stay in the moment. "She helped me understand something." Cody put his hand on the player's shoulder for a few seconds and then crossed his arms. He needed the boy to understand this next part. "You're a child of God. No matter what you see when you look in the mirror. No matter what you've done or might do in the future. God loves you. He's crazy about you." Cody grinned. "There's only one Aaron Baylor."

Cody wasn't sure Baylor wanted this heavy of a response. But Baylor was still watching him, still waiting. Cody continued, "See . . . value comes from within a person. Those who believe in God find their value in Him, what He wants for their lives."

The kid was quiet. Then gradually he started to nod and after a while he turned to Cody. "You believe that?"

"Bailey helped me see it . . . a long time ago." He lifted his eyes to the sunny California sky, those sweet yesterdays alive again. "She told me about the Bible. I began to read it and there it was in black and white. The truth about God's love. I've believed it ever since. It's what keeps drawing me back to the Lord."

Baylor smiled and shook his head. His eyes shifted to the ground and for a long moment he rubbed the back of his neck. "Deep stuff, Coach. Real deep."

"But true."

He turned to Cody, his eyes marked by the beginning of hope. "So you're saying I need to know who I am, how much God loves me. That's why I should feel good about asking Macy Withers to the prom?"

"That's why you'll feel good about anything." Cody grinned. "Playing football. Getting good grades. And yeah, even Macy Withers."

Baylor nodded again. A breeze drifted across the football field and for a minute they were both quiet. Baylor spoke first, "You and Bailey . . . it didn't work out, right?"

"It didn't." Cody steeled himself against the reality. "She married someone else."

Baylor winced. "Sorry."

"It's okay." Cody exhaled. "She married the guy she was supposed to marry."

"What about the blond girl who used to come to the games?" Baylor wasn't being rude or pushy. He seemed genuinely curious.

"Andi Ellison."

"Right." Baylor hesitated. "Weren't you engaged?"

"Twice." A familiar ache came over Cody. "It was my fault. I couldn't get it right." He forced a smile. "She deserved better."

Baylor stood and for a long time he looked at Cody. Then he shrugged, his heart clearly lighter than it had been. "I don't know, Coach. There's only one Cody Coleman."

Cody chuckled. "Touché." He pointed to the field house. "Go get your homework done. Practice in ninety minutes."

Baylor jogged off, but ten yards out he turned around. "Hey, Coach."

"Yeah?"

"Thanks." His smile lit up his eyes. "I'm gonna ask her. And hey . . . maybe it's not too late with Andi." He lifted his hands. "Just saying."

"Go on, Baylor."

Cody's townhouse sat on a quiet tree-lined street a few blocks off Hillcrest Drive, not far from the Oaks mall. If he had to live alone in Southern California, this was the place to do it. He had come to love his home — him and his dog, Riley. The town-house was lodged between a park and a botanical garden and as many open miles of trails in the Santa Monica Mountains as he could've ever wanted.

Quiet places he could go to think and pray on days like today.

Practice had gone great, better than he had hoped. Most of his starting lineup had enough experience and talent to go the distance in the fall. Maybe all the way to state. And his coaching staff was the same great group of guys he'd had last year. They knew each other's styles and play-calling, and the way they had clicked today was proof of the winning days ahead.

But none of that could rein in his wayward heart.

Ever since the conversation with Baylor, Cody had barely gone through the motions. There had been times in his life when football had taken off the edge, made the sad and lonely less of a burden.

Back when he and Bailey first went their separate ways, or when he lost his next girlfriend, Cheyenne, to cancer. Yes, he hurt and yes he lay awake at night asking God why things had gone so wrong. But at least on the football field he could see straight. His passion for the game was a respite from the pain that surrounded him.

Not so today.

It wasn't the loss of Bailey Flanigan or Cheyenne that wouldn't let up today. God had different plans for each of those girls. Cody couldn't argue with that. He was at peace with how things had turned out. No, the face he couldn't push from his mind today was the one Baylor had asked about.

The sweet face of Andi Ellison.

Cody parked on the street in front of his condo, went inside and greeted Riley. The black mixed Lab was three years old, and he lived for the time he spent with Cody. "Hey, boy . . . how was your day?" Cody bent down and patted the dog's head, scratched the soft fur behind his ears. "You ready for a run?"

Riley knew what that meant. He barked and ran to get his leash. When Riley wagged his tail, he did so with all his body. Like he might break in half he was so excited. "Give me a minute." Cody laughed. His dog was his best friend these days. The best thing about coming home.

Cody changed into his running clothes. Then he attached a specially designed running shoe over his prosthetic lower left leg. The missing limb was the result of an explosive device in Afghanistan. The phantom pain from his injury only hit him every once in a while now — and never while he was running. Out on a run it was easy to forget the injury had ever happened.

And today, Cody couldn't wait to get out there. Five miles on the mountain trails would help him sort through his feelings. He and Riley set out and from the first few steps the memories joined him. Memories he couldn't shake.

He didn't want to even if he could.

The past he shared with Andi Ellison was complicated. Again and again. They'd met in college, of course. Back when Andi had been Bailey's roommate. Back when Cody was too in love with Bailey to even notice anyone else. Andi was wild and rebellious back then. Her parents had been missionaries turned Christian filmmakers.

Andi wanted none of it.

She ran against everything she knew to be right and true and she spent her days at Indiana University on her own terms. Cody remembered the first time he understood how bad off Andi had gotten. He had found her on campus late one night, laying on the ground so drunk she was nearly unconscious. He helped her back to the dorm room she shared with Bailey, and he stayed long enough to make sure she was okay. For an hour Andi had mumbled things to Cody she'd never said before.

When the night was over, Cody knew two things. First, Andi's drinking was as dangerous as Cody's had once been. And second, Andi was in love with him. Back then it was easy to dismiss, easy to think she didn't really have deep feelings for him. Her confession had only been the alcohol talking. That's what Cody told himself.

Especially since back then his heart belonged to Bailey . . . and only Bailey.

Andi's behavior got worse after that. She took up with a foreign exchange student, a dark-spirited guy with wrong intentions. They dated for a few months and the guy found a way to get Andi to do things she never meant to do. Cross lines she had never imagined she would cross. Andi wound up pregnant. She told Cody later that only then did she realize what she'd done, how far she'd run from the faith she'd been raised with.

She had the baby — a boy — and put him up for adoption. Luke and Reagan Baxter adopted the child and Andi had a dramatic change of heart. She returned to God, made things right with her parents, and moved home. Not long after, Andi's family left Bloomington for Southern California.

It wasn't until much later, when Cody flew to Los Angeles for the interview at Oaks Christian, that he ran into Andi again.

This time things were different.

Sparks flew and the chemistry between him and Andi was undeniable. By then both Cody and Andi had been sober for years, and Andi was strong in her faith, trying her hand at acting. It made sense since her dad was a producer. After the interview at Oaks, Cody flew back to Bloomington but he and Andi talked every day.

A month passed before Cody made a decision.

He called Bailey, picked her up at her parents' house, and took her to Lake Monroe. They walked their favorite trail, and that morning he did what he had tried and failed to do for years. He ended things with Bailey Flanigan. He told her that no matter how close they had been, no matter how they had felt for each other or how much they still cared, it wasn't right between them. It never had been and it never would be. And he told her to find her way back to Brandon Paul. The guy who had given Bailey far more time and attention than Cody ever had.

His words that day were not because he didn't care about Bailey.

But because Brandon really was better for her.

And because of one other reason: Cody had fallen in love with Andi Ellison.

Cody breathed deep and kept running. Riley panted as he kept up beside him. A stream wound its way beside the trail at the top of the hill, a place where Riley could cool down and get a drink.

The past lingered in Cody's soul as he and Riley continued on the familiar dirt path into the mountains. He had taken the job at Oaks in part because he was certain that his future belonged to Andi. For the next year that's exactly how things had played out. They rode bikes along the path at Redondo Beach and they walked to the end of the Santa Monica Pier. They swam in the chilly surf and spent Saturdays in Santa Barbara, strolling the stretch of shoreline where artists and craft vendors set up their wares each weekend.

After a year, Cody talked to Andi's father. He wanted to do more than date Andi. He wanted to marry her. He was sure. Cody would never forget the man's reaction or the words he said that day.

"When you came into Andi's life, I had a chat with God," Keith Ellison told him. "God assured me you were the one." He chuckled. "Obviously that wasn't something I ever shared with Andi. But I believed I'd really heard from God." He smiled. "And now I know that I did."

The man had hugged Cody. "You're like a son to me. You always will be."

Andi's mother was also in agreement. Everything seemed like it was headed for the most beautiful happily-ever-after.

And when the time was right Cody took her to an early dinner at Bella Vista, the prettiest Santa Barbara restaurant perched high on a bluff overlooking a perfect stretch of the Pacific Ocean.

After the meal they walked along the water, hand in hand, and as the sun melted over the sea, Cody pulled a simple solitaire diamond ring from his pocket and dropped to one knee. He asked Andi to marry him and she said yes. The happy moment lasted only a few hours.

Later that night, back at Andi's house, they learned the terrible news.

As Cody was proposing, thousands of miles away in Indiana, a semitruck hit the van carrying Erin Baxter Hogan; her husband, Sam; and their four daughters. The family had been headed to Bloomington for a family reunion.

Only Amy Hogan — one of the little girls — survived.

The news rocked Cody's world. Years earlier, Bailey Flanigan's family had been best friends with the Baxters, which made them Cody's friends, too. At least back then. Which made the accident a little too close to home. Maybe it stirred up memories of Cody's days in Afghanistan, or maybe it reminded him of the frailty of life.

Whatever it was, he couldn't rebound.

Sometime after the accident he called Bailey and the two talked about what had happened that day, how the people of Bloomington were handling the tragedy, and how the Baxter family was doing. Toward the end of the call, Cody realized he was doing everything he could to keep the conversation going.

As if only Bailey could understand him, only Bailey could talk him through his angst and sorrow. Whatever confusion his heart had felt during that time, when the call was over he was no longer sure of his feelings for Andi. He let a week pass, and then two. But at the end of that month he knew he was wrong to keep walking blindly toward a wedding date.

He had lost his certainty. Lost his way when it came to Andi and the future he had imagined for the two of them. On a heart-breaking day late that summer, he drove with Andi to a secluded spot in the mountains. "I can't do this, I can't marry you," he told her. "I'm sorry." Tears filled his eyes.

"I need time."

Cody's feet pounded the path. He stared at the fading sunlight ahead of him. His decision back then had been both unnecessary and cruel. At least from the vantage point of today. He should've told her how he was feeling, why he was breaking things off. He should've talked about the accident and the sadness it evoked. Instead after he broke off the engagement, Andi had cried and asked him why, what had she done? What had he done? He had no good answers for her then.

He had none now.

Confusion, that's all it was. Heartache and hurt for the people he knew so well and a mixed-up sense of what the future held. Maybe he just needed someone to talk to. Someone other than Bailey. Either way, the wedding was off. And that was only the beginning of Andi's and his crazy, tragic love story.

The top of the path came with a view of the setting sun over Thousand Oaks, flickering lights from the residential streets, the haunting transition between day and night. Riley jumped into the shallow stream and Cody stopped for a few seconds to catch his breath. That's how his life had always been. As far back as he could remember. Flickering lights, catching him in the transition between day and night.

Mostly night.

Father, what's wrong with me? Why did I let her go? Twice?

An ocean wind from the other side of the mountain range drifted through the scrub brush and cactus plants that dotted the mostly barren mountainside. Cody stared at the vast sky. *Are You there, Lord? Do You see me?*

I see you, My son. You're never alone. I am with you. Always.

Peace flooded Cody's veins. There it was, the familiar voice of God. The sureness that no matter how quiet and lonely the nights, Cody was never truly alone. He let the assurance wash over him like sunshine on a winter day. God would see him through this season — no matter how long it lasted. Riley ran up to him and shook off the stream water, dousing Cody, head to toe.

"Thanks, Riley." Cody laughed and wiped his face with the back of his hand. "Let's get home."

He and Riley jogged back and Riley found a cool spot on the bathroom floor while Cody took a shower. Like he did every day after his late afternoon run. "Just you and me again tonight, buddy." Cody wrapped a towel around himself.

Once he had changed into sweats and a T-shirt, Cody found the most comfortable spot on the sofa. Maybe Baylor was right. Maybe it wasn't too late for Andi and him. He considered it for a minute and then dismissed the thought. No way. It was definitely too late. Things couldn't be worse between them.

Not just the broken first engagement, but his recurrence of post-traumatic stress disorder. The PTSD was like a snake in the grass, ready to strike at any moment. And so their relationship had suffered deeply. His episodes of anxiety and moodiness were something he hadn't explained to Andi. Didn't want her to know he was still struggling. A misstep for sure. A mistake. Cody sighed. If he had it to do over again, he would be more honest, more open.

But there was no going back now.

God had shown him so much since then, ways to handle the terrifying flashbacks and phobic fears that almost always came without warning. A guy at church had told him about a group for wounded soldiers that met at a home close to Cody's. For five months he attended two meetings a week and over time Cody learned how to deal with the episodes. How to live with them.

So why not call Andi and explain the situation? How messed up his mind had been and how much better he was doing?

He thought about it but after a while he let the possibility die and settled in with his book. She would never pick up. Not if he texted or called. In that way, there was nothing different about this night compared to the others. Riley lay on his feet as Cody read three chapters in C. S. Lewis's *Mere Christianity* and then the entire book of James in the Bible. Cody kept the TV off and turned in early. Like most nights lately as he fell asleep he saw the blue eyes of the girl he still loved. The one he missed with every breath — even if there was no chance he'd ever see her again.

The eyes of Andi Ellison.

2

Andi Ellison carried a box of wrapped turkey sandwiches into the temporary shelter set up for flood victims. Heat sweltered against her skin, and her white T-shirt clung to her back, but with every breath Andi knew this much:

She was right where God wanted her.

"Over here, miss. We're hungry! Please!" A woman in a torn dress waved her down. Huddled beside her were three young children. "Help us, please!"

"I'm on my way." Andi hurried toward her. "We have lots. More bottled water on its way, too." She stooped down and handed sandwiches to the kids. Then she locked eyes with the woman. "I'm sorry . . . for what you've been through."

"We . . . we lost everything." The woman was shaking. She looked small and lost, as much like a child as her little ones.

Andi kept her voice gentle. "Would you

like me to pray for you?"

Tears filled the woman's eyes. "Yes. Please." She struggled to speak. "We have nowhere to live." She shook her head, despair hanging from her like a cloak. "A police boat rescued us from the roof. Our house is gone. Everything inside it. All of it." Her voice broke. "I don't know what to do."

It was the same story Andi had heard over and over again.

"He sees you." Andi believed that with everything in her. She took the woman's hands. "God says that His Word will be a light unto our path. Let's just pray for that."

The woman nodded and hung her head. Beside her, the children held their wrapped sandwiches in silence. Andi prayed that the Lord would extend mercy to them in this terrible situation, that He would lead them to whatever was next.

As Andi talked to God, the woman nodded. Tears streamed down her pale, weathered face. "We were still coming back from last year's floods."

No words could make sense of the disaster. Andi squeezed the woman's hands. "I need to pass out the other sandwiches. I'll be around if you want to talk."

For the second year in a row storms had

parked over the Gulf Coast and created mass flooding in New Orleans and Baton Rouge. The entire region had again been declared a state of emergency. Andi Ellison had been dispatched to the area as part of a relief team that handled national disasters.

This was Andi's life now. She had taken a job with the Christian organization after she ended things with Cody. She couldn't stay in Southern California, couldn't risk running into him again and being reminded of their second failed engagement.

She hadn't been good enough for Cody Coleman. Before she broke up with him she found a live YouTube performance by country singer Hillary Scott of Lady Antebellum. She was singing "I Can't Make You Love Me," and every line . . . every single line had spoken straight to Andi's heart.

I can't make you love me if you don't . . .

Whatever the reason, however she had fallen short of Cody's forever love, she had to admit the reality of the situation. She couldn't make Cody Coleman love her. And so it had been time to leave.

After the breakup, knowing she was not sure what to do or where to go, Andi's parents had told her about a job opening with the disaster relief group. The next week Andi became part of their team. So far she'd spent time in Indiana after tornadoes hit the state and on the flood-ravaged East Coast in the wake of Hurricane Hermine.

With every day on the job, Andi was more sure she was right where she needed to be. Helping people recover from a tragedy they never saw coming. Praying with strangers and handing out food and water. Raking mud from the ruined remains of homes and businesses. Yes, this was where God wanted her.

But that didn't mean she loved Cody any less. She would love him until she drew her final breath. But the lyrics to the song were spot-on. She couldn't make him love her, she wouldn't try. Besides, she was getting comfortable with being single. She was making friends now.

Her new life was better than rejection.

She and God had a plan. Andi helped people all day and God helped her fall asleep at night. Not everyone got married, not everyone was supposed to. Life could still be good and rich and full and complete. The Lord was enough.

And when the loneliness crept in and her broken heart got the better of her, Andi pulled out her journal. So all the aching and hurting and loss of her own tragedy would have somewhere to go.

The sound of voices broke through the memory. She needed to keep moving. Andi took the box of sandwiches down the long aisle where the flood victims rested on cots. More rain was expected tonight — something the rivers and levees and bayous couldn't take. She and the others from the agency staff had an inexpensive hotel on higher ground. But at some point if it kept raining, none of them would be safe.

That didn't bother Andi.

Life wasn't safe. And no matter what happened God was with her. If she could get through saying goodbye to Cody Coleman, she could get through anything. Even a disaster like this.

"Sir." She put her hand on the shoulder of an older man. He sat on a thin cot, his eyes glazed over like the clouds outside the tent. "Are you hungry?"

The man stared at the ground. Andi had seen shock on the faces of disaster victims often enough to know the signs. She looked at his hands. Fingers trembling, and his teeth were chattering. Andi set down her box of sandwiches and jogged through the tent to the place where dry blankets were stacked. "There's an older man on Row One," she told the woman behind the table. "He's in Bed Eleven. He needs a medical examination."

"I'll put him on the list." The woman had worked with Andi on other disaster projects. The two of them and the rest of the team knew how to give their best in a situation like this. How to stay calm and collected and process the victims as quickly as possible.

Andi hurried the blanket back to the man. She opened it and eased it around his shoulders. He still didn't make eye contact, but his shaking fingers grabbed hold of the ends of the blanket. He pulled the edges around himself and turned to Andi.

"They . . . can't find her." His teeth shivered together with every painful word. "Have you . . . seen her?"

"Your wife?" Andi crouched down so she could look into his eyes. "Is she still out there?" Keep it positive. That was her training. She searched the man's eyes.

"Yes." His gaze drifted again. "She's out there. Somewhere."

Andi pulled a sandwich out of the box and handed it to the man. "Maybe if you ate something. You have to keep your strength up. She'd want that."

He cast her a frantic glance, the way a lost child might look. "You think so?"

Andi understood what was happening.

The man needed hope more than he needed a sandwich. "I know she would. You need to keep up your strength. You'd want that for her, right?"

The man nodded, never breaking eye contact.

"Okay, then." Andi partially unwrapped the sandwich and handed it to the man. "Let's pray for her, okay."

He clasped the sandwich and started to cry. Not the quiet tears of the woman Andi had met a few minutes ago. The man's tears came in sudden waves. Like the storm itself. He sobbed while Andi spoke. "Lord, You know this man's wife and where she is. Please . . . will You be with the rescue workers and help them find her? And will You protect her until they find her?"

Andi covered the man's hands with her own. His skin was cold and clammy. Definitely shock. She took a quick breath. "Comfort this man and let him know You're here. All things are in Your control — even this." She paused, her own emotion welling up in her throat. "We trust You, Lord. We do. In Jesus' name, amen."

"A–a–a–men." His eyes found hers one last time. "Thank you." He held out his hand. "Please . . . can I have a sandwich for h-h-her?"

Andi smiled. "Good idea." She reached in the box and handed him another. "She'll be hungry for sure. I'm Andi, by the way. What's your name?"

"Harry." He set the sandwich beside him and stared at it. "She'll be hungry. That's right."

"What's your wife's name?" Andi's tone said she didn't doubt for a minute that the woman would be found. "I'm sure she's worried about you, too."

"Her n-n-name is Patsy. Harry and Patsy. That's us." He looked at Andi again. "Thank you for thinking of her. I always think of her." He was still shaking, but he seemed calmer than before. "We've been married forty-nine years."

Tears filled Andi's eyes, and she blinked them back. She forced a smile because the man was still watching, still hanging on to any thread of hope. "I'm sure she loves you very much."

The man's gaze drifted and he touched the extra sandwich. "She does love me. Forty-nine years. She's all I have."

If Andi didn't move on, she'd drop to the ground from the heartache of it all. *Please, God, let them find her. Please.* She steadied herself and found her smile once more. "If you need me, I'll be handing out sandwiches." Andi hesitated. "Keep praying."

"Yes." He nodded again, his eyes still locked on some distant place or maybe some long ago memory. "I'll pray. I will."

The conversation, the sandwich, the prayer . . . all of it was a life rope for the man. Whether his wife was found or not Andi had given him a reason to hold on. And in so doing she had given herself a reason to hold on, also. Which was why she'd gone into relief work in the first place. As she helped others, she herself was helped. They were all trying to survive some kind of storm.

Whether it came with the wind and rain or not.

Andi picked up the sandwich box and moved to the next cot. She swiped her fingertips beneath her eyes and struggled to compose herself. The next victim needed her at her best. Tears came with the job, of course. But she had to find a way to hide them. People caught up in the aftermath of devastation and disaster desperately needed to be surrounded with strong people. Calm people. They needed workers with a solid plan for what happens next, people to listen to their terribly sad stories and pray with them. Workers who could get them food and water and shelter, so the shock would have a chance to wear off even a little.

Sometimes Andi waited till she got back to her hotel room before she let the tears come. People from her agency worked twelve-hour shifts every day as long as victims lived in their shelters. As long as they were needed. After a tragedy like the Louisiana floods, they would receive a month of paid leave. Time to recuperate and find restoration for their souls. So they'd have a well deep enough to draw from when the next disaster hit.

As far as Andi knew, they had at least another month before they'd have every flood victim placed in more permanent housing, before the next team could help everyone salvage whatever they could from their homes.

Today was one of the tougher days for Andi. She checked with the man at the front desk before she left. "What about the gentleman in Bed Eleven? Did they find his wife?"

The man's expression fell. "Not yet. He's been coughing, too. Probably inhaled water during the rescue."

Andi looked over her shoulder at the old man. He was still sitting on his cot, still looking straight ahead, catatonic-like, the blanket still around his shoulders. In his hands was the second sandwich — the one for his wife.

"They need to find her." Andi turned to the man. He was the crew leader this time around. "Can the medics start him on antibiotics?"

"They did." Her boss gave her a sad smile. "Get some sleep, Andi. It's going to get worse before it gets better."

She breathed in deep. Already the air was pungent with mold and mildew — the way flood areas always smelled. She swatted at a mosquito on her arm and met the man's eyes again. "I'll try. See you in the morning."

Andi boarded the shuttle that ran between the temporary shelter and the hotel where she and her co-workers were staying. A few seconds later, one of her co-workers — Caleb Rhimes — entered the bus and took the seat beside her.

"Hey." His eyes were warm, deep. "Long day, huh?"

"Always." Andi leaned her head back against the headrest. "So many hurting people."

Caleb studied her for a beat. "I watched you today. With that older man." He hesitated. "You're the most compassionate person I know."

51

His kind words were a balm to her ragged heart. "He can't find his wife."

"I figured as much." Caleb took hold of her hand and gave it a gentle squeeze. "I'm honored to know you, Andi Ellison."

"Thanks, Caleb." Andi smiled at him. Lately she enjoyed this work friend most of all. Their friendship might even be leaning toward an attraction. "You, too."

Caleb was in his late twenties, a dark-haired handsome guy from Amsterdam. Last winter he came to the United States to do mission work, something he'd always wanted to take part in. He'd worked for a church in Louisiana before being hired by the disaster relief organization a few months ago.

This was the first mission he and Andi had worked together.

As they exited the bus onto the rain-soaked sidewalk, Caleb hugged her and kissed her cheek. The way Europeans and Hollywood types do. But this time his lips lingered and their eyes met.

"You are the highlight of my days here." His breath was soft against her skin. "I want you to know that."

A rush of heat filled her cheeks. "Thank you." He made her feel beautiful and wanted. Something she hadn't expected to feel again after Cody. "Get some rest."

"You, too." He walked her to the door of the hotel and they parted ways at the elevator. Caleb's room was on the first floor, Andi's on the third.

Long before she reached her room Andi knew this would be one of those nights when the tears came all on their own. When she was helpless to stop them. Caleb was interesting, yes. But how could he be more than a diversion? She didn't want to live in Amsterdam, and he'd already told her that's where he was returning when his term of relief work was over. Amsterdam was his home.

Once inside she adjusted the air-conditioning. The housekeeper must've dropped the temperature to sixty-eight degrees. Andi liked her room warm — with a breeze if at all possible. This time around she didn't have a roommate, so she could keep the room how she liked. She raised the window and fresh air rushed over her. This far away from the flood zone, the night air smelled like sweet springtime.

She found her journal and her Bible in the nightstand and dropped to the chair near the window. Already tears trickled down her cheeks. Her eyes found a line of lights in the distance. *Please, Father . . .*

Harry needs his wife. Even for a few more years. If she's alive . . . please.

Andi closed her eyes and tried to stave off the wave of sadness. The irony of course was this: All day long she worked with people who had lost everything, even very nearly their lives. But in the process she had found hers. The victims needed her.

Which was more than she could say about Cody Coleman.

She glanced at her journal, the place where she could pour out her heart and soul and try — one more time — to understand what had gone wrong with Cody. He had loved her at one point. More than he had ever loved anyone.

Even Bailey Flanigan.

She believed that, because if she didn't, the heartache would bury her alive. What they shared was real. It had to be. The feelings she'd seen in Cody's eyes couldn't have been anything but the truth. Otherwise she would struggle to get out of bed in the morning.

Andi exhaled and opened her eyes. She read the Bible first — something she did every night. The way she figured it, she still had a lot of time to make up. Her days of living crazy had cost her much, days when she had walked away from God and His Word.

She had assumed the Bible to be some archaic book, a stodgy list of old-fashioned dos and don'ts. Real life, she had told herself, was out there waiting for her to grab hold of it. She'd had no use for the faith her parents had raised her with. It had never occurred to her that God's ways might've been instituted by a loving Father who only wanted the best for His children.

Not until Andi had her own son did she realize what she'd done. What had happened to her life, and how living her days without the Lord had gone so terribly wrong. She had chosen her own way and God had allowed it. But sitting there that day in the hospital room with her baby boy in her arms, knowing it would be the last time he would truly be her son . . . well, that was enough to get her attention.

After that she turned back to God with a vengeance. She found a quiet place every night where she'd spend an hour reading her Bible and praying. God became less of a power figure and more of a friend. Someone she could talk to about anything.

In the midst of that time, Andi followed her family to Southern California, willing to stay single. Forever if that was God's plan

55

for her. For the first time in her grown-up life, she'd been content. She was auditioning for one of her father's movies when she ran into Cody Coleman again.

A moment that changed everything.

At first Andi figured it was a meeting orchestrated by the Lord. Only He could've seen to it that they would be in the same place at the same time so far away from where they first met, in Indiana. But as time passed, as she became more aware that Cody would never love her the way he loved Bailey Flanigan, she was no longer sure that reconnecting with Cody was a miracle.

More of a mistake. Something she should've run far away from.

Because no matter how much Cody loved her back then, he loved Bailey more. He probably still did, no matter what she tried to believe. And that was the problem.

Andi could never be Bailey.

She turned to the book of James in the New Testament. James was a book of action — something Andi could easily connect with. She started at the beginning of Chapter One.

Consider it pure joy, my brothers and sisters, whenever you face trials of many kinds, because you know that the testing of your faith produces perseverance. Let perseverance finish its work so that you may be mature and complete, not lacking anything.

Andi stared at the words. *Pure joy, Lord? Watching that old man wait for his wife?* She wasn't angry or upset. Just sad. *Why not take them both at the same time? Why let a man like that survive alone?* She studied the night sky. *I trust You, God. I really do. But still . . .*

Gradually a realization began to take shape in her mind. She trusted God, even now. Something she hadn't done so easily six months or a year ago. Which could only mean one thing.

The testing of her faith *was* producing perseverance.

And one day, however far off, the joy would come.

Because God said so.

3

Some days John Baxter missed the intensity and energy of the emergency room, the urgency and desperation, the way patients had needed his expertise morning to night. He missed the life-and-death decisions and the way he'd called on God minute by minute to get through a single shift.

John would always be a doctor — one of the best Bloomington, Indiana, had ever known. But this beautiful April day he didn't miss the work. Now that he was retired, he and Elaine had time for their family, their children and grandchildren. Sweet precious time. They had hours for long walks and thought-provoking talks and trips to their small downtown.

Maybe it was his age, but in this season of life he found himself appreciating the little things. The parts of earth that might not be there once he got to heaven. Sunlight shimmering on Lake Monroe or the morning wake-up song of the swallows and blue jays and robins.

The smell of jasmine growing outside their front door or the vibrant reds and yellows and greens of the local-grown peppers and cabbage and beets, and the way they looked spread across a dozen wooden tables at the farmers' market — the way they looked today. He and Elaine had picked up enough for a new salad recipe they were going to bring to the family dinner at Ashley and Landon's this weekend.

John stood at the kitchen counter sorting through a bushel of the reddest bell peppers he'd ever seen. "Nothing like an Indiana bell pepper."

Elaine was unloading the dishwasher a few feet away. She smiled at him. "It feels good, doesn't it?"

"Buying peppers?" He winked at her.

"That." She laughed. "But this. Having time for the farmers' market. Time to make salad. The pace of life."

"I knew what you meant." He dried his hands on a paper towel and came to her. With practiced ease he slipped his arms around her waist. "Yes. It feels very good. Especially with you beside me."

Their eyes met and held. No matter how healthy they were the calendar told him they wouldn't have this season forever. He was grateful that she appreciated the time together as much as he did.

John was about to ask her about dinner when his cell phone rang. He stepped away and answered it on the second ring. "Hello?"

"Papa! I caught you!"

"Cole!" John covered the receiver and grinned at Elaine. In a whisper he announced the obvious. "It's Cole!"

"Tell him hi for me." She returned to the dishes, her eyes filled with a quiet sort of happiness.

"So, Papa, my mom and I are just leaving the high school and we wondered if we could come by your house. Just for a few minutes. I have a big favor to ask. Or maybe more of an adventure." Cole's excitement colored every word. "Something we can do together." He grabbed a quick breath. "If you have time, that is. If not, I completely understand, but I wanted to ask you in person."

John kept his quiet chuckle to himself. At sixteen, Cole was never at a loss for words. But then he never had been. Since he was a baby, back when Cole spent his days at his grandparents' house, the boy had been a talker. And one of the people closest to

John's heart.

"I have time. Absolutely." He raised his brow in Elaine's direction. "Come on by. We're just putting away groceries."

Elaine nodded her response to the unspoken question. Of course they had time for Cole and Ashley. Elaine's eyes told John that they could stop by whenever they wished.

The call ended and John returned to the red peppers. "Cole has a question for me. He'll be here in a few minutes."

"Nice that he can just stop by." She hesitated. "I wonder what he needs."

"No idea." It was another reason John didn't miss the working world. Being retired was God's way of letting him slow down and appreciate life — the small details and precious times like this. Being available for his grandson.

Five minutes later John was at the front window when Ashley's car pulled up. She and Cole stepped out and headed toward the house.

"They're here!" John waited a minute as they climbed the steps, then he opened the door. "What a nice surprise!" He hugged his daughter and grandson.

"Dad." Ashley's smile looked hesitant. She gave him an apologetic look, one she clearly didn't want Cole to notice. "Thanks for making time."

"Of course." He ushered them inside. The house wasn't large. Three bedrooms tucked down the hallway. A living room and kitchen. Just enough for Elaine and him. Nothing like the old Baxter home — the one where Ashley and her husband, Landon, were raising their family now. "Have a seat. Elaine made blueberry muffins earlier. Come in the kitchen. I'll get you each a plate."

"Yes!" Cole dropped his backpack by the nearest chair and hurried to the kitchen. "I was hoping. Elaine, I love you!"

Ashley laughed. "That boy is always hungry."

They followed Cole into the kitchen, where Ashley hugged Elaine. "Mmm." She pointed to the vegetables on the counter. "Looks delicious."

"For dinner Saturday." Elaine offered the plate of muffins to Ashley.

"No thanks." Ashley smiled at Elaine. "Landon's making dinner."

Ten minutes later they gathered in the living room. Cole took the lead. "Okay, this won't take long." He dug through his backpack and pulled out a crisp white envelope. "We're doing a class project in history. Sort of a heritage project. Where we came from, who we came from. Stories from long ago. That kind of thing."

John shifted in his chair. "Interesting."

"And the other day" — Cole took a small, square photograph from the envelope — "I found this." He turned it to face them. "And I knew exactly what I wanted to do my project on."

The floor of John's heart fell away. The photo was of his first wife, Elizabeth, sitting on their old white sofa, morning sunlight soft on her pretty brown hair. In her arms was a sleeping, two-year-old Cole.

John felt Elaine's eyes watching him and after a few seconds she stood and smiled at the group. "I'm going to finish up in the kitchen. Cole . . . Ashley. See you Saturday night."

As she walked past John she patted his shoulder. Then she was gone.

Cole seemed to sense the awkwardness that had suddenly come over the room. He looked at his mother and then at John. "Is something wrong?"

"No. Not at all." Now John understood Ashley's hesitancy when she first got here. He swapped a look with her and she managed the slightest shrug. John turned to Cole again. "I'm . . . I need to . . . Well, truth is, Cole, I haven't seen that picture in a long time."

Cole rushed ahead. "Grandma gave it to me for Christmas when I was little. On the back it says, 'I love you, Cole. Now and always.'" He looked at it again. "She has this amazing peace about her. In her eyes." He lifted his gaze to John's. "I really don't remember her." He paused. "I wish I did."

"Yes." Ashley looked from Cole to John. "I told Cole how the two of you had an interesting love story. How none of us would be here today if it wasn't for what happened between his grandparents back then."

John nodded. His breathing was back to normal, but his heart still pounded. He needed to talk to Elaine about all of this. If she wasn't comfortable with Cole's project, then John could steer the boy to another idea. An in-depth look at John's early days as a doctor or how Cole's great-great-grandfather had served in World War II, how the man had been one of the heroes at Iwo Jima.

Anything but his love story with Elizabeth.

Cole was still talking, explaining something about how his mom's comment that day led him to think that his grandparents' story would be perfect for the project. How he wanted to know more about the grandma he had loved so much when he was little.

Every so often John nodded. But he wasn't really listening. He couldn't concentrate. It wasn't because he felt uncomfortable about the project. It was because of the photograph.

Elizabeth had loved Cole with everything in her. Back then Elizabeth babysat Cole whenever Ashley worked. Their daughter's life had been complicated and lonely and Ashley had relied on Elizabeth to help.

Before dying of breast cancer, Elizabeth made a copy of the photo, framed it and gave it to Cole. A reminder of those early days.

John knew the photograph well. He owned the original, of course. The picture was part of an aging collection in a leather scrapbook tucked away on the bottom shelf of the living room bookcase. In a place where the kids and grandkids could easily access it whenever they wanted to remember days gone by. Life when they were little.

The years when John's first wife, Elizabeth, was still alive.

"You there, Papa?" Cole planted his elbows on his knees.

A cough and John found his focus. "Yes. Definitely. I agree." He made eye contact with Ashley and then looked at Cole again. "It's a great idea, Cole. Her story is very important."

Cole pulled what looked like a school planner from his backpack. "Not just her story. Your story. The two of you together." Cole opened the book. "I'm supposed to do four hours of interview research at least. Like, super-detailed."

"With me?" John blinked.

"Definitely." Cole looked at his planner and then back at John. "Mom says your love story could be a book. So that's what I'm doing my report on. How you fell in love, what life was like when you first started your family. All the details."

"If that's okay with you." Ashley was quick to interject. She raised her brow at Cole. "That's why we're here, right?"

"Right." Cole chuckled. "Sorry. I meant to say if that's okay. If you're not too busy, I could come here and talk to you, maybe once a week. Like an interview. Get all the details, you know?"

"Absolutely." John's heart felt strangely heavy. "All the details. Right." He remembered to smile. "I'd love that, Cole. Really. Let me get back to you tonight. Is that okay? Just to check my schedule."

Cole hesitated. "Of course." He closed his planner and returned it to his backpack. "I'll wait till then."

John was silent. Again an awkward feeling filled the room. Ashley seemed to sense it, too, because she took a deep breath and smiled big. "All right then. I'm sure it will all work out." She stood and gathered her purse. "We'll head home, and Dad, you can just call Cole whenever you know."

For a moment John thought about recommending the other ideas, but he stopped himself. Cole wanted *this* story, not something else. He would check with Elaine and make a decision. But even as Cole and Ashley hugged him and headed to the car, John knew this was less about Elaine and more about him.

Whether it would be good for him to spend four weeks reliving his love story with Elizabeth. He returned to his chair just as Elaine joined him from the kitchen.

He lifted his eyes. "You heard?"

"I did." She sat down across from him, a glass of ice water in her hand. "Want some?"

"No. I'm fine, thanks." He groaned and closed his eyes, lacing his fingers behind his head. For a while he stayed that way, sorting through the decision ahead. He opened his eyes and looked at Elaine. "What are you thinking?"

"You have to do it, John." Her smile reached the depths of his heart, her kindness a tangible force. "It's a beautiful story. All the grandchildren should know what happened with you and Elizabeth."

"But four weeks?" He kept his gaze locked on hers. "Four weeks of talking about Elizabeth and me? Our story?" John stood and stared out the front window. He turned and faced his wife. "I don't know."

Elaine hesitated, but only for a moment. Then her hint of uncertainty became a smile once more. She took her time as she spoke. "Elizabeth was your first love." There wasn't the slightest bit of jealousy in her voice. "I meant what I said. Tell Cole what happened. Let yourself go back, John. You and Elizabeth, that's part of the legacy of all the grandkids." She held his gaze. "Remember, Elizabeth was one of my closest friends. I want the kids to know her."

"Elaine." John went to her and helped her to her feet. He pulled her into his arms. "How did I get so blessed to marry you?"

"I'm the blessed one." Her eyes shone. "Life with Elizabeth . . . life with me. They are different. She's your past. I'm your future. There's room for both of us."

For a long minute he wasn't sure what to say. "Thank you." He searched her eyes. "For understanding." He kissed her forehead. "I'll tell Cole."

68

John found his phone and called his grandson. "Hey . . . looks like I'm wide open."

"That was fast." Cole laughed. "I was just praying you'd have time."

They decided the interviews would happen each Thursday. Cole's lightest homework day. "Next Thursday it is!" John kept his tone enthusiastic.

"Oh, I almost forgot." Cole's voice grew more serious. "I need pictures. Lots of them. I know you have that scrapbook, but I need pictures for my display."

"Okay." John tried to imagine the hours ahead, poring over photographs of Elizabeth and him. "How many would you say?"

"A lot. Maybe twenty-five. Thirty." Cole seemed to think for a minute. "Even a copy of a letter or two would be amazing. Anything you think might make the project more interesting."

John agreed to do his best and for another five minutes they talked about Cole's classes. He loved history, but math was giving him fits. "You'll get through it. You're a hard worker, Cole." He paused. "Just like your grandmother."

"Really?"

"Definitely."

"There you go. My first detail for my

report." Cole sounded like he couldn't wait for next week. "This is going to be great, Papa."

John agreed, but after the call ended, and after Elaine left for Bible study, John still wasn't sure. The house was quiet as he walked to their bedroom and flipped on the light in his closet. It wasn't a large space, but at the back, on the highest shelf, was an old cardboard box.

A box that held every letter Elizabeth had ever written.

Love letters for him, and letters of encouragement for the kids. Poems and a few journals she had kept through the years. A while ago, John had made copies of many of the letters and put together a scrapbook for each of their six adult kids. It was a time of deep reflection and remembering, a month when he almost felt like he had Elizabeth back beside him again.

Of course, there were a few letters the kids had never seen. Even now. Letters that spoke of a time between Elizabeth and him that their children knew little about.

John stared at the box. The last time he'd gone through it was before Elaine.

Spending time with the letters again meant letting Elizabeth's words wash over him and settle into the places of his heart that belonged only to her. It would open him all over again to a grief so great he hadn't known it was possible. The experience would be like ripping open a scar with the knowledge that this time around the hurt might never heal.

All so he could find a few letters that might work on Cole's project. He steadied himself against the doorframe of his closet and made up his mind. *The letters can wait,* he told himself. Plenty of time between now and next Thursday.

The photographs. That's what he could work on now. John walked to the bookcase and removed the album, the one that contained so many photographs of Elizabeth. He carried it to the same chair where he'd sat earlier. *Father, I'm going to need Your help on this.*

This is for My glory, son.

Chills ran down John's arms. The voice was familiar. Often when John was alone, talking to God, he heard a response. Words that appeared at the center of his heart, deep in his soul. But this time John wondered if he'd heard correctly. Cole's project was for God's glory? How could that be?

You'll have to show me, Lord. But until then I just need Your strength to get through these next four weeks.

71

The truth was this: Many years had passed since John had gone back to the beginning. Since he'd allowed himself the luxury of reliving those days when he and Elizabeth met and fell in love. Telling their story would take him there again.

And once there, John wasn't sure he'd ever want to leave.

4

It was all Baylor's fault. Or maybe it was his own. Whatever the case, Cody couldn't stop thinking about Andi Ellison. Not so much where she was or what she was doing. But how he had lost her, how he'd let her get away. And why he hadn't done something to stop her from leaving.

Ever since the talk with his player, Baylor's words stayed with him. *Maybe it's not too late with Andi. Maybe it's not too late.* The statement stayed with him even now, as he wrapped up the fifth day of spring training. Practice was going well. They were a week into it and already it was clear that next football season held promise.

But Cody wasn't consumed with thoughts of rushing yards and passing percentages as he left the Oaks Christian field that Wednesday afternoon. It was Baylor's words that filled his head. *Maybe it's not too late . . . maybe it's not.* Cody grabbed his bag from his office and flung it over his shoulder. He wore his sunglasses through the athletic building toward the parking lot.

He didn't feel like talking today. Get home, get Riley, and take another run. That's all he wanted. Time alone where he could talk to God and reckon with his wayward feelings. He walked with a purpose, and the glasses worked. Kids waved to him, but he got all the way to his car without a single conversation.

He took the 101 freeway two exits south and reached his townhome in ten minutes. Not until he had Riley on his leash and the pavement beneath his feet did Cody think again about the possibility. Another chance with Andi? The idea that she might even talk to him again? All of it was impossible. And now that he could hear himself think, he could easily understand why.

She had made the answer painfully clear when she broke off their second engagement. Cody didn't love her the way she wanted to be loved. That's what she believed. Cody was distracted and distant and whatever was causing his inability to connect with her, she couldn't live with the loneliness.

Not for one more day.

Those were pretty much her words that

day, the day they broke up for the last time. Since then Cody had run from the pain. Like he was running now. Whenever he thought about Andi, he replayed their last memory. It was over. She had ended things. Period.

So why couldn't he stop thinking about her?

Cody stopped near a stream and waited while Riley ran through the tall grass and sniffed at the trunk of a withered oak. The occasional break was for Riley's sake. Dogs went crazy if they didn't smell things, didn't get a chance to explore. Cody uttered the slightest chuckle. Maybe that was his problem. He needed to leave here, explore more.

Get Andi out of his head.

Cody was still breathing hard from the half mile run from his townhome to this spot at the base of the mountain. His T-shirt was damp. But not as damp as it would be once he and Riley reached the top of the hilly path. Today Cody might just keep running.

Riley returned to him, his tongue hanging out, eyes happy.

"Good boy, Riley. Good boy." Cody patted the top of his furry head. "You ready?"

They took off again, and this time every step seemed to draw him back. Which was just how Cody had hoped the late afternoon would go. He remembered breaking off their first engagement, and he remembered regretting his decision to do so. The fall and winter that followed had been crazy painful. He felt terrible, the way he felt now. Cody could remember thinking daily about Andi, where she was and why he had been so foolish to let her go. A few times after that first breakup he'd tried to call her but she never picked up.

Cody had made it through the holidays and into January without seeing Andi or her family. But then one Saturday morning in February, Cody had stopped at his favorite coffee shop and there she was. Andi Ellison. Sitting at a table by herself, her laptop open, headphones on. Long blond hair spilling down her back.

For the longest time, Cody had simply watched her, as the conversations and smell of fresh brewed coffee surrounded him. She looked more beautiful than ever. Still, something in her eyes was different.

Like the loneliness had hardened her heart a little.

After a minute, Cody walked up and took the chair beside her. She did a double take, and a quick gasp slipped through her lips. She pushed back from the table, removed her headphones, and stared at him. Her heart was beating so hard, he could see it in her throat. "Cody . . ."

"Andi." He looked at her, quiet for a few seconds. Waiting until she seemed less caught off guard. "I saw you and . . . I had to . . . say something."

Cody held on to the way he had felt that morning, and for a while he paused the memory right there. Riley was still padding along beside him, still loving the run. Cody, too. They reached the top, where the sun was sinking into the Pacific. Cody stopped just long enough for Riley to get his drink.

His memories were fueling him, so today Cody did what he wanted to do. He kept going. The trail ran along the top of the mountain range, so if Cody wanted a longer route, this was the way to get it. His heart returned to the memory. Andi and him that Saturday over coffee.

It seemed to take Andi a full five minutes before the color returned to her face. But even then her eyes looked closed off. As if she had nothing but walls where he was concerned. Her hands had trembled and her voice hadn't sounded like her own. That's how shocked she seemed to be at the sight of him.

Cody did most of the talking.

"Andi . . . I'm sorry. I was wrong." Cody hadn't been sure where he was going with the admission. But if he never talked to her again, he wanted the moment between them to count. He leaned closer. "I never should have broken up with you. I think about you, Andi. Every day. And I pray for you."

Cody hadn't been sure what part of his statement resonated with her. But as soon as he mentioned praying for her, the walls slowly began to drop. She looked at him more intently. The hurt in her beautiful eyes was obvious. Enough to suck the oxygen from the room. "You . . . pray for me?"

His eyes filled with tears. Did she think he was completely heartless? "Every day."

Neither of them said anything for a while. Andi folded her hands on the table and stared at her fingers. As if she was seeing the place where her wedding ring would be. Cody had known the conversation wouldn't last long. Andi was too hurt to talk. That much had been clear. Cody struggled to find something to say. "I've called you."

She nodded, but didn't look up.

"So . . . you don't want to talk? Not ever again?"

Only then did Andi lift her eyes to his. Tears pooled for her, too. "I can't, Cody. Don't you get it?" Anger flickered in her tone. "We were supposed to be married by now. I was going to be your *wife.*"

The defeat he felt in that moment was something he'd never forget. "I know that. It's all I want, Andi. All I think about."

She searched his face, as if she didn't believe him. Couldn't believe him. She gathered her purse and her laptop. "I have to go."

"Andi, please." Cody kept his voice quiet so they wouldn't make a scene. He stood and walked with her to the parking lot. "Just hear me out. I said I'm sorry."

When they reached her car, Andi turned and stared at him. "I can't do this again, Cody." Tears began to fall down her face. "Goodbye."

As she drove away, Cody knew he should've felt hopeless about the situation with Andi. But that day he remembered something Andi's dad had told him once. They were talking about two characters in a movie and Keith had said something that had stayed with Cody.

"The opposite of love is never hate," he had told Cody. "Hate cares too much. The opposite of love is apathy. People who don't care at all. That's the opposite of love."

Before running into Andi at the coffee shop that day, Cody had worried that she didn't care about him. That she was apathetic and had moved on, determined to forget him. But that wasn't true. Andi still cared.

Her tears were proof.

And for that single reason, the next day Cody called her. He didn't expect her to answer, but he had to try. The phone rang three times, and just before Cody hung up, he heard her voice. "Why are you calling?" She sounded tired and maybe a little afraid.

"Because." He closed his eyes, begging God for a chance. "I still love you, Andi."

The memory froze there.

Cody was almost home from his run and he needed to get cleaned up. He had promised his mom he would stop by tonight after dinner. Maybe she would help him understand why a single player's comment had set him back like this.

"Come on, Riley, boy." He and the dog went inside. Cody poured fresh water in the dog's bowl and took a shower.

An hour later he walked through the door of his mother's small house a few miles away. She met him just inside and they hugged. "So good to see you, Cody. I thank God every time."

Cody smiled. "Me, too, Mom." He grinned at her. "Mmm. Chocolate chip cookies?"

"Yes." She smiled. "I missed baking for you all those years when you were growing up." She led the way into the kitchen. "I won't miss it again."

Cody's mom had spent most of Cody's childhood in prison for dealing drugs. But she'd been out for several years now. She was a cashier at Costco during the day and at night she attended a number of Bible studies. His mom once said, "I'm as addicted to God as I once was to drugs. Only with Him I can never overdose and no one's going to throw me into prison."

Their lives were proof that God alone could heal a person's addictions. No matter the struggle. His mother's drugs and Cody's alcoholism. Both things of the past now.

They sat at the table with a plate of cookies and coffee. Cody ate one practically whole. "Mmmm. Still the best, Mom."

She beamed. "Whatever you don't eat you have to take with you. I sure don't need them around here!"

After a few minutes, the conversation drifted to Oaks Christian and Cody's football team. Whether it was his lack of enthusiasm about the upcoming season or something in his voice, his mom picked up on it.

She narrowed her eyes. "What is it?"

Cody tried to feign innocence. "What's what?"

"Something's wrong." She leaned back in her chair. "What's bothering you?"

He didn't want to trouble her, didn't want her worrying about him. But he did want her opinion. "One of my players said something the other day. It got me thinking." Cody paused. Then he told her about the boy's comment and how he'd been wondering about Andi ever since. He narrowed his eyes. "I guess I don't really know what happened after we got back together. Why we couldn't make it work."

For a long time his mother said nothing. Then she gave Cody a patient look. "She was right to leave. You were distracted, Son. You didn't treat her like the gift she is."

His heart sank to a new low. He'd been afraid she'd say this. "I loved her. I don't know why I was like that. I mean . . . I really don't know why."

Again his mom watched him, taking her time. "Was it Bailey?" She hesitated. "I always wanted to ask you. Ever since Andi broke things off this last time."

"Absolutely not." It was a question Cody had asked himself. Whether Bailey Flanigan was somehow at the center of how he had acted, how he hadn't cherished Andi. But every time his heart exonerated him. "No, Mom . . . It wasn't that. I'll always care for Bailey. I remember what it felt like to be in love with her. But those feelings changed."

"Hmmm." His mom gave a slight nod. "So what was it? Why didn't you treat her right?"

"It's complicated." He sighed. "And now . . . well, now I guess I'm upset because we didn't get closure . . . not like we should have. But she's finished with me. She won't return my texts. It's completely over."

"And you really don't know why?" She raised her brow.

"I think I know. The PTSD came back. Every nightmare made me more closed off to her . . . to everyone." He would always be upset with himself for how he'd handled that. "I should've told her."

"Cody!" His mom's face filled with concern. "You didn't tell her?"

Remorse came over Cody again. His mom knew how his mind would flash back to the days when he served in the Middle East. The day the vehicle he was riding in hit an explosive device. The horrible afternoon when he lost his lower left leg.

He had never kept any of his struggle from his mother, and for a while he even thought they were gone. But not long after he'd asked Andi to marry him for the second time, the episodes came screaming back. No warning.

Cody waited several seconds. He'd replayed those days dozens of times. Even though the episodes scared him. Even though they took him back to his darkest hours, and even though he hadn't wanted to burden Andi with them, always he came to the same conclusion.

He should have told her.

Whatever his reasons for hiding the truth from Andi, they were wrong. If they would've ended up marrying, he would have had to tell her someday.

He still prayed that God would take the PTSD away for good, so there would never be another night when he'd lay his head down on the pillow only to spend his sleeping hours in some desert village being shot at.

But if that never happened he would've had to share the truth with Andi. The way he would've wanted her to share her deepest fears and concerns with him.

Cody looked at his mother and shook his head. "I didn't tell her." He would've crawled over glass if it meant getting back to that time, back to the season when he still could've confided in Andi.

"Cody . . . no." His mom's expression was a pained mix of shock and hurt.

An angry frustration doubled inside him. "I thought I was being kind. Doing the right thing. I didn't want to involve her in my nightmares." He shrugged. Why did it always seem that his soul was hurting? "I figured she deserved more than that. I kept thinking . . . if I prayed enough it would pass and everything would be great with us."

A sigh slipped from Cody's lungs. "I know so much more now." He had learned techniques for dealing with the episodes. Memorized Bible verses that brought peace, practiced deep abdominal breathing, and disassociation, where he forced his brain to think of a vivid memory of the beach or a sunrise every time the flashbacks started. Not that Andi would listen to any of that.

He didn't blame her.

His mother reached across the table and squeezed Cody's hand. "Here's my advice. It'll always be my advice when it comes to Andi Ellison."

He expected his mother to tell him to let her go, to realize that it was time to completely and fully move on. He'd be thirty in a few quick years and it was time he thought about meeting other girls. Dating again.

Instead what she said practically dropped

Cody to the floor.

"You go after that girl. You call her until she answers her phone and if you have to, go and fly to wherever she is. And when you find her, you tell her the truth. How the way you acted had nothing to do with her and everything to do with you." His mother paused. "Where is she, by the way?"

Cody had thought about that, too. He actually didn't know exactly where Andi was. She worked for a disaster relief organization, but whether she was in the Midwest helping tornado victims or in the flooded plains of the Gulf States, Cody had no idea. He shrugged. "She's off social media. It's been a long time since anyone's talked to me about her. I have no idea where she is, Mom."

"Well then . . ." His mother stood and walked across the kitchen for the coffeepot. She poured them each a cup and then returned. As she sat down she looked straight at Cody. "Do what you have to do to find her, Son. You can't move on until you sit down with her one last time and tell her how you feel."

Again her words caught him off guard. He raked his fingers through his short hair. "She won't talk to me. I already know that."

"Only God knows." She smiled. "That's

what a certain son of mine used to tell me."

Cody let her words breathe life into the lonely deserts of his heart. After a few seconds, he nodded. "You're right."

"So you'll try?" Her voice was gentle. It was clear she wasn't pushing him to find his way back to Andi. She just didn't want him to have regrets. "At least call her?"

"I'll pray about it." He stood and stretched. "I need to go. Riley's waiting for me."

"My grand-dog!" His mom was on her feet getting a bag for the cookies. As she filled it she laughed. "I have to bring him a bone this weekend."

Cody took the bag of cookies and kissed her cheek. "That's why he loves you." He lifted the bag. "Thanks for these. Extra running this week for sure."

By the time he reached his car he was thinking of Andi again, how he could look for her. What it would take to have one last conversation with her, the chance to tell her how he felt. Cody was sure she would turn him down and he would be left feeling worse than before. But his mom was right about one thing. He'd never know unless he tried. And there was one thing in the way.

He had to find her first.

5

A stack of old photographs sat on the kitchen table, a monument to all that had once been. John filled the coffeemaker with water and tried not to look at the pictures. Today was the day. The first interview. Cole and Ashley would be here soon.

John glanced at the clock on the wall. The one Elizabeth had bought for him on their tenth anniversary. *Because time is our greatest gift,* she'd told him. John had kept it because, well, he and Elaine needed a clock. No sense getting another one. And none of the kids wanted it. A clock on the wall seemed no longer a necessity what with phones and watches and computers and microwaves.

The time was everywhere.

But today the clock practically screamed at him, reminding him of one very special truth: Though time had moved on, today it would take him back. All the way back to the beginning. John clicked the brew button on the coffeemaker and sauntered toward the old clock. It looked a little crooked. He adjusted it one way and then the other until it was perfect.

Can she see me, God . . . my Elizabeth? Does she know the journey I'm about to take? He paused. *Would You tell her I miss her, Father. Please, would You do that?*

John turned away from the clock and sat at the table. The stack of photographs contained images of some of the happiest moments he'd ever known, from the first time he locked eyes with Elizabeth to the birth of Brooke. That was all Cole needed. He had only asked about the beginning of their love story. How it all started. After Brooke, the story became always and ever happier.

Until Elizabeth's cancer.

A sigh worked its way up from John's heart. He'd been through every single photo. These were copies of the best of them — starting with their first picture together. The one someone had shot at the mixer, the dance where they met.

Elaine walked into the kitchen and smiled. He'd almost forgotten she was here, working on one of her handmade quilts in the next room.

"Coffee smells good."

"Thanks. I made hot chocolate for Cole."

"Good idea." She came to him and put her hand on his shoulder. "It's chilly. Nothing like a warm drink and a good story."

John studied her, looking for any sense of bitterness or jealousy. He saw none. "I want you to be part of the story. Stay, would you?" He took her hand. "Please."

"You know I want you to do this, right?" She took the seat beside him, a bit weary.

"Of course. You told me to do it." His heart beat faster and alarm filled his soul. *Where is she going with this?* "Are you changing your mind? Elaine . . ." He took hold of her hand. "Cole and Ashley will be here in ten minutes."

"I'm not changing my mind." Her voice was kind, but her eyes held a pain John had never seen before. "It's just . . . you've been distracted this week. Like you slipped back into some other time and sort of, I don't know . . . forgot about me."

"Elaine . . ." John felt a physical ache. He didn't want any of this to hurt her. "I'm so sorry. I never meant . . ." He wasn't sure what to say.

She was right.

John had spent much of the week going through the photos, remembering the beautiful and painful times that made up his and Elizabeth's story. "I'm sorry." His mind raced for something to say, something that would help ease the uncomfortable feeling between them. "If you stay . . . maybe this can be about us sharing the story. Not just me. You'd feel more included."

"John." Elaine angled her head and gave him a doubtful look, the sort of disbelieving look she might give if John had said he was going to sprout wings. "There's no way I can be included in your story. It's yours and Elizabeth's. Period."

This hadn't happened since John had married Elaine, a reason to go back and relive once more the details of his story. He searched Elaine's eyes. "I don't want this to come between us."

"It won't." She picked up the photo at the top of the stack — the one of John and Elizabeth at that first dance. Elaine looked at it for a long time and then turned to John. "You think I can be here while you go through these photos? While you talk about how young and beautiful she was, and how you would've gone to the moon for her?" Tears welled in her eyes.

John felt terrible, but there was nothing he could say. If he was honest with himself, now that she'd given him her blessing on this project, John was looking forward to spending time in the past. Where Elizabeth's memory still lived. "It all happened so long ago."

"It doesn't matter." Elaine set the photo down. She was quiet for nearly a minute, as if she was choosing her words with great care. "John . . . I love you. But I can't be here." For a brief moment a shadow of sadness seemed to fall over her. "I'll be okay. I'll find things to do, and this will pass."

He hoped so. But that's exactly what John was worried about; how long it would take to find his way back to the place he'd been before all this. The easy way of living and thinking and following God with Elaine by his side. The life they'd lived before Cole came by last week.

Life with Elaine was happy. Their days were beautiful and meaningful. Sure, he thought about Elizabeth every now and then. Her memory was a part of him. He could see her in the faces of their children. But he didn't *live* in the past.

After the next month, he wasn't so sure.

Elaine stood and kissed his cheek. "I'm going to Margaret's. She's working on a quilt, too. We're going to stitch together and catch up." A smile lifted the corners of her mouth. He could tell she wasn't angry.

"I understand." This was all John's fault. He'd have to work to remember her feelings, to not be consumed with the story he was about to tell. "I'm sorry, Elaine. I don't know what else to say."

"It's okay." Again, she put her hand on his shoulder. "I want you to talk freely. Like I said before, Cole deserves this story." She smiled. "After four Thursdays I'll probably have three quilts. Which is fine by me."

He stood and brushed his knuckles softly against her face. "You're amazing. If I haven't told you lately."

"Mmmm. Even if you have, I like it." She didn't seem in a hurry. They still had five minutes until Cole and Ashley would be there. She moved to the refrigerator and pulled out a covered plate of fruit. "Have you heard from Kendra lately?"

"This morning." John was thankful for the connection his family had with Kendra Bryant. She was the recipient of his daughter Erin's heart, and last Christmas Eve she and her husband, Moe, had met the whole Baxter family. The meeting hadn't been easy, but since then Kendra called once a week, just to update John. "She and Moe found a church they like. Their marriage is doing much better."

"How amazing." Elaine looked happier

now, more like herself. They would get through these weeks and everything would be okay. John followed Elaine as she gathered her purse and the fruit and her bag with the unfinished quilt. When they were at the door she turned to him once more. "We have to keep praying for them. Kendra and Moe."

"Definitely." John heard the sound of a car and looked out the door in time to see Ashley and Cole pull up. "They're here."

Elaine waited long enough to greet Ashley and Cole. John watched her, the easy way she had with both of them. Elaine and Ashley had come so far from the days when Ashley was so very troubled by John remarrying.

When Elaine was gone, Ashley cast John a wary look. "Is she okay?"

"She is." John moved toward the oversized chair beside the fireplace. He put the stack of photographs on the end table. "Elaine thinks this is important." He smiled at Cole. "I do, too."

"Good." Ashley's smile was marked with empathy. "I've been thinking about her. This can't be easy."

"It's not." John hugged her. Cole was rummaging through his backpack. Only Ashley could hear him. "We'll get through it. We talked this morning."

Ashley hugged him again. "Thanks for doing this. It means the world to Cole." She met his eyes. "And to me."

"Same here." John smiled at her, as they both took their seats. Cole pulled a notebook, pen, and a single piece of paper from his backpack. "I've been looking forward to this." He sat down and opened the notebook. "I printed a list of questions."

"Great." John's heart beat a little faster than before. "Where should we start?"

Cole positioned his pen over his pad of paper. "First, I forgot to ask you about an ancillary character." He looked up at John. "That means secondary."

John smiled. "Got it."

"I need at least one ancillary character to get an A." Cole raised his brow. "Someone besides family."

"Okay." John thought for a second. "Well, near the end of the story you'll hear about this one man, he was a Vietnam vet. He could be an ancillary character."

"Wow!" Cole checked his notes again. "That sounds perfect. We get extra credit if we interview that person."

"Hmmm." John could still picture the man, the deep lines in his forehead, the way he had been full of life and zeal for God. As if he'd never been a part of the war at all. "I lost track of him a very long time ago. But you could try!"

"Yeah, maybe Facebook." Cole took a deep breath. "All right, Papa. How bout we start at the beginning? Like when you first met Grandma."

A quick laugh. "Good idea." John leaned forward in his chair.

Where do I begin, Lord? Memories and thoughts swirled in his head. Nothing about their beginning had been easy — for John or Elizabeth.

Ashley sat next to Cole on the couch across from John. She hugged a pillow against her stomach, the way she used to do during family movies when she was a teenager. Her eyes looked nervous, like she wasn't quite sure what was coming.

And she wasn't. John was positive about that. Ashley and her siblings knew only the basic time line of their parents' story. They knew nothing of their crazy sad love story or how their beginning was so painfully difficult. Or how easily they could've missed coming together at all.

Cole was perched on the edge of the sofa, pen poised over the open notebook. "Okay. Ready."

An idea hit John. He had planned to start

with the dance, the night he first met Elizabeth. But that wasn't really the beginning. It wasn't the place where their stories started. John's mind raced. "Maybe I should talk about our early history. My life and your grandmother's life — before we met."

Cole stared at his notes for a minute. When he looked up his eyes brightened. "I'd like that. My teacher wants context. I can't write about your beginning without knowing the stuff that came even earlier."

Ashley leaned back, her arms still folded over the pillow. She was here as a spectator, clearly glad for the up-close seat to any story John might tell. Any reservation Ashley had shown before must've been linked to her concern for Elaine. Now that the story was about to begin, she was as interested as Cole.

"Well, neither of us had it easy in the years that led up to us meeting." John could see that better now. His kids and grandkids had never known the hardships he and Elizabeth had lived through. He was grateful to God for that.

John drew a deep breath. "My parents were both dead by the time I met your grandmother. And I had no siblings." John could remember how he felt, living without a family. "My dad died in the Korean War

97

when I was just nine years old. My mom passed away about three years later from pneumonia." He paused. "But everyone said she died of a broken heart."

Cole was writing as quickly as he could. After half a minute he looked at John. "I didn't know that."

"Me, either." Ashley stared at John. "Or maybe I knew. But I didn't realize you were so young."

"So . . ." Cole checked the notebook. "You were just twelve and both your parents were gone?"

"Yes." John could still feel the isolation of being an orphan. He had no aunts or uncles, no one to take him in. He leaned over his knees and folded his hands. "There was this one family, they lived across the street. Their kids were younger than me, but when the parents heard I was about to be a ward of the state, they stepped up and became my guardians."

"Wow." Again Cole was writing as quickly as he could. "What were their names?"

"Wesley. Jeff and Joan Wesley. Their boys were Bill and Steve."

Again Ashley sounded surprised. "The state just let them take you? With no home study from social services?"

"Things were different then." John nodded. "They were great people. Really. They became my family. And they were Christians. I'd never really heard much about God before that."

"You didn't believe in Him?" Cole looked shocked.

"My parents didn't believe. I'd never been to church." John shrugged. "But even after I moved in with the Wesleys, I didn't believe. I went to church with them, but I couldn't get past the obvious."

"If God was real, why did He take your parents?" Ashley sounded sad. "That's awful."

John nodded. "So that was me. Living with this family I had come to love, not a believer, and determined to get my medical degree. It felt like a way to make my life matter. Becoming a doctor."

"Hmmm. That's exactly the sort of context I need." It took Cole a minute to catch up with his note-taking. "What about Grandma?"

"She was younger." John lifted his gaze to the window, to the blue sky beyond. "Only nineteen." He hesitated. This next part was sad, too. "Your grandma's parents were very strict. They wouldn't let her date or dance or listen to popular music. And she certainly couldn't spend time with boys. Not at all.

Those were their rules and nothing could change their minds."

"So did Grandma believe in God?" Cole looked up from his notes.

The boy's question was a good one. "Not really."

"What!" Ashley straightened in her seat. "Are you serious? I never knew that!"

"It's true." This was only the beginning of what Ashley didn't know. "Your mother went through the motions. But her parents had made faith so unattractive that Christianity was just a religion to her. A system." He paused. "Not a relationship with God, the way Jesus describes it in Scripture. Like it's supposed to be."

"Wow . . . so sad." Cole looked at his list of questions. "Okay, then . . . how did you and Grandma meet?"

How did we meet? John's heart skipped a beat. He could see the dance hall and hear the music. The dusty smell off the old wood-planked floor filled his senses again. He reached for the picture on the top of the stack. For a few seconds he stared at it. Then he looked at Cole. "It was the fall of 1974. I was a second-year medical student at the University of Michigan."

Cole looked up. "U of M? The Wolverines?" His eyes grew wide. "I didn't know you went there, Papa."

"I did." He felt a sense of satisfaction. This wouldn't only be a time to relive his past with Elizabeth. These hours would teach Cole more about who his grandparents had been. Details Cole could tell his kids and grandkids one day.

"So that's why you're a Michigan football fan." Cole shook his head. "I guess I should've known."

"I have a number of favorite teams." John chuckled. "It'd be easy to miss the fact that Michigan is my alma mater. Undergrad and med school."

"I told you a long time ago, Cole." Ashley gave Cole a quick smile. "You must've been too young to remember."

"Probably. Anyway . . ." Cole looked at his notes. "So you were a med student at U of M."

"Yes." John glanced at the picture again. "Technically I shouldn't have been there that night. The dance was for underclassmen. But Bill Wesley asked me to go, so I did." He laughed again. "Five minutes after I got there, I was ready to leave when your grandmother walked in. Honestly, she was . . ."

As John spoke, he easily fell into the story. He was no longer sitting in the living room fifty years later. He was back at that dance hall once more, cup of punch in his hand, worn-out suit hanging from his thin frame.

And like that, the decades disappeared and the memory of that night came to life again. The way John had known it would. He didn't fight it, didn't work to stay in the here and now. If he was going to go back, then he wanted to relive it. All of it.

He breathed in deep and let the story come.

6

The Big Bopper belted through the tinny music system that night in Ann Arbor, Michigan. Tucked near the back of campus, the dance hall was a favorite spot for students. Dances were always packed and the hall stayed open till midnight. U of M held mixers there every other Friday night and this was the first of the school year.

The rule was the same each time. Only underclassmen could attend the dances. Period.

The idea that John might go to the dance came from Bill Wesley, a freshman that year. Bill begged John to come, mostly because Bill didn't think the night would go well if he attended by himself. That year, Bill was a skinny kid with bushy blond hair and pale skin. A few years and he would grow into his lanky frame, but still back then he was probably right about needing John.

Since Bill was like a little brother, John agreed.

He didn't doubt himself until he walked through the doors and saw the students. "That's it. I'm too old." John turned toward the door. He had to get out of there before one of the administrators saw him. "I shouldn't have let you talk me into this."

"No one cares." Bill grabbed his arm. "Everyone says it's a dumb rule. No one enforces it." He talked loud enough to be heard over the music. "Besides, you can't leave. You're my secret weapon. My ace-in-the-hole. The girls won't look twice at me if you're not here."

"The girls will find you. Have you looked in the mirror, Bill? You're a regular Casanova." John reached into his pocket for his car keys. "I'm out."

"John! Come on." Bill trailed him as they wove their way through underclassmen. "You're my wingman."

John looked over his shoulder at Bill. "You'll have to fly alone." He laughed and gave a shake of his head. They were almost to the front of the dance hall when the double doors opened and a group of girls stepped inside. A rainstorm had burst over Ann Arbor in the past ten minutes, and the girls squealed as they brushed the rain from their bare arms and dresses.

That's when he saw her.

There amidst the other girls was one that took his breath. He'd never know why she looked up at him at that moment, but she did. The raindrops on her eyelashes made her blue eyes sparkle, and John was instantly sure of one thing.

He'd never seen any girl more beautiful.

And just like that he was Bill's wingman once again. He stopped in his tracks and leaned toward his friend. "What a great dance, right, Bill? That's what I was just saying, right?"

"What?" Bill was a little slow on the uptake. He followed John's gaze and then he caught on. "That's Elizabeth. Prettiest freshman of our class."

"Definitely." John felt like he was in a trance, the ground beneath him less sure than before. "Elizabeth." The sound of her name on his lips felt right. Like he'd said it a thousand times before. "Come on. Let's get some punch."

John and Bill made their way back into the crowd, Bill celebrating the victory and John intent on one thing alone. Dancing with Elizabeth. Once they'd found their place near the drink table, John slipped his hands into his pockets and looked for her.

It didn't take long to find her, because she was doing the same thing. Their eyes met across the crowded dance hall just as the Beatles came on.

The words filled John's mind with possibilities. "All you need is love . . . all you need is love . . ."

Bill sang along beside him. "Come on, girls. Can't you see me over here?" Bill said the words loud enough for only John to hear. "A little love, please! Right this way!"

John laughed. Bill always made him laugh. But he wasn't sticking around for the private concert another minute. "I'll be back." He patted Bill on the shoulder. "You've got this."

John made his way through the crowd again until he was standing right in front of the pretty brunette. John looked at her wet dress and grinned at her. "If this is a new style, no one wears it better."

Her eyes shone brighter than the chandeliers that hung over the doorway. Elizabeth giggled and looked away briefly. As if she were surveying the room. When her eyes met his again she seemed suddenly shy. "I'll take that as a compliment."

"I'm John." He grinned at her.

She did the same. "Elizabeth."

"As for the compliment, that's how it was

intended." John bowed like a knight of old. "Would the beautiful Elizabeth like to dance?"

Instantly she crossed her arms and took a step back. "I can't. I'm sorry."

This wasn't going to be easy. John didn't care. He was too caught up in the nearness of her, the smell of her perfume to give up now. "You can't? Or you won't?" His tone wasn't serious. He angled his head. "Because I'll bet you're a really great dancer, Miss Elizabeth."

She laughed again, and once more she looked around.

John followed suit, trying to imagine what she was looking for. "If you're running from the law, I've got you. No one'll get past me."

This time she laughed out loud. She stopped looking around and focused her attention straight on him. "My parents won't let me dance. And even if they did, I can't do it. I . . . never learned."

John stared at her open-mouthed, the teasing still marking every moment. "They won't let . . . ?" His voice trailed off, as if he was too shocked to finish the sentence.

"No." She shook her head. Her eyes never left his, proof that she was enjoying the banter. "No dancing. Not for a minute." Her eyes sparkled and she batted her lashes.

"They'd kill me if they caught me here."

"Here? In this innocent dance hall?" He looked around. "What could possibly happen here?"

"You're crazy." She laughed again. "I told my parents I was at my friend's house. I wore one of her dresses and we snuck over. I'm serious." She raised her brow, still flirty. "They'd kill me."

"They won't kill you." John took her hand and led her toward the dance floor. "But what *will* kill you is not knowing how to dance." He stopped midstride and she had no choice but to bump into him. He turned and searched her eyes, their faces inches apart. "Good thing I'm here." He paused, so close he could smell the mint on her breath. "I'll teach you everything I know."

She looked breathless, as if the conversation and his confidence were all a little heady for her. John waited a few seconds, lost in her eyes, and then Chubby Checker's "The Twist" came on. John grinned. "Come on. The twist is easy."

"But I . . ."

"I'll show you." They were too committed now for her to change her mind. At least that's how it seemed. Besides, her protesting seemed more a matter of form than of substance. Everything in her expression told him she didn't want him to leave.

They found a spot on the edge of the floor and John took the lead. "Just do what I do." He leaned close to her so she could hear him over the song. The twist really was easy. The variations were endless. Elizabeth watched him, and after thirty seconds of laughing and looking nervous, she began to dance.

John wasn't a bit surprised that Elizabeth picked it up so easily. She had natural rhythm and looked better dancing the twist than most of the girls on the floor. When the music ended, John pulled her in for an impulsive hug. "That was perfect! You're a pro, Elizabeth. Look at you!"

She was laughing again, but she stepped back from him. Seeming careful to keep her distance. "I always wanted to learn the jitterbug. Could you teach me that?"

No sooner had she said the words than Glenn Miller's "In the Mood" came on. John couldn't believe it. Whoever was in charge of music definitely played quite a mix. The DJ couldn't have planned the songs any better. "The answer is yes, my dear. Follow me."

They spent the next five minutes laughing and learning and dancing. John had hold of her hands, and when the song ended, he let go and raised his fists in the air. "You're a natural. You've taken lessons all your life!"

"I haven't." She was out of breath, her cheeks rosy.

John would never forget the way she looked in that single moment. She was a wispy girl with long legs and pretty cheekbones. Her eyes shone beautiful bright blue against her long brunette hair, her white sleeveless dress swaying to the music. "You're the most stunning girl here, Elizabeth." John did a slight bow again. "I thought I should tell you."

"Why, thank you." She curtsied — proof that she'd done at least a little dancing in her friends' rooms. John took her hand and led her to the drink table. He poured her a glass of punch and he caught her looking closely at him. "My mother's right."

"What's that?" John handed her the drink and stood close so he could hear. "She must've told you tonight would change your life."

"She doesn't know I'm here." Elizabeth clutched her drink. "My mother says I'm not ready to date boys. I'm too young."

"And you think she's right?" John cocked his head, keeping himself from laughing.

"Yes!" She shook her head. "I've been dancing with you all this time and I don't

110

even know your last name."

"That!" John stroked his chin with his thumb and forefinger. "Yes, that could be a problem." He set down his glass and turned toward her. The whole experience was so surreal. He could barely remember his name. He locked eyes with her. "I'm John Baxter." He wanted desperately to kiss her. But he kept the few inches that separated them. "And you're the most beautiful girl I've ever seen."

"Hello, John." Her eyes were shy again. "And you're the most handsome guy I've ever danced with."

"Wait . . . I'm the *only* guy you've ever —"

"Come on." More laughter while she found a spot for her glass. "You have to teach me how to swing!"

The night was something from a dream. Every minute of it, every song was etched forever in his heart. As midnight drew near, the DJ came over the loudspeaker. "Last dance of the night! Grab your girl, and let's give it a go!"

The last song of the evening was one that would forever make him think of her. Whenever he heard it on the radio or at a wedding. It was their song that night, and it always would be.

The song was "Never My Love," by the Association. As soon as the first notes played, John took her hand. This time he wasn't in a hurry. His eyes melted into hers and he moved closer. So close he could feel her breath on his face. "What about a slow dance, Elizabeth?" He had never wanted to kiss a girl more than right then. "Can I teach you that?"

She swallowed, breathless. The teasing tone from earlier was now something deeper. A chemistry stronger than the two of them. "Yes, John." Her cheek brushed against his. "Show me. Please."

He led her carefully onto the dance floor this time. With everything in him he never wanted to let go of her hand. By then the first verse was halfway through. She stepped into his embrace and he eased his arm around her waist. "Feel the way my body moves." He whispered the words near the side of her face. "Keep my rhythm. That's all there is to it."

"I will." Their faces side by side, they began to sway and move to the music.

John wanted the song to last forever. He sang the lyrics quietly, so only she could hear. *You wonder if this heart of mine . . . will lose its desire for you. Never my love.*

A few times he caught a glimpse of her

face, and each time her eyes were closed. As if she were feeling the same way he was. When the song ended, it took every bit of John's willpower not to touch his lips to hers. Students began to file out of the dance hall, but John and Elizabeth stayed that way, cheek to cheek, lost in a slow dance they never wanted to leave.

Bill finally came up to him. "John . . . what are ya—" He stopped short. "Elizabeth. Your friends are leaving."

She jolted from the moment and like Cinderella from a fairy-tale dream, she pulled away. "I have to go."

"Wait." John's heart thudded in his chest. He couldn't let her walk away without getting her number. He needed to see her again. No one had ever made him feel this way. He found a scrap of paper and a pen. "What's your number? I want to take you out."

"You can't." This time she wasn't laughing. "I told you, John. My parents would never let me go."

There had to be a chance at least. John's mind raced. "Okay, then here." He scribbled his number on the paper and handed it to her. "Call me. Find a way . . . please."

She took it from him and slipped it into the pocket of her dress. Then just as sh

113

was about to run off, she came to him and hugged him. As they embraced he could feel her body against his, feel the way they fit together, and something else. He could sense the way she clung to him. She didn't want to leave, either. Whatever crazy chemistry had ignited between them, she felt it, too. "Goodbye, John." She whispered the words and then with one last look, she ran to join her friends.

John could barely draw a breath.

Bill walked up to him and waved his open hand in front of John's eyes. "Earth to John Baxter. Hello."

John laughed, but his heart wasn't in it. All he wanted was to stand here on this very dance floor and relive every second of the night. Every dance and laugh and touch and moment with her near him.

But the janitor pushed a broom onto the floor. "Time to go, people. Let's move it."

"Standing here won't bring her back." Bill rolled his eyes. "Let's get home, Mr. I-can't-stay-at-the-dance-another-minute."

John finally remembered to exhale. "She changed my mind."

"You think?" Bill chuckled. "Tell me all about it at home."

Back at the house, John didn't share any ut the most basic details. The night belonged to Elizabeth and him alone. He wouldn't share it with anyone.

Three days passed and all John did was think of her. He couldn't focus in class, couldn't imagine studying for an exam. He couldn't even get through a shift at the drugstore where he worked a few nights a week without feeling himself in her arms again.

Finally on the fourth day, the phone at the Wesleys' house rang. It was three o'clock in the afternoon. John didn't think anything of it until Joan Wesley lowered the receiver. "It's for you." She smiled and mouthed the words. "It's a girl."

John's heart skipped a beat. He took the phone as quickly as he could. "Hello?"

"Hi. This is Betsy." The girl paused. "I'm Elizabeth's friend." She uttered a shy laugh. "This probably seems crazy, but Elizabeth couldn't call you from her house. She asked if you could meet her in thirty minutes on campus at the bench across from the science building."

Only then did John realize he hadn't asked Elizabeth where she lived. He had assumed she had a room in one of the dorms. But he remembered Elizabeth's comments about her parents. "Does she . . . live with her mom and dad?"

"Yes. She can never call you from there." The girl sounded proud of herself. "I told her I'd help."

John felt a rush of relief. "Thank you, Betsy. You don't know . . ."

"Actually, I do." There was a smile in her voice. "What should I tell Elizabeth?"

"Tell her I'll be there. I'd meet her on the moon if that's where she wanted to go."

John rode his bike to the bench and got there fifteen minutes early. Sure enough, at 3:30, Elizabeth appeared on the path, also riding a bicycle. She wore a pale pink blouse and navy short pants. Her pretty hair was pulled back in a ponytail.

When she climbed off the bike he took hold of both her hands. "You get more beautiful every time I see you."

"Thanks." She looked into his eyes, and the fear from the other night was back. "My parents would disown me if they knew I was doing this."

"We aren't doing anything." He moved a step closer. "I just wanted to see you . . . to talk."

That wasn't what either of them wanted to do. The look in Elizabeth's eyes told him that much.

"There was another question I didn't ask you." She released his hands and sat on the bench. Like at the dance she was breathless, but he doubted it was from the bike ride.

He stood there, looking at her, taking in the vision of her. "Ask it."

"How old are you, John? The dance was for underclassmen."

True. John winced. He took the seat beside her and shifted so he could see her. She did the same and their knees touched ever so lightly. *Focus, John. You can't lose this girl.* He tried to think of the best way to say this. "I broke the rule."

"John." She shook her head and a quick laugh slipped between her lips. "How old are you? Thirty?"

"Wow." He chuckled and leaned back a little. "I hope I don't look that old."

"You don't." She laughed. "I thought you were a sophomore. Betsy told me you were in medical school here."

"I am. Yes. Second year." He shrugged. "There never seemed to be a good time the other night to bring it up."

"So you're what . . . twenty-four?"

"Just turned." He didn't blink, didn't look away. "And you?"

"Nineteen." She leaned her head back and groaned softly. "Now my parents will definitely kill me. I break the rules and go to the dance and take up with the only second-year med student there."

John knew he should be worried. She might be young, and she might be scared to death of her parents. But her words would stay with him always. *Take up with . . .* that's what she'd said. She had taken up with the only second-year med student. His smile started on the inside and took over his face. "We can find a way, Elizabeth. Age is just a number."

Her eyes locked on to his again and the afternoon breeze made the moment feel magical. "It is, isn't it?"

This time her words almost made him cheer out loud. She wasn't going to run. They would find a way. They had to.

Before they knew it they'd devised a plan. With Betsy's help they would meet here and he would take her wherever she wanted to go. Out to dinner . . . to Allmendinger Park . . . shopping at the mall, or just here. Sitting this way on a bench that would forever memorialize the beginning of their love.

Two weeks later the Wesley family left town for a long weekend at the lake. From the first night John wanted desperately to take her home, find a way for the two of them to be alone. A place where they wouldn't have to look over their shoulders for her parents.

They were at the park that evening, swinging side by side and talking about the rigors of medical school, when John couldn't wait another minute. He looked at her, taking his time. "My family's gone." He searched her eyes. "The house is empty."

Elizabeth didn't say anything. Her expression grew deeper, with the same sort of desire John had felt the minute she walked into the dance hall that first night. "I could . . . make you dinner."

She smiled. "You'd make me dinner?"

They were the best words John had ever heard. He took her hand. "Let's go."

They bought ground beef and potatoes and carrots at the store and drove to his house. The whole time John wondered if she could hear his pounding heart. He didn't want to do anything that would cross lines. He respected Elizabeth like he'd never respected any girl before. But once they set the groceries down on the kitchen table, he turned to her. "Elizabeth."

She faced him, breathless, her lips slightly open. "Kiss me, John. Please."

His heart felt like it would burst, but he kept his cool. He drew her close and wove his fingers into her hair. Then for the sweetest minute of his life he kissed her. One kiss became another and another.

She was a drug and he was forever addicted. He knew he would never feel this way about any other girl as long as he lived. But after that single minute he stepped back. It took a while before he caught his breath. "I . . . can't. We can't."

Her heart was pounding as hard as his. Again, he could see it in the hollow of her throat. "I know."

John took another few steps from her and moved closer to the groceries. "Let's . . . let's figure out dinner."

Elizabeth nodded. "I'll help."

"Stay there." He held up his hand. "Give me a minute." His laugh was as much the sound of his body trying to cool down as it was his way of keeping the mood light.

They managed to make dinner and share a conversation about her parents and their many rules and John didn't kiss her again. Not even when he dropped her off a few blocks from home later that night. After all, her parents thought she was at Betsy's house. The last thing he wanted to do was shame her, even in the slightest.

Not just because it was the honorable thing to do. Though John would've spent the whole evening kissing her if he could've. But he also didn't want her parents to see guilt in Elizabeth's eyes. If they did, they might learn about him and find a way to break off what John and Elizabeth had just started. And that was a risk John simply couldn't take.

Because he didn't want Elizabeth merely for a night.

He wanted her for his entire life.

7

A shift had happened in Cole's heart. Ashley noticed it halfway through the interview. At first Cole's mood had been lighthearted. Curious of course, but the boy had no idea what a rebel his grandfather had been back in the day. Ashley had tried to tell him before the meeting today.

"Papa was very different in his early days," she'd told Cole as they drove to her father's house. "Just so you know."

"That's fine." Cole hadn't really registered the fact.

It had taken her father's story to drive the point home.

Now Cole was quiet, pensive. He didn't say anything as they climbed into their SUV and pulled away from her father's small Bloomington house.

Ashley waited until they were out of the neighborhood before she interrupted the silence. "See, Cole? Grandma and Papa's story is deep. There's heartache in it, too. Coming up in the next few weeks." She glanced at Cole. "I wasn't sure how much he was going to share, if he was going to get into the specific details."

Cole nodded, but he didn't look at her. "I'm glad he did." He kept his eyes straight ahead, as if he were seeing into the past, all the way back to the day Ashley's parents first met.

One more try, she thought. "I learned things today, too. I mean, of course I knew their story. The basic facts. But this afternoon was very special for me. I'll remember it always."

This time Cole angled himself so he could see her. "Could we go by the cemetery? On the way home?"

Ashley felt her heart melt. "Yes, of course." He had never before asked. Like most kids, he wanted nothing to do with death. Didn't want to be reminded that life wouldn't continue on in this wonderful predictable routine of days and weeks and seasons and years.

Death wasn't something Cole had ever talked about. Especially after losing his Aunt Erin and Uncle Sam and their girls in the car accident a few years back. Ashley was sure that to Cole, cemeteries were creepy.

Too much life to be lived to think about dead people.

But here was Cole wanting to spend a few moments contemplating a very great loss. One he probably hadn't thought about since he was a little boy. One that might not have come to the surface at all if it weren't for the photo. The one that gave Cole the idea for the project.

Ashley accepted the silence. Cole was so like her. His sense of adventure and his love for life, his passion for God, his determination with sports, and his propensity for the arts. The boy who had taken up drawing in the past year would always have a hold on her heart. The fact that after just an hour hearing her father's love story, he was so moved he wanted to go to the cemetery.

Proof that Cole was deeper than most boys his age. He saw meaning in the mundane and now, what had started out as a school project had clearly woven its way into his soul.

They parked near the place where so many of their loved ones were buried. Without saying a word, Ashley walked beside Cole to her mother's tombstone. The words were simple. Her name etched clearly for all to see that Elizabeth Baxter had been here . . . and she had gone, far too soon.

Cole bent down and traced his fingers over his grandmother's name. He laid his hand on the dates at either side of the dash. "She died of cancer, right?" A quick look over his shoulder at Ashley. "That's what happened?"

"Yes." Ashley felt tears in her eyes. "She was very young." Without hesitating, Ashley lowered herself to the ground and sat cross-legged next to Cole. "At least to me she was. Barely in her sixties."

Again Cole didn't say anything. He stared at the tombstone as the springtime breeze fell, gentle against their faces.

Only her father could tell the heartbreaking details of their love affair. Her dad alone knew their early days, the story that was the foundation of the entire Baxter family. But Ashley could fill in details that surrounded her mother's death. Especially since Cole clearly wanted to know. She took her time, letting Cole process whatever he was feeling.

When she finally spoke, she used a soft tone. They were the only two people in the cemetery, so there was no need to talk any louder. "Grandma lived long enough to see me get married. That was something we all prayed for."

Cole smiled, but his eyes were sad. "That's

nice." He sat down on the ground beside her and picked at a few pieces of grass. "But it's still so sad, Mom. Like . . . she should be here."

Tears stung at Ashley's eyes again. She swallowed hard and waited until she could speak. "I know. I feel that way, too. God's ways are not ours, Cole. That's what Grandma used to say." Ashley sniffed a few times. "Grandma wanted so much to live. She wanted to see all you kids grow up and graduate from high school and get married. No grandma ever loved her grandchildren as much as she did."

A few seconds passed and Cole wiped a single tear from his cheeks. "I wish I could remember her." He turned his teary eyes to Ashley. "That was the hardest part today, Mom. The more Papa talked about her, the more I wanted to remember her. I wanted to give her a hug and tell her how glad I was that she and Papa fell in love. I kept wanting her to be there, next to him."

Ashley closed her eyes for a moment and then looked at Cole. The familiar ache swelled and filled her heart. "I wanted that, too."

Years had passed since Ashley had wept over losing her mother. Really let herself feel the loss and remember the feeling of her mom's arms around her. But Cole's transparency brought the hurt straight to the surface. It was all she could do not to break down.

"Isn't that weird?" He searched her eyes. "Seeing your dad with Elaine? After your whole life of your parents together with each other?"

Her answer didn't come quickly. She exhaled and stared at the distant trees, the blue sky behind them. "It was weird at first, definitely." She blinked and dabbed her fingers beneath her eyes. "I thought he should stay single the rest of his life. Or at least wait a lot longer."

"Because after a love like he had with Grandma, how could he love someone else?" Cole looked directly at her, like he was genuinely trying to understand.

"Exactly." Ashley could feel her tears ready to burst through. She breathed the sweet spring air, the smell of jasmine nearby. "I was the last one of the brothers and sisters to understand. It wasn't until your little sister died that Elaine and I found our way to a friendship."

The sun moved out from behind a passing cloud. Cole squinted against the light. "What happened?"

"Well . . . I wanted Sarah Marie's life to

matter. Even if she only lived a few hours."

"I remember being there at the hospital. Everyone singing around your bed and taking turns holding her." Fresh tears filled his eyes. "I remember holding her."

Ashley pointed to the adjacent tombstone. "She's buried there. Beside your grandma."

"I saw that." Cole used his thumb and forefinger to wipe his tears. "I don't remember what Elaine did that day."

It was something Ashley would never forget. "She brought me a baby girl outfit. The sort of thing you would do for any other baby girl. But Sarah Marie . . . no one thought to bring clothes for her because they knew . . . they knew she wasn't going to live."

Cole looked at the grass for a moment and then back at Ashley. "I never thought about that."

Ashley couldn't fight her tears anymore. They trickled down her face as she remembered that day. "Leading up to her birth, I'd been thinking how all I wanted was my mother. I wanted her there beside me, to comfort me and tell me everything was going to be okay. My mom would've understood that I needed at least something normal to mark Sarah's birth. Something other little girls would have. It was one of the hardest parts of that time, not having my mom with me."

"That's so sad." Cole reached for her hand. "I want you there for all those big moments. When I get married and when I have my kids one day."

Ashley brushed away her tears once more. This moment was another way Cole was different from other boys his age. Deeper, sensitive. She drew a shaky breath. "So there I was, thinking how much I missed my mother, when Papa and Elaine walked into the hospital room."

Ashley could easily remember the way she felt that day, how she'd been overcome with sadness until that single moment. "Elaine walked up and handed me a wrapped gift. Inside was the sweetest little pink outfit." Ashley closed her eyes again, overcome by the memory.

Without saying a word, Cole put his arm around Ashley's shoulders. For a while they sat there, side by side at the foot of her mother's tombstone, and just let the sadness be. How kind of God to give them this time together. Time that clearly was important to both of them. Ashley needed this, a moment when she could just sit with her son and remember the losses of yesterday.

And the way they still hurt today.

Ashley leaned her head on her son's shoulder. He was taller than her now, and becoming a man like Landon. Just the way Ashley had always prayed he would. Here and now she drew strength from him, just knowing that he cared about the things that hurt her. Knowing that they hurt him, too.

"That was a turning point with Elaine and me." Ashley sat up straight again.

Cole stood and walked to the nearby tombstone. "Sarah Marie." He looked back at Ashley. "She lived only those few hours?"

"Yes. Not even a day." Ashley smiled through blurry eyes. "But what a full and rich life she had."

Cole sat down beside her again and plucked absently at a few more pieces of grass. He looked deep into Ashley's eyes. "So Grandma is taking care of Sarah Marie." It wasn't a question. "She's not here with us grandkids on earth. But she's with the girl cousins in heaven."

Again it was hard for Ashley to see through her tears. "Exactly. And Erin and Sam. All of them together."

"Like your painting."

"Yes." One of Ashley's paintings depicted her mother and all the Baxter family who had passed on. It hung in the entryway of Ashley and Landon's house. "Those already home in heaven."

Cole nodded. He didn't say anything for a minute or so. Then he took a deep breath. "I think I understand a little better." He brought his knees up to his chest and looped his arms around them. "It's just . . . at first as Papa told his story, I kept think-ing how it wasn't fair. She was the one he loved the most. His first love." Cole stared at his grandma's tombstone again. "She should still be alive."

This time Ashley put her arm around Cole's shoulders. "You understand a little better, why it took Papa time to agree to all this."

"Definitely." Cole brushed a few pieces of grass off the edge of the stone. "All this storytelling will make him miss her more. Maybe more than ever."

"Right." Ashley thought for a minute. "Maybe we should pray for Papa. That this won't be too hard for him. We still have three more visits to hear his story."

"True." Cole looked at her. "You wanna go ahead?"

"Sure." Ashley prayed that her dad would remember the details of his love story with her mom, but that in the process he wouldn't get so lost in the sorrow that he couldn't be happy today. "Elaine needs him,

131

and he needs her, Lord . . . so please help Papa stay happy about the life he has now. Even as he gets a little sad about the life he lost when he lost Mom. In Jesus' name, amen."

A quiet fell over them. There was nothing more to say.

Cole helped Ashley to her feet and the two of them returned to the SUV. The afternoon was one Ashley would never forget. She would always remember these hours with Cole, and the way he had wanted to spend time at the cemetery with her. She could hardly wait to tell Landon.

On the drive home, Cole turned on the radio and almost at the same time Kyle Kupecky's hit song "This Is Not the End" came on. It was Ashley's favorite. Sometimes when she was alone in the car she'd sing it at the top of her lungs.

Like it was her anthem.

Cole loved it, too. He had a better voice than Ashley did and he knew every word. "This is not the end . . . the night is dark but the stars are shining . . . This is not the end, so keep your faith and trust His timing."

Ashley's eyes were dry now. The song, a reminder of a very powerful truth. Cole was still singing along.

"And if you fall . . . land on your knees, reach out to heaven and you'll see . . . This is not the end."

They were halfway home when the song ended. Cole turned down the radio and looked at her. "What about your love story, Mom? You've never told me what happened with you and my dad."

Suddenly Ashley couldn't draw a breath. She kept her eyes on the road, pretending to be too involved in driving to really hear what Cole said. *No, Lord . . . please don't let him ask this. Not now. Not after such a beautiful day together.*

"Mom?" Cole made a sound that was more confusion than laughter. "Did you hear me?"

"What?" Ashley gave him a quick look. "Sorry. My story? Right . . . What do you want to know?"

"Well . . ." Cole raised one shoulder and let it fall again. "I'm not sure. Everything, I guess. I don't want to be all old and one day my son's in high school and he wants to do an interview and that's how long I have to wait to know your love story."

"Thanks, Cole." She allowed a sarcastic laugh. "All old, huh?"

"Not you." He chuckled, clearly realizing how he must've sounded. "I'm just saying.

133

I'd rather know now. Family stories are important. They're part of our legacy. Our history."

"Like your assignment." Ashley kept her voice cool, but her heart was racing. She never wanted him to ask this. Never wanted to go back to those days again. *Please, God . . . not my story. Please, no.*

"Right. But not for school, you know? Just you and me, talking about what happened with your story."

Ashley gripped the steering wheel so tightly she wondered if it might come off. Panic wrapped its strong fingers around her throat. Ashley chided herself. This was ridiculous. Just because he asked didn't mean she needed to break into the story here on the drive home. She forced her tone to sound casual. "Sure, Cole. We can do that sometime. Absolutely."

"Really?" Cole studied her. "You seemed like you didn't want to talk about it."

"Not at all." She smiled at him and relaxed her grip on the wheel. "Maybe after you finish your project sometime."

"Okay." Cole seemed satisfied. "Maybe we can go eat somewhere and you could tell me then. I really want to know more. The details."

The details. Ashley shuddered. "Of

course."

With that, Cole turned up the radio again. It was another song Ashley loved. Francesca Battistelli's "Holy Spirit." A song about the Spirit of God being welcome in whatever moment might be happening.

Even a moment like this.

Where Ashley was practically having an anxiety attack thinking about telling Cole the truth about his father. What kind of man he had been. What sort of situation had led to Ashley getting pregnant. And how she almost . . .

She couldn't let herself go there. And though the song spoke of peace, Ashley couldn't shake the anxiety. *Help me, God. I can't talk about the past with Cole. I can't do it.* The panic consuming her was unrelenting. And as they pulled into the driveway she felt desperate for just one thing. The peace that passed all understanding, and the only source of that peace.

The Holy Spirit of God.

8

Cole had a mountain of homework to finish, but first he made time for their family dinner. His dad had cooked for them — the way he had promised to do every Thursday while Cole interviewed his papa. Tonight was spaghetti. Cole walked up to the pan on the stove and stirred the sauce. It looked a little watery. Nothing like his mom's sauce.

But that didn't matter. His dad was buttering the garlic bread, so Cole pulled the Parmesan cheese from the refrigerator. "Want help?"

"Sure. Just don't let me burn the bread. I'll never hear the end of it from Janessa."

Cole laughed. "True." His little sister Janessa loved garlic bread.

His dad waited by the oven, potholders on his hands, and looked at Cole. "Mom says you stopped by the cemetery."

"We did. I needed to think about everything. Like why Grandma isn't here when

Papa loved her so much."

"I know." His dad seemed to let that sink in. "I wonder that, too, sometimes."

"God's ways are not our ways." Cole felt the corners of his mouth lift some. "That's what Grandma used to say."

"She did. I remember that." His father checked the bread and then turned to Cole. "Your mom said today was really special." He smiled. "You're a good son, Cole. Including her in your project this way."

"Thanks." Cole loved times like this, talking to his dad, feeling the connection between them. "I didn't realize it would make me feel so many things, hearing Papa's story. Then talking to Mom at the cemetery."

His dad pulled the bread from the oven. It was golden brown. "Perfect."

"Yes. Janessa will be thrilled." Cole laughed again.

Once the bread was safely on the counter they moved to the round table just off the kitchen. When they were facing each other, his dad looked straight into his eyes. "Mom says you talked about Sarah Marie."

Cole thought back to his little sister's grave marker. "She had such a short life."

"In some ways that was the miracle of her time here." His dad folded his hands and set them on the table. "So many people were praying for us, believing for a miracle. When she died we all were shown the truth. That the miracle was even knowing her at all." He smiled. "You know?"

"Yeah." Cole nodded.

"Because all life is precious to God." His dad was quiet for a moment. "And it should be precious to us. No matter how long a person lives."

"And now she's with God . . . waiting for the rest of us." Cole leaned back in his chair.

Cole thought about the conversation with his mom earlier. "I like that she's with Grandma and Aunt Erin and the rest. Mom and I talked about that. It's nice that God lets them all be together."

His dad's smile gave an easy view to his soul. "God loves us more than we can ever understand."

The door opened and the other kids burst through, all talking at once. Something about Janessa catching the biggest tadpole of the afternoon and how Amy had helped her and how Devin was proud of the girls for not being sissies.

The quiet conversation between them was over, but Cole didn't mind. He'd had his time, his chance to share the importance of today with his dad.

After dinner he excused himself to his room. He had a few hours of homework still. No time for tadpoles today. Something else that stirred the depths of his heart. His dad used to say there would always be precious lasts along the journey to being a grown-up. The last time that they ran across the lawn . . . the last time that they looked for tadpoles in the pond.

It was his way of teaching them to appreciate every day.

Which was why before he started his homework he thanked God for today. The time with his papa and his parents. It was a day Cole would remember always. Like the day that was coming sometime soon. When his mom would tell him about the love story between her and his father. That would be a beautiful day for sure.

Because his mom was one of the most loving people he had ever known.

Ashley waited until the kids were in bed before she found Landon in the TV room watching the Indiana Pacers. She sat next to him and rested her head on the back of the sofa. The day had been so much more emotional than she had expected. Sure, she'd known her heart would get involved

139

in hearing the story of her parents' beginning.

But she hadn't expected the beautiful time at the cemetery, and she certainly hadn't expected the bomb Cole dropped on the ride home. She closed her eyes and tried to imagine how she would even begin to tell Cole his story.

"You okay?" Landon took her hand in his. He slid his fingers between hers and ran his thumb over her thumb. The way he always did when they were together.

She opened her eyes and sat up straighter. "After the cemetery today Cole asked me a question. On the way home."

"A question?" Landon turned down the TV and faced her. "What sort of question?"

Ashley felt sick to her stomach. How would Landon feel hearing this news? She felt a chill run down her spine. *Help Landon understand, dear God . . . this has nothing to do with Cole's feelings for him.*

"Ash?" Landon released her hand and ran his fingers through her hair. "I'm here, baby. What is it? What did he ask?"

She couldn't put this off another minute. She took a deep breath. "He asked me about my story . . . about his father and me." She searched his eyes. "He wants to know, Landon. I'm not sure what to tell him. I mean . . . I never wanted to go back to that time and now, where would I even —"

"Ashley." Landon put his hand along the side of her face. "Honey, it'll be okay. Maybe it's time to share some of the details. He's almost seventeen."

Her fears were so great she didn't want to speak them. But she had to. Landon was the only one who would understand. "If he knows what I did . . . he might see me differently. Things might never be the same."

Understanding filled Landon's eyes. "You're thinking of your brother, Luke."

He was right. Luke had been her best friend growing up. But after she came home from Paris with a baby, her brother was disappointed in her. Angry, even. Luke thought Ashley had ruined the Baxter family name, and for a while it seemed their relationship might be over. Then Luke's girlfriend wound up pregnant. Luke's world was rocked for a while, but in the midst of a rebellious time for him, he had reached out to Ashley.

Today they were closer than ever.

Landon still had his hand alongside her face. "You're afraid what happened with Luke will happen with Cole. If he knows how it was with you and his father. Honey,

141

that would never happen with Cole."

Ashley began to shiver. She wanted Landon to be right, but still . . . "What makes you so sure?"

"Honey, for one thing, he already knows at least some of his past. He knows I'm not his biological father. Which could only mean one thing."

"I had a baby with some other man."

"Exactly."

Ashley stared at her wedding ring. Landon had always been proof that God loved her. That He hadn't given up on her because of her terrible choices in Paris. Instead of throwing her away, God had brought her Landon. She lifted her face to his. "Why would Cole want to know *that* story?"

"Because it's part of his past." Peace warmed Landon's expression. "You don't have to tell him everything. Not now . . . and maybe not ever. Just enough so he understands how much you love him. How you wanted him . . . and how his presence eventually brought you back to God."

The shivering eased off and Ashley leaned closer and slipped her arms around Landon's neck. "Thank you." She whispered the words near his face. "I needed to hear that."

"It's the truth." He brushed his cheek

against hers and then he kissed her.

There would never be a time when she wouldn't feel butterflies in her stomach when Landon kissed her. She still couldn't believe he was hers.

But the butterflies quickly disappeared as she remembered one more troubling thing. She didn't want to say it, but they'd come this far in the discussion. "Also . . . I guess I can't believe he could even use the word *father* to describe a stranger he doesn't know." She slid back a little so she could look at him. "That's an insult to you, Landon. It feels completely wrong."

This time Landon smiled. For a while he just looked into her eyes, melting her heart and making her know that everything would be okay. Not just for her and Cole, but for all of them. "Ashley, baby." His smile remained while he spoke. "I will always be Cole's dad. His father. No one could ever change that. No story or truth from his past."

Relief came over Ashley like a warm blanket. What an amazing man Landon was, that he could have a conversation like this and not be threatened in the least. "That's really how you feel?" Her voice broke a bit, but she held back her tears.

"Of course. And like I said it only makes

sense Cole would want to know about his beginning. He's studying heritage in school." Landon leaned closer and kissed her again. "Everyone has a beginning. Sometimes it's a beautiful love story — like your parents'."

She kissed him this time, longer than before. "And sometimes it's a broken story" — another kiss — "that God turns into a masterpiece."

The passion between them never dimmed. It only grew deeper, like the connection they shared. Landon put his hands on either side of her face. "Exactly. And that's what Cole will take away from your talk. Whenever you have it."

Ashley still dreaded the moment. But at least now she didn't feel sick about the possibility. "Thank you. For always making sense of my crazy emotions."

He turned off the TV and stood. She did the same. "Happy to oblige."

"Tell me we're going to bed. To finish this upstairs." She gave him a look that said there was no place she'd rather be.

"Yes." He kissed her once more and took her hand, leading her to the stairs. "Especially now that we're done talking."

Cole finished his homework sometime after

144

eleven o'clock, but his mind was too busy to fall asleep. He couldn't stop thinking about his papa's story. What would the other three weeks tell him about their history? His heritage?

One thing he kept coming back to was his papa's mention of the Vietnam vet. As far back as Cole could remember, he'd been fascinated by war and the sacrifice of those who served.

In history class Cole had already studied Vietnam, how soldiers had come back from war to people spitting at them and disrespecting them. Cole knew that if he had been alive back then he would've made sure each soldier got a proper thank-you. That's something his papa always said. People deserved a proper thank-you for a job well done.

The soldiers that went to Vietnam were only boys, hardly older than Cole. He wondered what the man had to do with his papa's story. He already knew his papa didn't serve in Vietnam. So how did they know each other?

And what if Cole could find the guy? How cool would it be if his ancillary character was a vet? It wouldn't be easy. His papa had already said he'd lost track of the man a long time ago. Still . . . Cole wanted to try.

Cole got ready for bed, climbed under the sheets and stared at the ceiling. The longer he thought about the idea, the more it seemed like the perfect addition to the story. He was required to do interviews with at least one other person besides the main source. It could be someone in his immediate family, so Cole had planned to talk to his mom. After all four hours of interviews were finished.

But if he could find the Vietnam vet, that would really be something.

He would wait until tomorrow and he'd call his papa, just for a few quick questions. What was the name of the man? Where did he live the last time his papa had talked to him? That way he could start looking for him. Cole would do it as a thank-you for his papa. For helping with his project. And deep inside, Cole had the sense he'd find the guy.

Because the feeling stirring inside him was certainty.

As if somehow God was going to make this happen.

Cole could hardly wait.

Wilson Gage settled into his La-Z-Boy recliner and popped the top on another cold one. His sixth of the night. He focused his eyes on the television and tried to remember what he was watching. Something on CNN. A special on the current administration. A checkup. Or a report card.

He couldn't remember.

His eyes blurred and he struggled to make sense of the show. But it was beyond him, like most things these days. Too many head injuries, the doctor told him.

Not from football. He barely even got to play football before he enlisted and was whisked into the war. No, the head injuries were from his days in Nam. Times when he had been slammed to the ground by a grenade or the afternoon when his jeep took a round of friendly fire. The driver had jerked the wheel and the men inside had flown twenty feet in every direction.

Keep fighting, his commander told him. *The headache will go away.* But it never really did. Oh, sure, he could get by at first. His determination to find life again after the war was too great to let a little thing like a headache get him down. But these days he had trouble remembering. Trouble processing.

Which was maybe a good thing. He was eighty now.

It wouldn't be long.

For so many years, he worked on and off

in construction. Trying to forget the things he saw in Vietnam. He didn't believe in God. Not anymore. Not since Scarlett died three years ago. He pictured her beautiful face, her sweet voice. Scarlett had loved Jesus, yes she had. She was in heaven now, no doubt. Hanging with the good crowd. Wilson could've been there one day, too.

But God hadn't answered his prayers.

When Scarlett got sick, Wilson dropped to his knees every morning, every night begging God to heal her. She was all he had after the war. The only reason he wanted to live through Vietnam. The only reason to come home again.

So of course, when God took his Scarlett that was the end of Wilson's faith. Why believe in a God who didn't care? That's what he figured. Better to pop a cold one and drift away in a drunken haze.

But lately Wilson had to admit something.

The years weren't slowing down. He wasn't getting any younger. One of these days not too far off he'd wake up to his final sunrise. The head injury or the drink or the calendar . . . something would catch up with him. And that would be that.

Then what?

Several years ago he'd heard a preacher put it succinctly. A person would die just once. They'd face Jesus — every one of them — and a verdict would follow. Heaven or hell? Everyone would go to one place or the other.

He used to believe he was going to heaven, but now he was sure he was wrong. Nothing but hell for him. He was already living it.

He squinted at the TV and took another swig of beer. Then another. The next one finished it off, and Wilson crumpled the can in his hands. The sound always reminded him of the jungle. People hiding behind trees, climbing into military vehicles. It made him feel afraid and bulletproof all at once.

The way he'd felt back then.

On the television people on the news were arguing. Screaming about taxes or tax hikes. Something. Wilson picked up the remote and turned it off. After half a dozen beers he couldn't concentrate anyway. He leaned his head back against the chair and kicked the footrest out. Maybe he'd sleep here tonight.

He looked around and his eyes fixed on the cross, the small wooden one that hung near the front door. Scarlett had given it to him — back before she passed. Even though he didn't believe anymore, he kept it because it reminded him of her. "You with me, God? Do you see me?" His words slurred and they sounded loud, even to him.

Then Wilson had an idea.

"Okay, God, I believed in You once. So if You're there . . . if You're really there, then can You show me? Give me a sign, God. Please give me a sign."

As soon as the words left his mouth Wilson wondered if they were the wrong kind of thing to say. God might not want him throwing out a request like that. Asking for a sign.

Wilson thought a minute. Maybe if he offered something in return.

"Here's the deal, God. You show me that You're real. That You're here and You care about this old vet . . . and I'll stop drinking. I will, God. Right there on the spot. I promise."

For some reason Wilson waited. As if God might actually talk to a lowly old drunk like him. The house remained silent. Wilson kept his eyes on the cross until they started to feel heavy. Yes, he would sleep here tonight. In the shadow of the cross.

If God wanted to give him a sign, there couldn't be a better place than this.

9

Spotlights shone in every direction as Bailey Flanigan Paul stepped out of the car and onto the red carpet next to her husband, Brandon. Bailey was seven months pregnant, but she didn't look it. Her pale pink sequined chiffon dress did a great job of covering it up. Not that they were trying to hide her baby bump.

But tonight wasn't about that.

Bailey took her place next to her husband for their official arrival at the Hollywood premiere of Brandon's newest movie, *The Chance.*

Dayne Matthews had produced the film, so once Bailey and Brandon could make their way inside Grauman's Chinese Theatre they would connect with Dayne and his wife, Katy.

"How's our little girl? Kicking much?" Brandon leaned in and whispered even as he smiled and waved for hundreds of cameras on each side of the carpet.

"All the time." Bailey smiled for the cameras even as she kept the conversation going. They had found out that the baby was a girl. Something they had both secretly hoped for.

Brandon put his arm around her shoulders. "You cold?"

"I'm fine." Bailey grinned at him. Her gown wasn't enough to keep her warm. The dress had cap sleeves and felt nearly weightless on. But with Brandon beside her she didn't feel the chill in the night air. He lowered his arm and offered it to her. She took it and whispered to him, "As long as I have you."

He ran his fingers over hers. "You always will."

With practiced experience they made the walk, taking their time, smiling at the sea of photographers. Bailey could handle this. She was past her days of nausea. The second and third trimesters were definitely better than the first.

"You're handling this like a pro." Brandon winked at her as they reached the carpet's halfway point. He talked with his face set in the sort of smile the cameras expected. They'd shared moments like this before, but tonight was special because of the movie's message. And because their baby girl was making the walk down the red carpet with them.

"Not as much a pro as you." Bailey kept smiling, shifting her gaze for the cameras as they walked. She glanced at Brandon, laughing a little. "Which is fine with me."

Just before they reached the grand double doors one of the marketing assistants stopped them in front of *The Chance* backdrop. A dozen hired photographers snapped studio shots as they posed.

"Go ahead," the marketing director shouted. "Interact. Look natural."

"This is the fun part." Brandon spoke softly, his flirty voice for Bailey alone. He turned and kissed her. Then he whispered close to her face, "You're gorgeous. If I haven't told you." He kissed her again to the sound of the clicking cameras. "I still can't believe God gave me you."

"Okay!" The bark of the marketing director interrupted the moment. "Move on, please."

Brandon laughed again. "Never changes." He took Bailey's hand and they walked inside the theater lobby.

"Hey, you lovebirds!" Dayne Matthews walked up and hugged Brandon. Their producer friend looked beyond thrilled about something. "So . . . good news! We've added another three hundred screens. That puts us equal to any movie this year."

"Really?" Brandon looked from Dayne to Bailey. "We prayed for that."

"We did." She loved moments like this, when God answered prayers even in this crazy world of moviemaking.

Katy walked up and Dayne put his arm around her. "We prayed, too . . . that nothing would hold the film back, and that people would be touched."

"Reporters want to talk to you both." Dayne nodded toward the front of the lobby. "Shouldn't take long."

The four of them walked toward the interview area, and as they passed through the crowd Bailey took it all in. She was glad she and Brandon spent barely any time in LA now. Most auditions for faith-based films were in Atlanta or Nashville, and when Brandon needed to meet with studio executives in California, he could do so by Skype.

But tonight's celebration was important and appreciated. Bailey was glad to be here in person, because they had all worked hard to create this movie. In the interview area, one of the reporters asked them about their other life, the one in Bloomington.

"We promised each other we'd make

Indiana our home," Brandon answered first. "We've kept that promise . . . and it's working well for us."

Bailey explained that she and Brandon had developed nearly an entire city block of downtown Bloomington, an area they called the Arts Center. They had created a beautiful theater as part of their B&B Productions.

Brandon shared that half the block contained discounted office space for local missions and ministries. "And our new coffee shop and café are constantly busy." He sounded passionate as he finished answering the question. "We committed this dream to God when we married. And now it's coming true."

The reporter seemed satisfied — though Bailey wondered how much of Brandon's answer she would use. The two of them could've talked for hours about their life in Bloomington. Not only the Arts Center, but their personal lives in Indiana. The blessing that she and Brandon could raise their little girl around family, and still see her brothers' football, baseball and basketball games.

Life was rich, indeed.

Even moments like this when Bloomington felt very far away.

When the interview was over, Bailey and Brandon walked with Dayne and Katy into the theater and they took their seats. Brandon held Bailey's hand and she savored the feel of his fingers against hers. Tonight was important. A way of acknowledging a job well done.

When the time came, Dayne stood and walked to the front. He wore a fitted navy suit, looking the part of Hollywood royalty.

Brandon leaned close to her. "I smile every time I think of his story."

"Me, too." Bailey watched Dayne as he found the wireless mic. He tapped it a few times, but it wasn't working. Bailey kept her voice low. "He's such a different person now."

A smile lifted Brandon's lips. "I know."

Of course, Dayne's transformation had been years ago. Today many people might not know or recall his early wild years of fame. But his true fans would always remember his story. How Dayne had been the oldest son of John and Elizabeth Baxter, given up at birth and raised by adoptive parents — missionaries overseas. John and Elizabeth never knew their son's adoptive parents had died in a plane crash when he was just eighteen years old. Or that he had grown up to be Dayne Matthews, the actor. They never imagined Dayne would find them days before Elizabeth died of cancer.

But he did.

The story could've made its own amazing movie. Dayne had lived dangerously back then, known for his good looks and wild behavior.

But finding the Baxters had changed everything for Dayne. He had told Bailey and Brandon that though he would always love his adoptive parents, he considered himself a Baxter. He always would.

At the front of the theater, a couple of tech guys finally got the mic to work. "There we go." Dayne faced the audience. "Welcome, everyone." He smiled at the tech duo. "I think we all know who the real stars are. We're nowhere without tech support."

A chorus of easy laughter filled the theater. Bailey looked around and chills ran down her arms. Every seat was taken, and an electricity filled the air. She wondered if everyone felt the same way she did. Like something very special was about to happen with this film. The story might not only entertain those who saw the movie, it might actually change culture for the better. Bring into focus what was really important.

Forgiveness.   Redemption.   Second chances.

Dayne waited until the crowd quieted. "I want to thank a number of people who helped make *The Chance* the amazing movie you're about to see." He smiled, obviously comfortable in front of the packed house. "But I decided to do it this way instead."

He paused and looked slowly at the hundreds of faces in front of him. "If you were an assistant, a grip, someone who carried coffee or moved cords or served us in any way during the making of this movie, would you please stand."

Gradually a couple dozen surprised attendees rose to their feet. The applause started loud and stayed that way. No one looked more appreciative than Dayne. "You, my friends, are the most important people here."

"Love this." Brandon squeezed Bailey's hand and whispered, "Class act."

Dayne asked those standing to remain that way. Then he asked others to join them. Those involved in directing, in producing, the actors, the set designers, family members and friends who lent weeks of support, and so on until everyone was standing. Dayne added his applause to the mix, and when everyone had returned to their seats he squared his shoulders to the crowd again, as if he were taking in the moment. "I thank God for each of you. Really." His smile

158

softened. "Let's pray."

Dayne asked God to bless the night, and even more to bless the film. "Let it touch this generation with truth. Let it remind us that whatever the division, with God there can be healing. Racial healing. Relational healing. Marital healing. Even a healing with God. In Jesus' name we pray. Amen."

Brandon leaned close to Bailey and whispered, "He makes me want to be a producer."

"You'd be fantastic." Bailey brushed her face against his. "I love this, by the way. Being here. It's so different from other movies."

The next two hours flew by and Bailey found herself laughing at some parts and wiping tears at others. The entire theater seemed moved.

When the film ended, the crowd erupted with applause, and as the theater emptied into a reception in the lobby, Bailey and Brandon celebrated with full hearts. The feeling that something special was about to happen with the movie remained with her on their flight back to Indiana.

When the plane landed, Bailey leaned her head on Brandon's shoulder. Her doctor had told her she could fly this late in her pregnancy because she was healthy. But still she was tired. She yawned. "I'm ready to be home."

"Me, too." He put his hand on her knee. "You need your rest. Lots going on. Besides, I miss our regular life."

She smiled at him. He knew her so well. "Exactly."

In two days they'd hold auditions and callbacks for their next community theater show. Rehearsals would start in two weeks, and a few days after that they would join Bailey's family and most of the Baxters for the first big barbecue of the season. The party would be crowded — filled with family and friends — just the way it always was with the Baxters.

Bailey smiled. She loved how anyone could show up at one of those summer dinners.

She could hardly wait.

Bailey was just beginning to unpack when Andi Ellison called. A quick smile and Bailey answered it on the second ring. "Andi!" The two of them were still best friends. They talked at least every few weeks, but it had been more than a month this time.

"Hi there." Andi sounded muffled. Like she wasn't in a good service area. "How was the premiere?"

"This one's going to change lives. I really believe that." Bailey sat down on the edge of the bed. "We found out what we're having!" Her voice brimmed with excitement.

"What? Tell me! I'm dying over here!" Andi's voice sounded clearer now. "Wait! Let me guess."

"Okay . . ." Bailey paused. "Boy or girl?"

Andi hesitated. "Okay . . . let's see. Well, every time I pray for you I feel like I'm praying for a girl. That's my guess."

"You're right!"

"I am!" Andi squealed. "Bailey! You're having a little girl." She sounded like she was half crying, half laughing. "That's the best news ever!"

"Thanks." Bailey loved the way her friend celebrated her. Never mind that Andi's life hadn't always gone how she had planned. Andi sounded nothing but thrilled for Bailey. She stood and returned to the suitcases. There had to be three loads of laundry between her things and Brandon's. "I wish you were here. We haven't had coffee in forever."

"We haven't. I hate that about this job."

Ever since Andi had started her job, Bailey hadn't seen her once. Andi was doing great work. But she missed her friend. There was

161

a time when every visit Bailey made to Los Angeles, she would get together with Andi.

Now it had been six months since they'd seen each other.

Bailey wasn't sure she should ask the next question. But it was on her heart, and she and Andi didn't keep anything from each other. "Have . . . you heard from Cody?"

The silence on the other end told Bailey she might've made a mistake. But when Andi finally responded, there was no anger in her voice. Just the familiar hurt. The way she always sounded when she talked about Cody Coleman. "Not for a long time. Months." She sounded broken by the fact. "Then the other night he called."

The baby kicked a few times and Bailey felt the muscles in her belly tighten. She made her way to the bed and sat down again. "What did he say?"

Andi sighed. "I didn't answer the phone."

"What?" Bailey felt her stomach relax again. The occasional tightenings were nothing to worry about. That's what her doctor had said at their last visit. She searched for the right words for her friend. "Andi . . . you need to take his call." She hesitated. "What if he's changed? Maybe he has something really important to tell you."

Again Andi made no response. Bailey

wondered if they'd been disconnected. "Andi?"

"I'm here. I just . . . I don't know what to do. He's broken my heart so many times." She hesitated. "And . . . well, there's this other guy. His name's Caleb."

"Caleb? I haven't heard about him." Bailey felt a twinge of uneasiness. She couldn't imagine Andi and Cody not getting back together. Now or somewhere down the road.

Andi took a quick breath. "He works with me. He's from Amsterdam." Her sigh filled the phone line. "I mean, I can't see moving to Europe. But what if *he's* the guy?"

Bailey was slow with her response. She was glad her friend trusted her with this new information. "So . . . he's moving back to Amsterdam?"

"In a year."

"Got it." Bailey tried to gather her thoughts. "Okay, well . . . I guess I still see you and Cody together. Crazy as that might feel."

Andi was quiet.

Bailey had committed herself, so she continued. "I'm just saying . . . I don't know what's gotten into Cody the last few years. I really don't. But I'll never forget sitting across from him years ago, the last time we

163

walked around Lake Monroe." Bailey could see him still. The depth of emotion in his eyes. "When he told me he was in love with you, I knew something immediately."

They'd been over this. But Andi must've wanted to hear it again. "What did you know?"

Bailey smiled. At least Andi was listening. "I knew he'd never been more in love in all his life." She hesitated. "Because never in all the years when Cody and I were friends did he ever look at me that way."

Andi seemed to let that sink in. "Really?"

"Yes. With me . . . Cody was in love with an idea. An ideal. He thought I was this perfect girl and that if we dated, he could erase his past and be this perfect guy." Bailey understood this now. The complicated history between Cody Coleman and her. "But he was wrong about all of it. I wasn't perfect. And he couldn't be perfect, either." She paused. "He must've known that deep down. Because he never felt good about himself around me. Only God could give him the sort of fresh start he needed during those years. Not me."

"Wow." Andi seemed encouraged. "I've never heard you say it like that before."

"I've had time to give it some thought." Bailey stood again. With all her heart she believed Cody was still in love with Andi. Not that Bailey had talked to Cody. But because she knew him that well. "Anyway . . . maybe answer his call next time." Her voice was kind. Not pushy. "Okay?"

"Maybe." Andi's voice was soft. "Hey, I need to run. The food truck's here with more water bottles. It's so weird how everything everywhere is flooded, but one of the greatest needs for people is water. Water to drink, water to shower in. Water to wash their clothes."

Bailey hadn't thought about that. "Where are you now?"

"In the . . ." The connection grew fuzzy and Andi's voice cut out. "I'm still working the flood in the Gulf States. The storms keep coming. It's so bad here, Bailey."

"That's awful." The pictures on the news looked devastating. "Are there people living in tents?"

"So many." Andi hesitated. "Every shelter is full. And we're short on funds. Praying for people to help us out. The news hasn't shown anywhere near how bad it is."

Her statement wasn't meant to be a request for money. Bailey knew Andi better than that. But it was the first time she'd considered donating to the organization. Bailey and Brandon already gave to Compassion International and several ministries in their own community and internationally.

But what about the organization Andi worked for?

The group was always first on the ground when disaster struck. Bailey tucked the thought away. They wrapped up the call and Bailey knew she had to talk to Brandon about helping with Andi's relief efforts.

Bailey couldn't make Andi give Cody Coleman another chance. Couldn't make her friend's life easier or make the hurt go away. Couldn't help her know what to do with this Caleb guy.

But Bailey and Brandon could at least do this. And she could pray for Andi. That despite every kind of hurt she felt she would do something that might seem impossible.

Respond the next time Cody reached out.

10

School would be out for the summer soon, and Cody had a decision to make. He had found a private boarding school on a ranch in Montana for teens with emotional disorders. Anxiety issues, abandonment. Struggles with anger and abuse. Maybe not PTSD exactly. But still Cody could relate.

A few days ago, he sent an email to the school's headmaster, explaining his credentials and asking if they had a teaching and coaching position open. This morning he heard back from the man. His words had played in Cody's mind all day.

Cody walked through the door of his townhome just as Riley rushed up to him, tail wagging. "Hey, boy." He stooped down and patted the dog's furry head. "You missed me? Is that what you say?"

Riley stayed with him as he moved into the kitchen and started the coffeemaker. Then, like he'd done a dozen times since he'd printed the email, Cody pulled the folded piece of paper from his pocket and read it one more time.

Dear Mr. Coleman,
Yes, I've heard of you. I read about your story in *Sports Illustrated* a few years back. I was impressed, but more with your character. We do have a position open and I would love to meet with you at your soonest convenience to discuss whether this might be a fit for you.

The man had included his personal cell phone at the bottom of the message. Cody folded up the paper again and slipped it back into his pocket. He took a chair at his kitchen table and stared at the wall, at a Bible verse that had hung there since he moved in.

"For I know the plans I have for you," declares the Lord, "plans to prosper you and not to harm you." — Jeremiah 29:11

Cody believed God had good plans for him. The question was whether moving to Montana was part of those plans.

"It would force me to forget about Andi." He looked down at Riley. "Right, boy?"

The chair was hard-backed and not very

168

comfortable. Part of a set he'd picked up at a garage sale for twenty bucks. He leaned back and barely noticed the wooden spindles digging into his shoulders. They didn't matter. Cody was too consumed with the decision in front of him.

If only God would give him a sign, let him know which way to go. Stay at Oaks Christian and keep seeing Andi's memory everywhere he looked. Or start a new life, one free of her haunting his every hour.

God, just tell me what You want me to do. I'll follow Your lead. The prayer came from the depths of his soul, the way it had too many times to count today. Cody waited. Just in case the Lord might have an answer this time. But there was only the sound of the coffeemaker signaling the end of its brew cycle.

He poured himself a cup and walked to the living room, where he dropped on the sofa. Maybe a little TV would help clear his mind. Riley jumped up beside him and settled in against his leg.

"I can count on you, Riley. Wherever we go from here, we go together."

Riley looked at him, eyes faithful, devoted.

"That's right. Good boy, Riley." Cody flipped on the television to Fox News and was about to turn the channel when he caught the headline across the screen. LOU-ISIANA FLOODS DEVASTATE REGION AGAIN. Cody leaned forward in his seat and lowered the remote. Again? How had he missed this?

The anchorwoman was saying something about thousands of people being displaced, and floodwaters that had only partially receded. More storms were possible in the next few days.

Poor people, Cody thought. He couldn't imagine losing a house to flooding. The network cut away to scenes of devastation. Homes sitting in the middle of the road after having been carried off their foundations. Others reduced to piles of ruined lumber and rubbish. The next cut was a tent shelter.

"Volunteers and relief workers from all over the country have come to serve the victims of this second year of flooding." The reporter stepped aside to reveal a number of helpers taking bags and boxes of food from a truck and handing them to residents of what was obviously a temporary shelter.

At that moment, a girl with long blond hair came from the tent and easily pulled herself up onto the bed of the truck. Cody stood and stared at the screen. The girl had her back to the camera, but her graceful movements, the lithe way about her . . . it

170

almost had to be her.

Cody watched the girl slide down from the truck, brush her hands on her jeans, and come up to the reporter. Cody was right. He set down his coffee and took a few steps closer to the TV. The girl was Andi Ellison. He kept walking until he was close enough to touch the screen.

"Andi . . ." He whispered her name. As if she could see him through the glass, as if she could hear him. He reached out and touched the frame of the television, mesmerized by her face, her beautiful eyes. "I'm here."

The reporter motioned to her. "We have here one of the relief workers, Andi Ellison." The woman looked at Andi. "How long before people will be back in their homes?"

Andi tossed her hair over her shoulder. Her cheek was smudged with mud and her shirt was dirty. Like she'd been working for days on end. "Many of these people will never be back. We're still finding houses that were a complete loss." The depth and care in her blue eyes was deep and soulful. Never mind how dirty she looked. Andi took his breath all the same. *Most beautiful girl I've ever seen.* Cody wondered if he was the only one who thought so. "They'll need to find transitional housing before any fundin becomes available and they can rebuild. It'll be a process."

The reporter looked concerned. "So many people affected." She shook her head. "And what's the greatest need at this time? How can people help?"

"Well." Andi looked over her shoulder at the truck. "People can donate money or food to the few organizations down here making a difference." She looked at the reporter again. "And one of the things we're definitely short of are new socks."

"New socks . . . just regular socks?" The reporter seemed surprised.

"Yes." Andi looked anxious to get back to work. "In a flood zone, socks are always wet. These people would feel a lot better just knowing their feet could be dry for the night. It's the first thing people need after food and water."

"Thanks, Andi." The reporter looked into the camera. "You heard it here, folks. They need our help . . . if you can donate money or food, please do so. And if you can make it down to one of the temporary tent shelters, bring a few pairs of socks."

A quick thank-you to Andi, and the network cut back to the anchorwoman in the studio. And like that, the girl Cody had been missing for so long was gone. Again.

172

Cody hurried to the sofa and grabbed the remote. He hit the rewind button and took the program back to the point where Andi exited the tent and began helping in the truck. He played the segment again, and then a third time. Just before the reporter asked Andi the last question, Cody hit the pause button.

For a few seconds, Cody stared at her. Just took in the sight of her like a dying man in the desert getting his first drink of water after far too long. He had missed her so much. More than he had admitted to himself. The way her hair blew in the wind outside the tent, and the shine in her blue eyes.

His mother was right. He couldn't let her go. Couldn't up and move to Montana without at least trying to make things right between them. Whatever it took. Cody kept the TV there, frozen on her face. And as he did, a realization hit him.

Hadn't he just asked God for a sign? For an answer to what he should do next . . . how he should proceed? Minutes later he turned on the television only to see Andi Ellison interviewed?

A warm certainty started in his heart and radiated through his body. Of course this was a sign. It had to be. Not only that, bu now he knew where Andi was working. She'd been tending to victims of the latest Louisiana flood.

Surely he could find her now.

His heart began to beat harder than before, until after a minute it was pounding in his chest. As if it were telling the rest of his body to make a plan, kick things into action. Make a phone call. Whatever he had to do to reach her.

Cody pulled his cell phone from his pocket and called the principal at Oaks Christian. Five minutes later he had the time off. He'd have to finish working with his players, but he could leave next week. Once he got to Louisiana, he could spend the next four days looking for her. Day and night if that's what it took.

Cody rewound the segment again and this time he let her voice melt into him, deep into the places of his soul that had so desperately thought about her and cared for her and missed her.

Finally he clicked the television off and rushed to find his laptop. Ten minutes later he had a round trip to Louisiana. As soon as he clicked the purchase button, his racing heart slowed some. Another call to his mom to arrange for Riley to be dropped off he morning of his flight and suddenly everything was in place.

He was going to find Andi.

With every minute since he'd seen her on the screen, Cody had felt an increasing certainty. He missed Andi even more than he thought. She was the other half of his heart, and he could only pray God would open doors in the days ahead. That He would lead Cody to find her, and once he did, Andi might want him back again.

One more time.

Because Cody knew something he hadn't known before seeing Andi on TV. He not only missed her. Cody still loved her. He loved her with all his heart and he couldn't imagine letting her go ever again. Not now that he'd seen her.

He could only hope that somehow, some way, Andi would forgive him. And that if Cody found her, she would remember something that Cody hoped had been true for years now.

The hope that just maybe she still loved him, too.

11

A week passed in the blink of an eye and suddenly Thursday was here again. Like she'd promised, Elaine didn't stay. Once again she went to her friend's house to work on her quilt. John saw now that her being gone was the best choice for all of them. He could give himself fully to the story — the way he had last week — and not worry how Elaine might feel about it.

John had decided to hold on to the copies of the photos until he was completely finished with the interviews. That way he could refer to them while he told the story. Last week he had shown Cole that first photo, the one from the dance. And also a picture Bill had taken of the two of them on their bench near the science building. Another one showed John and Elizabeth sitting on their bicycles after a ride around Ann Arbor's downtown area.

There would be more today.

He met Cole and Ashley at the door and this time he didn't struggle with where to begin. The next part of their story was as breathtaking as it was beautiful. The hard part of the story would come over the last two weeks. But even then, the pain of the past was part of the reason John and Elizabeth's story was so amazing. God had taken the broken pieces of those long ago yesterdays and made them into a foundation for the entire Baxter family.

A foundation built on faith in God and love for each other.

When they were all seated, John held up a photograph. "This is the Wesley house. Where I lived. It's where your grandma made me dinner that first night."

Already Cole seemed to understand where the story was going. "Did you go back to the house alone again after that?"

"We didn't. Not right away. I couldn't put her in a compromising situation." John almost winced as he said the words. The compromising would come later. First it was time to share some of the happiest days of his life. He titled this next part something that made Cole and Ashley smile.

Falling in Love.

Like before, as he began to answer Cole's questions he felt himself drawn back in time. Until it was like those days were happening all over again.

In the most beautiful way.

They needed a plan to see each other. John knew he couldn't bring her back to his house. The outcome would be disastrous. Stopping had been nearly impossible last time. If they began kissing again, John wasn't sure he'd find the self-control.

Two days later they met at their campus bench and made a plan. Elizabeth would tell her parents she needed all day Saturday to study with Betsy at the library. She would go to Betsy's house, and Betsy would drive her to John's.

Then John would whisk her away to Independence Lake Park, a scenic spot ten miles from campus. They could spend the day together and her parents would never know. John looked for her reaction as they talked about the idea.

"I don't know." Elizabeth faced him. Her hair was in a ponytail again and she looked young and afraid. "Meeting on campus is okay. I have to be here anyway, you know? And you might just be a friend." She looked down and then lifted her eyes to him. "Leaving here . . . going somewhere like that, just the two of us . . . I could never explain that."

She paused. "If they find out . . ."

"They won't." John didn't want to push. He rested his arm on the bench and watched her. "We don't have to go. I don't want you to worry."

She slid closer to him, her eyes holding his. "You won't let us get in trouble, right? My parents can never know."

John thought about that. One day her parents would have to know, because John couldn't imagine losing Elizabeth. And if they stayed together, then he'd have to face her parents one day. Even if they hated him and . . . He refused to finish the thought.

Elizabeth was waiting for his answer, looking to him for strength and certainty. He pushed his hesitancy down deep within him. "Never. I'll protect you from them and anything else, Elizabeth. While you're with me you'll be safe. Always." It was a response he would later regret. One he would've done anything to make true.

He wanted with everything in him never to let her down.

In the end they decided to take the Saturday adventure. He could tell Elizabeth was nervous because while he drove scenic Whitmore Lake Road north to the park, she fell completely silent. John parked the car and looked at her. "It'll be okay."

Elizabeth nodded, but didn't say a word. John took the picnic basket and blanket from the trunk and came around to help her out. He had the entire day planned, but first he needed her to trust him. He managed to carry the basket and blanket and still reach for her hand. Her fingers felt cold against his touch so he found a spot in the sun on the sandy shore.

Once he had spread out the blanket he turned to her. "Come here."

For the first time since they left Ann Arbor, Elizabeth smiled. Not the smile from the dance or the way she'd looked when they kissed at his house. But a smile racked with anxiety.

Even so she did as he asked. She wrapped her arms around his waist and pressed her head against his chest. "I'm so cold."

"You're scared."

"Yes." She lifted her eyes to his. "I love my parents, John. I just wish . . . I wish I could . . ."

He waited, but she didn't seem to know what to say, how to finish her thought. "You wish you could tell them about me?"

Her eyes clouded with frustration. "Yes. Exactly. They're nice people."

John had a dozen reasons why they weren't nice people. Anyone who would keep their

180

daughter in a prison of threats and unreasonable rules and blame their behavior on God didn't deserve a girl like Elizabeth. But he kept his thoughts to himself.

"You aren't saying anything." She blinked a few times. "They're not terrible. I mean it."

"I'll meet them one day." He stepped back and forced a lighter mood. He did one of his bows, the same kind he'd done when he taught her the twist. Then like a proper Englishman, he pretended to remove his top hat and dip it, grand gesture and all. " 'Hello, fine madam and sir,' I'll tell them. 'If it meets your approval, I'd like to court your daughter.' " He winked.

Her ripple of laughter set the day's course in a better direction.

" 'What's that you say? How long would I expect to court her?' " John raised his hands and spun in a slow circle. " 'Fine madam and sir, for a very long time indeed. Till the moon and sun cease to shine . . . till the oceans become dry land.' " He came to her again and took her face in his hands. His words mixed with the slight breeze off the lake. " 'Until I take my last breath.' "

"John . . ." Her voice sounded like she had forgotten where they were or why she was afraid.

"I'll tell them, Elizabeth." His laughter faded. All that mattered was each other, and this single moment between them. "Just give me a chance."

Then, like the evening in his kitchen, he kissed her. Here, there was no music. Only the wind in the trees that surrounded the park. To John, the sound might as well have been a symphony. The rest of the day was like something from a movie. They left the blanket and picnic basket and rented a canoe. Together they paddled around the shore of Independence Lake, laughing and talking and pretending the world was on their side. On the far shore, away from the people gathered along the beach, Elizabeth spotted a baby bear. He was standing on his hind legs, leaning against a pine tree, batting his oversized paws at something up the tree trunk.

Every sound, every image, every second of their time was like the greatest gift. The reality waiting back home seemed to fall away, and for that one Saturday, Elizabeth was completely his. After the canoe ride, they hiked the trails that wove their way around the outer edges of the lake, and at one point they stopped and sat on a bench, out of sight from anyone.

It felt like they were the only people in the world.

"Tell me your dreams, Elizabeth." John couldn't get enough of her. Sure, he wanted to kiss her. He wanted more than that, if he were honest. But beyond that he wanted to know her, to meld his heart with hers until it was impossible to know where one ended and the other began.

She tilted her face to the vast blue sky and breathed in the fresh air. "I don't think we have enough time."

John smiled at her. "Try me."

Her eyes shone with a freedom she had clearly not felt earlier. "Okay . . . It's a long list." A raw, youthful anticipation lit her expression and she stood — the empty trail her stage. "I want to play the piano and sing. Not just everyday sort of singing, but in a room with people who pay to watch. I'd like to make a record. And I want to act, too. Shakespeare and musical theater. Or maybe star in a movie."

He raised his brow. "Ambitious. I love it."

"That's not all." She giggled. "I want to be a lawyer, and lock up the bad guys so no one has to worry about violent people who get out of prison too soon."

"That's important." John slid to the edge

of the bench, mesmerized by her. "What else?"

"Modeling. I'd love to be a model. With the prettiest dresses in all the land. And I'd like to be a teacher and a painter. Oh, and a doctor. So I can help people." She grinned at him. "A doctor like you're going to be, John. We can work at the same hospital."

"We will. Absolutely." He hung on her every word. There was no other girl like her.

She spread her arms out as far as she could reach. "And I want to have a big family. A house full of kids with laughter and love and music. Everyone will see me with all these children and they'll say, 'Why, there goes Elizabeth. She's the best mother to those kids.' "

John couldn't stop smiling. He was dizzy from her monologue. He stood and moved toward her. This time when he put his arm around her waist and pulled her close the motion felt as natural as breathing. He wanted to tell her they wouldn't say, *There goes Elizabeth.* They'd say, *There goes Elizabeth Baxter.* But it was too soon. He couldn't let his heart get ahead of him.

Couldn't risk her running scared.

Instead he held her loosely and together they swayed to the gentle sound of the lake water lapping against the shore. "I can dance with you anywhere." He allowed his face to brush against hers. "Know why?"

"Why?" Her voice was like the wind around them. Soft and surreal, like maybe she wasn't here and John wasn't dancing in her arms on a dirt path.

"Because . . . you're the music, Elizabeth." He eased back, his eyes finding hers again. "I love you." His words came without permission. As if his heart was speaking for him. "I'm in love with you."

Her smile started slowly and then filled her face, her eyes. "I thought I was crazy. We only met a few weeks ago."

John laughed. "We're both crazy." He put his hand against her cheek. "You feel it, too, don't you?"

For a long while she only looked at him, as if she didn't want to interrupt the beautiful moment with words. Finally she breathed in, her eyes holding his. "Yes, I feel it. I love you, too, John."

He looked down to make sure his feet were still on the ground. He'd never been so happy in all his life. "We'll figure this out." He kissed her once and then again until his passion for her became more than he could bear. "Okay." He steadied his breathing. A step back and then another. "Let's keep walking."

They were both breathless. Elizabeth laughed and played with her ponytail. She placed her hand in his as they started on the path. A few steps and she stopped, her eyes bright. "I forgot one thing."

"One thing?"

"That I want to be someday." She giggled. "I want to be a firefighter."

He loved her. Everything about her. "You'd be the first one, then."

"Wait." She held up her finger, laughing harder now. As if she was giddy from all the feelings. "Not all the time. Just for a day. So I can see what it's like to wear that heavy uniform and have the power to put out fires."

"You're wonderful." He put his arm around her shoulders and they kept their pace slow, their steps in time with each other. Like another kind of dance. He glanced at her. "A firefighter?"

"Since I'm giving you the list," her eyes sparkled up at him, "I don't want to leave anything off."

"I see that." He wanted to kiss her again, but he didn't dare. His resistance was only so strong.

They returned to the blanket John had spread out earlier and finished their afternoon with a picnic near the edge of the lake.

All around them families sat at wooden tables and couples cozied up on blankets, lost in each other. Little kids laughed and ran across the grass, and all of it seemed like a painting. Like the lot of them were only here to provide the perfect backdrop for John and Elizabeth.

On the way home, the plan was that he'd take Elizabeth back to Betsy's. Elizabeth's parents had agreed to her staying the night at Betsy's house as long as she was home early for church.

John looked at his watch. But he already knew they were running an hour early. His house was empty again; the Wesleys had once more taken the family to the lake for the weekend. The possibility took root in John's mind and wouldn't let go. He shifted in the driver's seat, thinking of a way to ask her. She could come over for an hour. Nothing more.

Nothing good can come from it, he told himself. *Don't ask her.* But he could already feel his strength waning. And then, as if she could read his mind, Elizabeth looked at him. "We're early."

He clenched the muscles in his jaw. It wouldn't hurt. Not if they kept the visit short. A quick glance her way. "I was just thinking that."

She nodded and turned her attention to the road ahead of them. They were almost to Ann Arbor.

John could feel the words fighting their way out. Elizabeth wasn't going to take the lead on this. He swallowed. They'd be careful. Everything would be okay. "My family's gone again." He kept his gaze straight ahead. Whatever duplicity might lie in the depth of his eyes, he didn't want her to see it.

"When do they come home?" She stared at her hands. Her tone told him she was battling her feelings, same as he was. The anxiety over needing to be back at Betsy's versus the other need . . . the greater need.

The chance to be together for another hour.

He reached across the seat and took her hand. With the decision between them as heavy as their unspoken desire, he worked his fingers between hers. The feeling stripped away every last ounce of his defenses. The touch of her skin against his, a sort of tipping of the scales so that there really was no decision to make.

"Maybe . . . you could come over? We could watch TV or listen to music." He cast her a weak smile. "Just be together."

Elizabeth was a naïve nineteen. She looked

young because she was young, and John already knew he was her first kiss. Now as she turned her eyes to him, he could see that she wanted to be with him. But more than that, she trusted him. Her shy look told him so. "I'd like that, John." She hesitated. "I'd love it."

They wouldn't cross lines. John would make sure of that. Just to have her alone, without other people around them. The two of them laughing and talking and dreaming without distraction. He thought some more. Okay, so maybe they might kiss. Just once or twice. Nothing too intimate. Yes, this was a good choice. John was sure. Nothing inappropriate would happen. He felt himself relax.

The rest of the ride home he entertained her with stories from his classes. "So we're dissecting a frog. Like I had to do in undergrad." He chuckled. "And all I could think was, *How is this going to help me treat patients in an emergency room?*"

She laughed and he could feel her relax a little. "Not a lot of frogs rushing into the hospital."

"Exactly."

They laughed until they arrived at his home. He held her hand as the two of them walked inside. "I'll get you water." Definitely water. The Wesleys didn't keep beer in the house. Except . . . The week before, one of the Wesleys' friends had joined them for a cookout and brought a six-pack. As far as John knew, four of the beers were still in the fridge.

Not a good idea, he told himself. Besides, Elizabeth was underage. He wouldn't consider giving her something to drink. He poured her a glass of water and then opened the refrigerator. A pop, maybe. Coca-Cola or a root beer. Something to keep him busy while they sat together. So he wouldn't think about how very alone they were.

But when he opened the door, when he looked at the drinks on the second shelf, the only one that looked good was the Budweiser. He hesitated. He could have one. Elizabeth wouldn't mind. Kids at U of M drank, after all. It wasn't like she'd judge him for it. He grabbed a can and walked back to the living room.

Elizabeth was sorting through the music. She looked up when she heard him and glanced at his drink. "Beer?"

"Just one." He handed her the water and raised the can in her direction. His grin kept the situation light. "I'm old enough, you know."

She seemed to process that. "True." She

190

laughed. "I keep forgetting how old you are."

"How old?" He mouthed the words. They both laughed. John pulled the tab on the beer and joined her near the shelf of eight-track albums in the corner of the room. He took a swig. The pungent liquid hit the spot. The day at the lake had made him thirstier than he had known. "What do you want to hear?"

Elizabeth looked through the choices. "Hmmm . . . Here!" She pulled out the Beatles. "You have *Sgt. Pepper's Lonely Hearts Club*? I listened to it the other day at Betsy's house."

"Sure. A few months ago." He chuckled. "Looks like we're playing that one."

They sat next to each other on the sofa and for forty minutes they talked about their peers at school and laughed at some of the university's more difficult professors and listened to the Beatles. John wasn't really paying attention, but one beer led to another, and then a third. He drank on occasion, but not every weekend the way some of his friends did. By the time he started his fourth, John was feeling it.

"Be careful." Elizabeth's laugh faded as he began to drink it. "You'll get sick."

"I'm fine." He smiled at her and set the beer down. The album was over, so he walked back to the corner of the room. "This one's my choice."

The buzz was coming on, warming his core and blurring the edges. He flipped through the music until he found the right one. Exactly what he was looking for. *Billboard Top Pop Hits: 1967.* "This." He held it up and grinned at her. "You'll love it."

"It reminds me of our first night." She tipped her head back as she laughed. "I'll never forget you teaching me how to dance."

Like a magnet to steel, John returned to her. He took his beer, finished it off and set down the empty can. Then he held out his hand. "Miss . . ."

She giggled as she took his fingers. "What are we doing?"

"Practicing." He helped her to her feet. "Ready? This one's a swing." He slid the sofa and chair back to give them room. And like that they were twirling around the living room. Elizabeth was a natural. She could've added dancer to her long list of career possibilities.

The next song had something close to a jitterbug beat, and by the time it was over, they were both out of breath, laughing and ready for a rest. "I'll get you more water."

"John . . ." She steadied herself, brushing a few strands of hair back from her forehead. "I should go. I'm already late."

He leaned on the wall so he wouldn't look wobbly. The beer was hitting him hard. Giving him permission to kiss her the way he couldn't do if he was sober. His smile came easily. "Just a little longer." He went to the kitchen, and this time he poured water for both of them. Enough beer. As he handed her the glass he clinked his against hers. "As soon as we finish the album."

The next song was midtempo. John raised his eyebrows. " 'The Twist.' Come on!" They set their waters down.

"I should go. It's getting dark out." Elizabeth's words didn't match the light in her eyes.

"You'll be fine." He thought about turning on the living room lights, but it was better this way. The night sky giving them their own personal dance hall. Music filled the room and they twisted until John's dizziness sent him straight into her arms. "I twist better *with* you."

"John . . . are you drunk?" She laughed again, but didn't seem worried.

"On you." He worked to keep from slurring his words. The song was ending, which was a good thing. John didn't feel like twisting. The next track was the reason he had picked the album. The first notes and Elizabeth's eyes found his.

" 'Never My Love.' "

The air between them changed. The laughter faded, and in its place came a passion that — if they were honest — had been there all along. Just beneath the surface. John held her so their bodies were slightly closer than before.

When the lyrics began he sang them straight to her, like the music had been written for them alone. "You asked me if there'd come a time . . . when I'd grow tired of you. Never my love."

She began to sing, too.

But then the words died on their lips and they stopped singing. He swayed with her but the dance was no longer the point. John wanted to kiss her more than he wanted his next breath. Here in the living room. The two of them with the lights off and only a dim remaining sliver of daylight filling the air. Just one kiss.

He felt Elizabeth move still closer. The song played on around them, only now John could feel her soft breath. Just one kiss. His lips found hers and the moment lasted longer than he intended.

He caught his breath, but then he was

kissing her again. Another time and another. The buzz made him feel like he was floating. Or maybe it was Elizabeth making him feel that way. He was tilting, swaying. Already he couldn't think straight. If they didn't stop . . .

"Elizabeth . . ." He took a step back. All he wanted was to be in her arms again. "You have to go." A ribbon of fear worked its way through his desire. He needed to get her home. Needed to get a grip.

"Yes." She sounded certain. It was time to go. But she came to him and this time she started the kiss. After a minute, John no longer knew the name of the song playing in the background. There was Elizabeth and only her. She took a moment to breathe and her eyes found his. "But . . . you've had too much to drink. You can't drive."

"I can't?"

"No." She kissed him again. "I'll sleep on the couch. And you can take me in the morning."

His lips were on hers once more. "You . . . you have to call Betsy."

"Okay."

He was swaying again, the drink still having its way with him. "Here." With unsteady steps he led her to the couch.

They both sat down, and as if he was helpless against gravity, he lay down and stretched out. She did the same. "You have to go to your room."

"Yes." He meant to sit up again. He wanted to sit up. But he wanted to kiss her more. Kiss her here, lying beside her. They fit so well on the sofa, his body against hers. "I have to go."

They kissed and after a minute she whispered, breathless. "Go, John."

"Okay." His lips moved over hers. "Goodnight, Elizabeth."

They were the last words he said for a long time. He kissed her and kissed her again and he could feel his hands finding their way to places they never should've gone. Ten minutes passed, then twenty and John felt like it was a dream. The most wonderful breathtaking dream.

The next thing John knew it was morning.

He and Elizabeth were lying tangled up beneath a blanket and she was asleep. She had never called Betsy and he had never stopped. Never gone to his room. And in that instant a realization hit him. One that would haunt him every day for the next year. For the rest of his life.

In a moment of weakness he had ruined everything.

12

Commotion broke out at the front entrance to the tent where Andi was still working. She was passing out water bottles when she heard people shouting and clapping. Happy voices, the type that were rare after a disaster.

Andi followed the sound up the aisle and at the same time she saw an older woman being escorted by a smiling Caleb into the temporary housing. The woman's clothing was ripped and her hair was matted. She was shaking, her eyes wide and frightened.

"Patsy, you're going to be just fine." Caleb pointed toward the adjacent aisle of beds. "Your husband's here. I'm sure of it!"

Her husband! Was this really her? Harry's Patsy? Andi felt her heartbeat double as she watched. Setting the water bottles down, Andi turned and looked in Harry's direction. He was curled on his side, napping. She had to get to him. She took the quickest route to Bed Eleven and watched as Caleb walked the woman closer.

His dark eyes met hers and he grinned. With his free hand he gave her a thumbs-up. "This is her!" He mouthed the words as he drew near.

Harry had become a favorite for both Andi and Caleb. Every day the two of them talked with Harry about Patsy and where she might be and how she must be missing him. Andi had prayed, but Caleb insisted the woman couldn't be alive. It had been nearly two weeks since Harry was brought to the tent.

But now there was no doubt. Caleb and Patsy reached Bed Eleven and then it happened. The weary woman stopped short and began to cry. Hands over her face, she stood there in the middle of the temporary housing and wept.

Patsy had found Harry.

Andi gently nudged the older man's shoulder. "Harry!" She spoke in a voice soft but urgent. "Harry, wake up!"

His eyes flew open and before he was fully awake, he kicked his legs to the floor and sat. "Did they find her? My Patsy?" They were always the first words out of his mouth after a spell of sleep. *Did they find her?*

"She's here, Harry." Andi pointed to the

woman standing there. "That's her, right?"

Harry drew a soft gasp. "Patsy . . ." He stood as Andi helped him to his feet. Her name was a whisper on his lips.

Then in the most beautiful moment, Patsy lowered her hands from her face and their eyes met.

Harry began to walk to her. "Patsy, you're home!"

She walked a little steadier with Harry in sight. Andi stepped back with Caleb as the older couple fell into each other's arms and embraced, both of them crying.

"It's a miracle." Caleb's arm brushed against Andi's. "They found her at a neighbor's house. I guess the neighbors had already evacuated, and when Patsy and Harry got separated in the floodwaters, she swam across the street."

Andi wasn't sure what she was enjoying more. The reunion playing out before her eyes, or the nearness of Caleb. She tried to concentrate. "Unbelievable."

"I know." Caleb stood a little closer to her. "She stayed on the kitchen counter and drank water from the sink. When the waters receded a bit, she ate canned tuna and apples from their cupboard."

"By herself?" Andi couldn't imagine the desperation the woman must've felt.

"Yes." Caleb looked at her and their eyes held. "After a week, she moved to the wet sofa." He shook his head. "It's extraordinary that she isn't sick."

Extraordinary. Andi smiled. She liked that about Caleb. The way he had such command over the English language. Caleb went on to explain that Patsy had already been evaluated by a doctor. "Their home is gutted. Rushing water must've poured through the place all day. The swim across the street was all that saved her life. That and the food and water."

Andi felt a certainty in her heart. "And the prayers." She grinned. "It *was* a miracle, remember?"

He chuckled. "Touché."

Caleb's faith was different from Andi's. He believed in God, but didn't believe God interacted with His people.

Harry and Patsy were still clinging to each other, hands locked together. Andi couldn't hear them, but she didn't need words to understand the beauty of their reunion. *That's what I want someday, Lord. A man who will look at me like that.*

Just as quickly as the thought landed, Andi let it go. She enjoyed Caleb, and maybe one day they might find a way to date. If he chose to stay in the United States, or if she felt like moving to Amsterdam. But for now she didn't dare dream of having a love like Harry and Patsy's.

She looked at the old couple again. Still . . .

They moved up the aisle and as soon as they reached the workstation, Caleb grinned at her. "By the way . . . you got the assignment you wanted."

For a few seconds Andi hesitated. "Not the animal shelter?"

"Yes!" Caleb hugged her and the two of them swayed together for a bit. Then he pulled back and searched her face. "Me and you . . . the two of us!" His accent was so thick she could barely understand him. But she was getting better at it. "They like us there for work after lunch."

Andi felt joy rush through her. Even though she had no doubt helping people was exactly what she should be doing, there were times when it drained her, left her unsure when her next smile would come. Working with lost animals would give her a break, and a little of the happiness she needed. And working with Caleb . . . well . . .

"This is the best news." She hugged him again, quicker this time.

"God is good, yes?" Caleb reached out

and squeezed her fingers. "That's what you would say."

He held her hand for a minute, which made Andi's head spin a little. Caleb liked her, she had no doubt. And now that they'd be working more closely together, anything was possible.

She studied the man in front of her. He looked more handsome today than yesterday. His voice was balm against her tired soul. In fact, now that she thought about it, her heart hadn't drifted to Cody in a few days.

Caleb was waiting for her response. "Yes, God is good." She felt the sparkle in her eyes. "All the time."

Seventeen dogs and eleven cats were housed at the temporary animal shelter. Andi and Caleb arrived with instructions to check the animals for injuries, give them vitamins to ward off illness, clean their cages, and spend time with them. As much as possible.

Andi looked across the array of crates. "Poor babies." She headed through the door. By the looks on the animals' frightened faces there was no time to waste. "Let's get started."

The room stunk and as soon as the animals heard her voice, half of them started crying or barking. The cats were generally wide-eyed and silent. Terrified, their lives turned upside down.

Caleb loved animals. He and Andi had already talked about that. He stopped at the first crate. A beleaguered poodle cowered at the back of it. "Every day more owners find their way here for picking up their pets." He shook his head. "But many of the people are still stuck in a shelter. Most think their dogs and cats are lost forever."

After taking some food, treats, and vitamins from a table set up near the door, Andi moved to the next cage. She bent down and peered inside. Trembling against the side of the cage was an older black Labrador mix. He had gray around his mouth and chin, and he looked at Andi with the most trusting, concerned eyes. They seemed to say, *My parents are missing. If you could so kindly help me find them . . . or just pet me. Either way.*

She smiled at the dog. "It's okay, boy. We'll find your family." The cage was unlocked, so she opened it and patted the top of the dog's head. "You hurt, boy? How'd you make it through that flood?"

Tentatively the dog stepped out of the cage and nuzzled up against her. He made the slightest whimper. Andi stood and the

Lab came to her. He wouldn't put weight on his left leg. "Oh, no." Andi kept her tone kind, comforting. "We'll help you. It's all right."

She petted the dog some more and gave him vitamins and a good brushing, being especially careful with his left leg. Then she filled out a record of the dog's condition and disposition. *Lord, let his family find him. Let him get help. He's such a sweet dog.* She sighed. This job would be good for her heart, but it wouldn't be easy.

Five cages down the row she felt her heart skip a beat. Inside was a female German shepherd and snuggled up beside her was a single puppy, not more than six weeks old. "Oh, honey . . ." Andi dropped slowly to her knees so she could see the two animals better. "What happened to your other babies?"

Caleb was working the far side of the room. He turned to her and sighed. "That's all the rescuers found. They think the rest were lost."

Andi looked again at the poor mama. The cage was a mess, and so were the dogs. "I'll clean you two up, don't worry." She opened the door and slowly put her hand inside. "I'm not going to hurt you."

The female dog stood and shuffled out of

the cage. Like the Lab from earlier she dropped down to the ground and put her head on Andi's knee. Her eyes lifted to Andi's.

Andi looked intently at the mother dog. "I know." She patted the messy fur on the mama's back. The animal definitely seemed sick. Her nose was warm and she was panting harder than the other dogs. Andi had a bad feeling about her. She kept her tone calm and kind. "I'm sorry, girl."

The dog closed her eyes and lay still.

The puppy wagged his tail and followed his mother. *Just like a child,* Andi thought. *He has no idea how bad things are . . .* The small dog frolicked around a bit and then found his way to his mama for some food. She might be wrong about the pup's age. He might only be five weeks. Not quite old enough to be weaned, but old enough to survive if . . .

She couldn't finish the thought. Again she ran her hand along the mother dog. "Your baby needs a good home. And he'll get one." She found the dog brush and started working it softly over the mama. "I'll make sure."

Andi and Caleb worked all afternoon, seeing to it that every animal had a cleanup and lots of love. Not all of the animals were sick — a few kitties were playful, and many of the dogs, too. They gave Andi plenty of reasons to smile. But by the time they went to leave their supervisor announced sad news.

The mama German shepherd had died. Sometime in the last hour. Death and loss were a part of her job. But the announcement hit Andi harder than she expected. She felt tears on her cheeks before she even realized she was crying. Then an idea hit her. "I'll take the puppy."

"You'll take him?" Caleb looked at her, a slight smile on his face. He brushed his knuckles against her cheek, as if he couldn't take his eyes off her. "That's a beautiful gesture, Andi. From a profoundly beautiful human."

Her heart skipped a beat, the feel of Caleb's touch still working its way through her. *Stay focused,* she told herself. She sniffed a bit and smiled at him. "I promised his mama."

Andi asked, and her supervisor agreed. "He's too little to leave alone in the cage. He'd cry all night."

Me, too, Andi thought. If she had to imagine the puppy here by himself. "I'll keep him in a box at the hotel and bring him here each day until we find his family."

Andi filled out some paperwork stating that she would release the dog as soon as the owner showed up. The supervisor provided Andi with puppy food and a pair of bowls, along with a small collar and a leash.

As they left the shelter, Caleb stopped her halfway to the shuttle. "Andi, you're sweeping me off my feet. Like no other young woman ever has."

Young woman. Andi smiled. No one had talked to her this way. His words were so different. So European. Combined with his accent, his words made Andi dizzy with attraction. More now than ever. "Thank you, Caleb."

He looked from the puppy to Andi. "When we get back to the hotel, might I have the pleasure of taking you and the puppy out to dinner?"

She smiled, basking in the warmth of his expression. "Yes." She patted the little puppy's velvety soft ear. "Indeed, fine sir. The two of us would like that."

Dinner was casual. Pizza at an outdoor restaurant across the street from the hotel. Caleb was kind, a brilliant conversationalist, for sure. Andi caught herself wishing the meal would never end.

"Tell me about Amsterdam." She allowed a little flirt in her tone. "I want to picture you there."

He grinned. "I thought you'd never ask."

The puppy slept in his box while Caleb told her about the Netherlands and his flat on the edge of the city. "It is a refined culture. One that finds great joy in the arts." He let his eyes hold hers. "You'd love it, Andi."

Only after the puppy woke up and started crying did they agree it was time to turn in. Caleb picked up the puppy and handed him to Andi. She cradled him near her chin. "I won't get attached." Andi said the words more to herself than to Caleb. "He's the cutest ever, right?"

"He's a handsome fellow, yes."

When they reached the lobby, Caleb hugged her and this time he ran his hand along the back of her head. When his mouth was near her ear he whispered, "This night was exquisite. Thank you."

Exquisite. Yes. Andi had to remember to inhale. She searched his eyes. "For me, too."

She thanked him for dinner and pulled herself away. Which wasn't easy. Because all she wanted to do was find a pair of chairs and sit with him, get to know him better. Let his voice wash over her and his brown eyes look deeply into hers.

Enough, Andi, she told herself. *He'll go*

back to Amsterdam and you'll never see him again. She tried to gather her senses as she took the elevator up to her room. Caleb had caught more than her attention. He had caught a piece of her heart. She steadied herself once she was inside her room. She took the puppy from his box. "Hey, little guy. I won't let anything happen to you." She held him up and pressed her cheek against his fur. "I promised."

The puppy sniffed her, making a series of whimpers as he did.

"I know." She nuzzled his face. "We'll take a walk tomorrow morning, okay?"

This time the puppy yawned.

Andi found a towel in the bathroom and set it in the box. Poor baby. He had no idea his mother was gone. As long as he had someone to care for him, he was happy. Something about the little puppy made Andi think of the baby boy she gave up for adoption. Little Johnny Baxter, the child being raised by his adoptive parents, Luke and Reagan Baxter.

Andi thought about him often, wondering if in some way the child missed her. But the truth was, he had the most wonderful parents. Andi heard updates from Luke and Reagan a few times a year. Johnny was thriving. Andi had done the right thing. And now

209

this little pup had the right parent, too.

Her.

Once the puppy was asleep in his box, Andi took her journal, sat near the window and began to write. Never mind that Cody was part of her past, or that Andi would break off their second engagement again if she had it to do over. She still felt a little unfaithful after her day with Caleb. She stared at the empty page and then — almost as if her heart was doing the talking — the pen began to move.

Dear Cody . . . His name still felt familiar on her tongue. In her soul. She sighed and continued. *I'll never send you this letter and you'll never see it, but still I have to write it. This job stirs up incredibly deep thoughts, times when I feel like coming back to my hotel and crying for hours. Today it was a dog that died.* She thought about Caleb, how he cared about the loss the same way she did. *Anyway, all of it makes me wish you were here.* She scribbled out that last part and tried again. *All of it makes me remember you. The way we used to be. Back when I could just sit next to you and share with you. Feel your arm around my shoulders.*

You were always the best listener, Cody. Your heart heard the things I said and you would do anything in the world to help me. A

Bible verse or a hug, a walk along the beach. I felt safe with you. You loved with actions. . . . At least you used to. Before the end. She read what she'd written. *What happened? I still don't understand how it all faded away. Maybe I never will.*

Her pen flew across the page, her thoughts clear. *Sometimes I wonder where you are, and whether you think of me. Whether you're mad at me.* She hesitated. *Please don't be mad at me, Cody. You were distracted. Confused. I don't know, but I know this — I couldn't give you my life unless you really wanted me.*

She felt again the full weight of walking away from him. Leaving Cody was one of the hardest things she'd ever done. She closed the journal and stared at the fading light outside. Eventually her heart would heal and she could move on. Maybe to someone like Caleb.

Maybe sooner than she thought.

Andi watched the way the city lights lit up a few stray cumulus clouds. Dozens of puffy white clouds had dotted the heavens the day she broke things off with Cody for the last time.

He had been finishing work at Oaks Christian, always the last one to leave after a football game. This one was on a Saturday afternoon, and Andi had been in the stands. Although Cody didn't know that. He thought she was having lunch with her parents.

In reality she'd already had lunch with them, already told them she was going to break off the second engagement. She had their blessing, because of how he'd treated her. How he'd been so shut down emotionally.

Andi still couldn't believe the roller coaster of emotions they'd both gone through from the time he found her in that coffee shop after their first broken engagement. He had offered to pray for her. That's what had drawn her back into his life.

Back into his heart.

They ended up talking the next day, and hours later they met at the beach and talked until nearly midnight. He took her to dinner the next evening, and like that they were a couple again. During that time her parents had moved back to Bloomington for a year. Cody told her he was taking her to Indiana for a surprise birthday party for her mother.

Instead it turned out to be a surprise engagement party.

With all their family and friends watching, Cody asked her — a second time — to be his wife. What else could she say but yes?

She loved him as much then as she had before.

It should have been a match that outshone the moon and stars. But a few months after they got back to Los Angeles, Cody began to withdraw. She'd be talking to him and he'd stare off at the sky. Like she wasn't even there. Sometimes he'd be on his phone. Too busy to look up or notice her.

After a season of that, Andi had her answer.

So after that Saturday football game, Andi waited till everyone had cleared the bleachers and all the players had gone home. When she saw Cody return to the field carrying his gear bag, she walked down the stairs and met him.

She could still hear their conversation now.

"Andi?" He had stopped and set his gear bag down. "I thought you were at —"

"My parents and I . . . we went to lunch earlier." She removed her sunglasses and looked into his eyes. "I need to talk to you."

Even now when she looked back on the moment she was sure Cody had no idea what was coming. He took her hand and led her to a nearby sideline bench. "What is it? You look serious."

"I am." She blinked back tears and for a long time said nothing. She studied his face, his expression. Memorizing the way it felt to sit beside him, to be his fiancée. One last time. Finally she drew a slow breath. "Cody . . . it isn't working."

His cheeks grew a shade paler and alarm colored his expression. "Andi." He shook his head. "What are you talking about?"

"Us. You and me." She looked at her left hand, at the diamond solitaire on her finger. Then she lifted her eyes to his. "Lately . . . it's like you don't see me, Cody. You're distracted. You look past me." She hesitated. "Sometimes you and I are at dinner and you look out the window, like you're seeing other worlds, other . . . I don't know."

"That isn't true." Cody took her hands. "I love you with everything I am, Andi."

Even then Andi had believed him. "I know you do." She savored the feel of his touch. "But you're not excited. You're not anxious to marry me. At least I don't feel it."

"But I do want to marry you . . . I think about it all the time."

"You're thinking about something else." She paused. "Or someone else."

Cody stood and paced a few feet. He looked shocked. "There's no one else. This is crazy, Andi."

"It's not crazy. My parents see it, too." She waited a few seconds. No way she was going to bring up Bailey. But she couldn't help but think of her. Andi's best friend had been Cody's love for years. Sure, Bailey was happily married. But Andi still wondered if Bailey was the reason her fiancé had been distracted. The doubts in her heart wouldn't go away.

One of Andi's favorite movies was *Scrooge,* the musical. The one with Albert Finney. In that old film Abigail comes to visit Scrooge in his countinghouse. Scrooge barely looks up as Abigail explains that he has replaced her with his love for money. Her words to him replayed in Andi's mind. *And so I release you with a full heart, for the love of him, who you once were.*

That's how Andi had felt that day at the football field with Cody. With her heart breaking in half, Andi worked her hands free from his grasp. She removed her engagement ring and handed it back to Cody. "I can't marry you." She kissed his cheek and stood. "I'm sorry. You're not who you were, Cody. I don't know what happened but . . . I can't marry you."

That day, standing there with the engagement ring tucked in his hand, Cody said only a few words. "I'm sorry, Andi. I love you still. I always will."

Then Cody had done something tha

stayed with Andi to this day. Something that reminded her not to dare answer the phone when he called. Not ever.

He let her walk away. Just watched her go.

Something he never would've done if he cared.

Andi let the memory break apart. She opened her journal again and once more read what she'd written. *Cody, I still pray for you. I still miss you. I still love you. And one of these days I'll stop writing you these letters.*

That's when I'll know that I'm over you.

Her cell phone rang and she answered it on the first ring without checking caller ID. "Hello?"

"Andi, it's Randolph." The director of the disaster relief organization.

She hadn't talked to him since she was hired. "Yes, sir?"

"I wanted to thank you myself." He sounded very satisfied. "Your friends Bailey and Brandon Paul made a significant donation today. I thought you should know." He went on, explaining how the group would now continue serving hundreds of displaced citizens. Even buying Bibles for people homeless and hurting.

When the call was over, Andi sat on the otel floor next to the sleeping puppy. She had barely mentioned the organization's financial struggles to Bailey. And now this. Back in college, Andi had often been jealous of Bailey. Not only of Bailey's ability to live out her faith but mostly of the way Cody looked at her. Cody, the only boy Andi had ever loved.

Andi looked out the window again. The clouds were gone. *If Cody loves Bailey after all this time, would you set him free, Father? Please . . . Bailey's married and that's just . . . it's wrong. Please, God.*

Possibly she was mistaken. But Andi doubted it. The good news was that over time she and Bailey had become more than former roommates. They were real best friends. They talked on the phone all the time and they prayed for each other every day. Besides her parents, no one knew Andi better. She loved Bailey Flanigan Paul with all her heart.

Even if maybe Cody still did, too.

13

Cole had been quiet, and Ashley didn't want to think about the reason. As the days passed, she blamed it on the depth of the story her dad was telling them, the way he and her mom had made small choices that led to actions neither of them ever intended.

But that Wednesday, Cole found her outside working in the rose garden and he confirmed her fears. He stood a few feet away and waited until Ashley looked up. "Mom . . ."

"Yes, Cole?" Ashley wiped the back of her hand across her forehead. Her knees trembled a little, but she hid it. "Everything okay?"

"Yeah, except . . ." He narrowed his eyes, like he'd never been more confused. "Why are you avoiding me?"

"Avoi—" Ashley straightened and set the clippers on a nearby stepladder. She peeled off her gloves. "Cole . . . I'm not avoiding you."

"You are." He wasn't smiling. A long breath came from his lips. "Mom . . . I asked you two weeks ago about your love story . . . the one between you and my dad. And every time I bring it up, you change the subject."

Ashley's mind raced. What could she say? Never mind her talk with Landon. Never in her wildest imagination did she think Cole would want to know about her time in Paris. "Honey." *Think, Ashley . . . God, give me the words.* She coughed a few times.

Cole waited for a long beat, his expression marked by hurt. "Tell me, Mom. At least tell me why you won't talk about it."

"I will talk about it. I promise." It was the only thing she could think to say. "Let's wait until after you finish the project with Papa."

Again Cole hesitated. He sighed, and the sound was heavier than bricks. "Yes, ma'am. If that's the way you want it." He wasn't being rude. But clearly he was upset. "It doesn't seem like it would take that long. You could tell me now. Right here."

"I realize that, Cole. But there's an order to things in life." Ashley worked to keep her voice even. "In this case, I believe it's best to wait." She searched his eyes. "You have

219

to trust me."

This time something must have clicked with him, because his expression softened. "Okay." He took a moment, as if he needed to gather himself. Then he managed a slight smile. "Love you, Mom."

"Love you, Cole." She watched him turn around and head back to the house. *How can I tell him? What will he think of me when he knows the truth?* His words rang again in her heart. *Love you, Mom.* What scared her most was simply this:

After he knew the story of his mother and father, he might say those words a lot less often.

Or maybe not at all.

The sunset over downtown Bloomington stretched deep pinks and pale blues across the Indiana sky in a way that made Ashley thankful for home. She and Landon had finished an early dinner and were walking along Main Street, stopping to admire the window display at the art gallery where her paintings were sold.

A damp cold hung in the air, but Ashley felt warm with Landon next to her, his arm around her. They studied her most recent painting, positioned under the lights. "It's perfect, baby." Landon smiled at her and kissed her forehead. The painting was of a three-year-old towheaded little boy who looked a lot like Cole when he was that age.

"Mmm." Ashley was still lost in thought from the conversation she'd had with Cole earlier. "Innocent."

"Yes."

"That's what I love most about it. Kids are only innocent for so long."

Landon looked at her. "Deep."

She managed a slight smile. "I guess that's how I'm feeling."

"Cole's still pretty innocent." Landon faced her and took her hands in his. "Everything okay?"

"Not really." Ashley didn't want to talk about it. "Let's keep walking."

Landon looked at her for a long beat, but then he led the way, his pace slow, thoughtful. The town was nearly empty that evening. They could take their time. "Want to tell me?"

Ashley filled her lungs with the cool air. "I'm not sure where to start."

This date night with Landon was supposed to be happy. They hadn't been alone like this for weeks. She wanted to hear about his job at the fire station, the dynamics of the team, the work he was proud of and the funny things people had said or done.

Anything, so long as they didn't talk about Cole.

"It's okay, Ash. Whatever it is." Landon had the most calming disposition. He always had. He looked down at her and smiled, a smile that came straight from the center of his soul. "I'm here. No rush."

"Thanks." She gave his hand a gentle squeeze and exhaled slowly. "It's Cole. We talked today." She had no choice but to tell him what had happened earlier. She'd given herself away. The painting gave her little option. If she'd known the gallery would have that piece in the window they could've walked the opposite direction.

Now, though, she had to take it as a sign. The time had come to share her fears again. Even if the conversation would be uncomfortable for Landon. Even if it hurt him. She would have to tell him eventually.

She slowed her pace. "Cole asked me about his father again today."

"Okay." His tone remained easy. "That's not surprising. Since you two are still interviewing your dad."

"I know. But . . ." Her stomach hurt just thinking about the conversation she would have to have with her older son. "Today was different. He wasn't only casually asking about him. He really wants to know. Like what was my story, and what happened. All the details."

"That's what he said?" Landon sounded surprised.

Ashley thought back to earlier that day. "Maybe not in those words. But he definitely wanted to know. He keeps calling it my *love story.*" She stopped walking and turned to him. "He accused me of avoiding him."

Landon hesitated. "Cole?"

"I mean, he wasn't rude. But he can tell, Landon." She looked at the sidewalk. Then she found his eyes once more. "He knows I don't want to talk about it." Tears blurred her vision a little. "*You're* his dad. I guess it's weird to me that he even wants to know about some other guy. The man's a stranger. He never cared about Cole at all." She hesitated. "Of course I don't want to tell him that."

For a while Landon just looked at her, searched her eyes. His expression was beyond kind. Like he would've done anything to take away her fear and concern. "Is it his father you don't want to talk about? Or your relationship with the guy?"

His words cut through to the place where Ashley had been hiding. Tears spilled onto her cheeks and she felt Landon draw her into his arms. All the shame and guilt and regret from her past came rushing at her like floodwaters, pulling her in, drowning her. "I can't." She muttered the words against her husband's chest. "I can't think about it, Landon."

"Baby." He smoothed his hand along her hair. "It's all right. You don't have to tell him everything. Of course not."

Ashley could barely breathe for the way the past pulled at her. "I was such a wretch, Landon." She couldn't look at him. Not right now.

"Isn't that the point?" His voice was a caress against her wounded conscience. "I once was lost but now am found. Right?"

The sidewalk was empty, but Ashley didn't want to have this conversation here in the open. She sniffed. "Can we find our bench?"

"Of course." He put his arm around her shoulders and they turned at the next street. Down a ways was a small grassy area. Too small to be a park. There, up against a tree, was a bench Landon had purchased for her last year on their daughter Sarah Marie's birthday. Ashley loved how Landon always remembered it, always found a way to celebrate it.

Even just between the two of them.

The bench had their little girl's name and birth date engraved on a small plaque at the center. It was a place they came to talk about deep things. Whether any of their kids were struggling in school or if there was trouble between their family members. Sometimes they came here to pray, and other times just to sit in silence. Each drawing strength from the other.

They sat down and Ashley leaned close to him. "Thank you." She still loved the smell of his cologne, after all these years. The way it reminded her of his strength and courage and dedication. Landon was the definition of a man, the way a man of God should be. "I love this bench. I always will."

"Me, too." The breeze from earlier had stilled, and the stars shone bright overhead. "Your life in Paris . . . it was how a lot of people live all the time. Life without God."

The thought stayed with her. Life without God. Yes, that was why she'd done such foolish things. Why she'd gone to Paris intent on throwing caution to the wind and why she'd taken up with a married artist. Even thinking about it made her want to throw up. Life without God, indeed. "I made so many terrible choices."

"You chose to have Cole." It was the one

truth she sometimes needed to be reminded of . . .

Ashley tried never to think about that awful day, the morning she sat in an abortion clinic about to do the unthinkable. God alone had sent her running out of the office. She'd come home pregnant and scared and all by herself, and her parents had loved her through every moment.

"How can I tell Cole all of that?" She felt cold. Her teeth began chattering. New tears sprang to her eyes. The tide of regret rising again. She looked up at Landon, her words a tortured whisper. "He'll hate me."

"Ash." Landon kissed the top of her head. "Cole could never hate you. That girl you were then, that's not who you are now. And even back then you listened to God. Otherwise Cole wouldn't be here."

The possibility sent a shudder through her. He was right. As awful as that time was, she needed to focus on the truth. Yes, she had been sitting in an abortion clinic ready to end her child's life. But even then all she could think was that no matter how bad she might be as a mother, it wasn't her baby's fault. When they called her name Ashley ran out of the clinic. As fast as her feet would carry her.

Yes, God worked good out of all situations. Even that one. "I have him. That's what matters."

"Exactly." Landon held her close again. "One day you might tell him those details, but not now. He's still very young." Landon was clearly in no hurry. He seemed to let his last words sink in. "Just tell him the basic facts. Tell him you're not proud of the past, but that God redeems all stories for people who love Him."

Ashley would rather swim with a school of sharks than tell Cole anything about his father. Still, Landon was right. "At least he'll know." She wiped her fingers beneath her eyes, sat up straight and looked at him. "How do you do it, Landon?"

"What?" His eyes shone in the light of the moon.

"Make me believe it's possible. That I could even think about having that talk with Cole."

"I'm your other half." He worked his fingers through her hair and touched his lips to hers. Their passion was never more than a kiss away. Like always. "I feel what you feel." He grinned. "Makes it easier to remind you of the truth."

Yesterday's anxiety receded. Ashley could breathe again. "I told Cole it would have to wait until after he finishes interviewing my dad."

"Good idea." Landon brushed his fingers over her cheek. "So Cole can focus on your parents' story for now."

"Yes." Ashley sighed. More relief. Landon agreed with her on the timing. She searched his eyes. "You're so good for me."

"That's funny." Landon held her face in his hands and kissed her again, longer this time. His eyes were smoky when he drew back and smiled at her. "I was just thinking the same thing."

Cole had a few questions for his mom — not about her love story, but about his papa's. He was in his room, sitting at his desk going through his notes. The story was sad. But Cole knew that tomorrow it would get sadder.

His eyes drifted down the pages from their last visit. The thing was, he didn't need notes to remember what his papa had told him during the first two interviews.

He'd remember the story forever.

On the first page he had written that Grandma Elizabeth was pretty. Very pretty. It was weird thinking of her that way. Trying to imagine his grandma and papa young and beautiful. But of course, they were.

They hadn't always been this age.

Cole read his way down the page, and found a note that caught his attention. *Too much beer.* Papa had drunk too much beer the night everything changed. Cole wondered if that was why there was never alcohol at their family get-togethers.

Not only that, but his parents never drank and neither did the families of his aunts and uncles. Was it all because of his papa's experience that night? Cole added that to the list of questions.

Then his eyes fell on another note. *Vietnam vet.* He had the man's name now. Wilson Gage from Indiana. His papa had told him when Cole called last week. Cole grabbed his laptop from his backpack. Might as well make the search now. So there'd be enough time to hear back from the man. That way he'd have his second source.

Cole thought it might take awhile to find him. Lots of grown-up men didn't use Facebook, for one thing. He typed "Wilson Gage" in the Facebook search bar and four possibilities came up. Cole clicked the first one. The man was in his twenties. Wrong Wilson Gage. The next one was even younger. But the third one lived in Michigan. A quick look and it was obvious the man was a vet.

Maybe, Cole thought. The man's last post was from three months ago. Odds were low he'd respond before Cole's report was due. But it was worth a try. He opened a new message and kept his letter brief.

Dear Mr. Gage,
My name is Cole Blake and I'm working on a heritage project for my school. I'm doing my report on my grandfather's story. It happened a long time ago and I'm learning all about it. He said a Vietnam vet from Indiana was an important part of the story.
Are you the Wilson Gage who lived in Indiana and helped a man named John Baxter in the 1970s? If so I'd like to interview you.
I'm not completely sure what happened, my grandfather hasn't gotten to that part yet. But I wanted to write now, so we could make a connection. I get extra credit if I interview another person who was part of the story.
So please could you write back and let me know if it is you? And if you want to do an interview, I can get some ques-

tions to you. Thank you, and God bless you.

Sincerely, Cole Blake

Cole hit the send button and closed his laptop.

He yawned and returned the notes to his backpack. His parents weren't home yet, but he was tired. School would come early. It always did. As he was falling asleep that night he thought again of the former soldier. Maybe the letter would encourage the man. He had to be pretty old now, and Vietnam vets weren't treated very good when they came home from the war. *Lord, if it would make that man feel important, could You please help him to look at his messages? Also, I could use the extra credit. Thanks, God. I really love You.* The details of how the man had helped Cole's papa were bound to come the next time they talked. Same with the part about what happened next with his papa, and how in the world his grandparents had managed to stay together through it all.

Cole could hardly wait for tomorrow.

14

Cody Coleman left early for the airport, for one reason. He wanted to spend an hour on the beach. Long enough to consider the trip he was about to take. Long enough to wonder exactly how he was supposed to go about convincing Andi to return to him. This was his last chance to gather his thoughts and pray, and the beach was one of his favorite places for that.

It had been a week since he'd seen her on TV. The waiting had just about killed him.

The sun was up over the Santa Monica Mountains, splashing morning light on the ocean. He pulled off at Will Rogers Beach and took a spot facing the Pacific. At first he was alone, but then a car pulled in and parked on the other side of the lot. That's when Cody noticed the pale blue lifeguard station.

Plastered on the side was a ten-foot piece of paper. Written across it was a beautiful, simple message.

Kaylee, will you marry me? Love, Trey

Then Cody saw something else. There had to be a dozen bouquets of red roses sitting along the short block wall that separated the parking lot from the sandy beach. And one more message on an easel set up between the block wall and the lifeguard station. The sign read:

This will be the view . . . each brand-new day with you.

Someone was getting engaged here. Right now. Cody slid down in his seat. Should he leave? Twenty yards away a couple was getting out of the car. She had long blond hair like Andi and he was tall with dark hair. Cody could see that she had a blindfold over her eyes. Obviously she didn't know what was coming.

Cody didn't want to attract attention to himself, so he stayed and watched, unnoticed. The signs, the flowers, the setup. The guy was a romantic, for sure. Cody sort of wanted to see how the moment turned out.

Must be pretty sure she'll say yes, Cody

thought. The way he'd been sure when he asked Andi Ellison to marry him. Both times. He tried not to think about it. The guy — who Cody guessed was Trey — led the girl — Kaylee no doubt — to the flowers that lined the wall. Then he took the blindfold from her eyes.

Cody couldn't hear them, but he could see Kaylee's surprise. She was still clearly remarking over the sea of flowers when Trey led her to the easel. Now the girl was starting to get it. She put both hands over her mouth and then hugged the guy.

He was grinning so big, Cody had to smile, too.

Cody watched as Trey led the girl toward the lifeguard station. Only when they reached a spot with just the right view did she see the enormous sign. She took a few seconds to read it, and as she did, Trey dropped to one knee and pulled out a ring.

Kaylee must've said yes, because the two were instantly in an embrace that looked familiar for one reason. It was the same way Cody and Andi had held on to each other when they got engaged. When they were together.

The guy slipped the ring onto her finger and they held each other again. Just as the sun came up over the mountains behind them. The two kissed, lost in the moment.

This was Cody's chance to find another beach. He'd waited long enough, and now that the surprise was over he needed to leave. A few parking lots down, he found a spot by himself. He rolled down the windows of his car and stared at the ocean. He had four days to find her and change her mind.

Open her heart to me, please, God. After the mess I've made of things, I can't do this on my own.

With Me all things are possible, My son.

The words practically seemed audible. Cody loved when this happened, when God spoke to him in moments like this. Almost like a father. The encouragement made Cody more excited to go.

He watched the morning beach come to life, the seagulls as they began their dive for fish and the occasional jogger running along the shore. Suddenly Cody remembered a Bible verse from his reading time yesterday. It was from Lamentations. God's compassions are new every morning.

Just like the beach. And working at Oaks Christian. Like his mother's new life since she'd been out of prison. Everything had the chance for new life, because God's grace and second chances were new every morning. Now Cody could just hope they'd be new for him and Andi.

Ideally, sometime in the next four days.

The road was rough beneath the Humvee, making Cody's job harder. He sat shotgun, his AR-15 loaded and ready. Insurgents were moving into the streets at the edge of the city. Cody and his fellow soldiers had orders to get there and clear the buildings, anywhere the enemy might be hiding.

Cody looked around at his buddies, three of them across the backseat, and the one driving. They were his best friends. The five of them ate together and slept in the same tent together. Whenever they had a mission, they traveled together.

But for some reason Cody couldn't remember their names.

He was about to ask the driver, when it happened. An explosion ripped through the jeep and suddenly blood was everywhere. Blood and body parts and screams, flying through the air, consuming Cody. He was still in the air, still spinning around above the desert floor, still surrounded by bloody body parts, and all of it was happening in slow motion. Only something was different now.

Something was terribly wrong with him.

Don't look down, Coleman. Don't do it. But the bodies of his friends cried out at him. *Look what this war did to you, Cody . . . You have to look . . .*

And his friends were missing limbs. One of them no longer had a head. And finally their voices won out and Cody stared at the place where his legs used to be. They were both missing. The body parts flying around the air were his own. I have no legs! He screamed the words. *Someone help me! Someone catch my legs and put them back where they belong. I need them!*

No matter how loud he screamed, no one listened. No one seemed to hear. So Cody tried to reach out and catch his legs himself. *If I can just reach them, everything will be okay.* He stretched out his hand for them, but his body wouldn't cooperate, like his arms weren't working at all.

Again he heard the frantic voices of his friends. *See what this war did to you, Cody. See what it did.*

Cody felt terror run through him. He didn't want to look, didn't want to know what had happened to his arms and hands. But he had no choice. He had to look hard through the blood still swirling around him, but as he did, he saw for himself.

His arms were missing. Both of them.

And then, with his own blood and body parts still spinning around him, Cody released a guttural scream like nothing he'd ever heard. He couldn't breathe, couldn't feel his heartbeat, and then it occurred to him.

He must be dead.

God, how could this happen . . . I'm not ready to die. I was supposed to marry Andi Ellison. Please, God . . . put me back together. Please . . .

"Sir?" The voice was pleasant, kind.

Cody could still see the horrors of the accident, still see the faces of his nameless friends calling out to him, telling him the war was a waste of his time. Telling him it wasn't worth it.

"No!" Cody heard himself cry out. He jerked back and then opened his eyes. A flight attendant was looking straight at him. It mattered, the work they had done in Afghanistan. It did.

The woman had her hand on his shoulder. "Sir . . . can you hear me?"

Where was he? Cody sat up straighter, his breaths coming fast and hard, like he'd been running ten miles. "What . . . what happened?"

"You're on a flight from Los Angeles, sir. You were shouting out." She looked concerned. "A dream, maybe?"

He was on a flight. That's right, he was headed to Louisiana to see Andi. In a quick move, he felt his arms and legs. They were still there, all but his lower left leg, which he'd lost in Afghanistan for real.

Yes, he must've been dreaming. Another episode. A reminder that in some ways he would never fully leave Afghanistan, never be completely removed from the day when his convoy ran over an IED, killing everyone in the vehicle but him.

All his friends from that time gone.

Cody settled himself. *Deep breaths. Take deep breaths.* His mind turned automatically to Philippians 4. The way he'd been trained in counseling over the past few months. *Do not be anxious about anything, but in every situation, by prayer and petition, with thanksgiving, present your requests to God. And the peace of God, which transcends all understanding, will guard your hearts and your minds in Christ Jesus . . .*

He realized then that the woman was still watching him, still worried. "Are you okay, sir?"

"I am. Thank you." People in the rows ahead of him were turning around and looking his way. "I'm sorry. I . . . I must be really tired."

Cody's racing heart began to settle down. *Do not be anxious about anything, but in every situation . . .* He turned and looked out the window and let the Scripture run through his mind again and again. It had been more than a month since his last bout. The episodes were unpredictable. He could never know when one would hit.

He adjusted his camouflage baseball cap. The one he'd gotten while he was on active duty. Maybe he needed more rest. That could be it. Another thing he'd learned in the group meetings.

"Hey there." The voice came from beside him. Cody was sitting in an aisle seat, so he looked up and saw a soldier in full fatigues, maybe in his late twenties. The guy was headed back to his seat, probably from the restroom.

"Yes, sir?"

The man took another step and faced Cody. "Army, right?" He nodded to Cody's cap.

"Yes, sir. Served in Afghanistan." Cody reached out his hand. "I'm Cody."

"Beck." The two shook. "I figured you had served." He glanced at Cody's prosthetic leg. "What with your injury." The man looked straight at him. There was something otherworldly about his pale green eyes.

240

"That dream you just had? It's the PTSD, right? The nightmare just now?"

"Yes." This was one of the worst parts of PTSD. The inability to control the nightmares. He hated the question, but there was only one way to answer it. "They won't leave me alone. Even now. Years later."

"You're going to be okay. I wanted to tell you." The soldier gave him an understanding smile. "Even if you still have episodes, God is with you. And they'll fade in time. Really."

Cody nodded. "I've heard that. I'm going to a support group." He sighed. "Praying God takes it away. The nightmares. The fear. They're tough, for sure."

"Yeah, they are." The soldier tipped his cap. "Keep praying. God has good things ahead for you."

"Thank you." Cody watched the guy head back up the aisle.

Strange, Cody thought. The entire conversation was as if God, Himself, had sent the guy. Just to give Cody a healthy dose of encouragement. Which he definitely needed. Because sure, the wicked dreams were exhausting and vivid. They made Cody feel like he couldn't breathe. But the nightmares were just part of PTSD.

It was the other part that made life hard.

The part he had kept from Andi after they got engaged the second time. The way he couldn't eat at a restaurant unless he had his back against a wall, or the way crowds sometimes made him extra quiet. Even the crowds at his own football games. The noise would pick up and all Cody could see were the people. Masses of people. And suddenly he would become keenly aware of his surroundings, and less aware of the people he loved.

People like Andi.

She'd been around him at moments like that, and he hadn't explained what was happening. Why he was quiet or anxious or distant. No wonder she'd broken things off. Cody looked out the window again and thought about that second engagement. He could remember feeling how all of his life had led up to that trip to Bloomington.

She thought they were having a birthday party for her mother. Instead Cody had been planning a surprise engagement party for Andi. He could remember feeling how all of his life had led up to that trip to Bloomington.

Now all of his life led up to this one. The trip to Louisiana.

He looked at the upsides of a hundred white puffy clouds. He could remember

Andi asleep beside him. Back then, all he could think was how in seventy-two hours — on a Saturday afternoon — despite the struggles between them — he would ask Andi Ellison to be his wife. Again.

And now he was praying for another chance.

His last chance.

He relaxed once more into the airplane seat. Now he could only pray she would say yes one more time. Andi, whose heart was pure gold. The girl who had slipped into his life like a summer breeze in the dead of winter, giving him hope like nothing ever had. They were survivors, the two of them. People who, because of choices and circumstances, had given up on their dreams of finding true love.

Until each other.

A rush of anxiety came at Cody. There was nothing sure about the days ahead, no way of knowing how Andi would react. She wouldn't take his phone calls, after all. Odds were good she wouldn't want to see him. But even so, he had to come, had to see for himself if there was even the slightest chance she'd hear him out.

Cody drew a slow breath and tried to relax. God was here. He could feel that, too. *I've made a mess of things, Lord.* He lifted his eyes to the vast blue beyond. *Through it all You never left me. You were always there, guiding me, providing for me. Making the answers clear.*

If Andi did talk to him, if she was willing to give him another chance, the situation would still be awkward. Who gets back together after two failed engagements? Cody tried to picture calling Andi's father some-day soon. They would talk for a few minutes about Cody's football team, spring training, and how the coming season looked.

But before long Cody would have to get to the point. Yes, he'd asked before, and yes, he and Andi had struggled through two broken engagements. Cody hadn't meant to hurt her, he would explain. He had his reasons. But now he was convinced he knew better how to love her. Better how to handle the trauma that still plagued him.

He'd never been more sure in all his life.

Andi's father would probably hang up on him, too. Or maybe not. Maybe he would actually be happy for Cody and Andi. The man had always loved Cody, and he'd said that he believed God had crossed their paths for this purpose.

Months after Andi broke up with him the last time around, Cody had run into Andi's father at Ralphs supermarket in Thousand Oaks.

The conversation that day was as real now as it had been back then. Keith had come up to Cody just as he was about to enter the checkout line. "Cody Coleman." His tone held an understandable hesitancy.

Cody had turned around and there he was — the man who would've been his father-in-law. "Keith. Hey." Cody shook the man's hand. "It's been a while."

"Too long." He paused. "How are you? Really?"

Cody stepped out of line so the two could talk. For several seconds Cody didn't say anything. Things were too far gone for small talk. "I . . . I miss her."

It felt like they were the only two people in the store. Keith nodded. "She misses you, too."

That had shocked Cody. "She . . . hasn't taken my calls."

"Andi's hurt." The man seemed to stand a little straighter, the way any daddy might when his daughter's heart was involved.

"I handled everything wrong." Cody hadn't known what to say. "I've never . . . been more sorry in all my life." He shifted, uneasy. "If I could do it all over again, I would." *And the two of us would be married by now,* Cody had thought to himself. "How is she?"

"She's fine. She enjoys her work." Keith hesitated. "Keep trying, Cody. She does miss you."

Okay, so Andi's father still cared about him. Still wanted to see them together. At least he had back then. Cody looked across his seatmates at the vast blue outside the window. He didn't like to think about the terrible broken engagements between them.

None of it had been Andi's fault.

Now if only he could find her and explain himself. He would tell her about the terrible dreams and strange episodes. The way he had wanted to protect her from the realities of his postwar trauma. At least then she would know that his distance toward her wasn't because of anything she had done.

He was in love with her then and he was in love with her now.

Cody felt overwhelmed. *What if she turns me away? How am I supposed to go on without her?* He closed his eyes. And suddenly the words of the soldier — Beck, right? — came back to him. *You're going to be okay . . . God has good things ahead for you.* Yes, that's what he needed to believe.

God was on his side, and he wasn't going to let PTSD stand in the way. Sure, he might have episodes. But he'd learned new ways of coping, and Andi would only help. Andi's face and voice filled his heart. She cared about people in pain. That's why she was making her living working in disaster areas.

Please, God . . . help her to see me in a new light. Let her listen to me, please. He missed her more than ever, with every breath. And something else . . . something Cody knew he would never find with any other girl. Andi Ellison made him feel ten feet tall.

Now he just prayed that Beck's words were right.

That God did indeed have good things ahead.

15

By the time Cody landed in Louisiana, rented a car and set out toward the flood zone, it was late afternoon. Still enough daylight to find her, but not much. Cody didn't care. He would've walked a hundred city blocks in the pitch-dark if it meant seeing her tonight.

As soon as he hit the edge of the disaster area, Cody felt his stomach turn. The torrential rain and flooding had been swift and certain. Entire neighborhoods were wiped away. Even now, with waters clearly receding, there were stacks of debris everywhere. Cars flipped on their sides, pieces of houses tangled up with broken trees and trash.

A police officer had given Cody the address of a temporary shelter. No guarantee Andi was there, but it was the first place Cody intended to look. As he drove, on either side he could see people helping each other. Many of them had shovels, and they worked to collect the piles of wood and garbage and broken belongings from what once must've been manicured lawns. Enormous bins sat in the streets and people everywhere were doing their part to fill them.

He had heard on the news that most of the workers were volunteers from local churches. Those leading the cleanup were mostly from Christian relief organizations like the one Andi worked for. All of it made Cody thankful for the church. The Bible commanded people to be the hands and feet of Jesus, to help the poor and serve others.

The scene playing out on either side of him as he drove was exactly what God must've imagined. Cody wished he could get out and help. But he had to keep going. Had to find her before the next few days disappeared.

Andi wasn't at the first evacuation center he went to, or the second. Then someone told him about the temporary animal shelter. The man thought Andi might be working there. Cody's heart pounded as he drove to the address and stepped out of the car. He stood there a moment, studying the place. It was an oversized aluminum shed packed with crates and cages.

The door was open and Cody could see

people moving around.

Then he saw her. She was working in the shed. A tall blond girl whose graceful movements could only mean one thing. He had found her. Cody straightened and felt his courage double. *I need You, God . . . help me do this.*

Clouds had gathered overhead and everything around him was soaking wet. The heavy branches from the nearby trees, the muddy ground, and the shed. All of it was drenched. Cody wore a navy blue rain jacket, which he pulled tight around himself.

The whole time he never took his eyes from her.

For a moment he paused as she brought a puppy to her face and nuzzled it against her cheek. Cody couldn't hear what she was saying, but watching her was enough. She loved animals, so working here was perfect for her. He was about to call her name when another worker, a guy, came up to Andi and stood close to her, the two of them admiring the puppy.

Cody took a step back. What was this? He watched another minute until the guy went back to whatever he'd been doing before. Were the two of them more than friends? The way they laughed and looked at each other, it almost seemed like it. Rocks filled

Cody's gut. Maybe he should turn around and head to his hotel. Think this through before he made a fool of himself.

But then he remembered the words the Lord had whispered to him. *With Me all things are possible, My son.*

Yes, that's right. Nothing would ever be impossible with God on his side. And God was on his side. Even now. That didn't mean he'd get the answer he wanted, but it meant he had to try.

He was too committed to leave now.

The shed was only ten yards away, and as Cody took a few steps closer, Andi must've heard him or seen him from the corner of her eye. Whatever caught her attention, she turned and faced him. And then she froze in place. After several seconds she set the puppy back in its cage and came out to meet him.

Cody didn't move. He waited while she walked toward him, her steps measured, like she was in a trance. Her eyes locked on his and she never looked away, never even blinked.

A hundred emotions and thoughts whirled in Cody's mind. How beautiful she looked and how different from the last time they'd been together. There was a strength to her now, strength mixed with confidence. As if she were exactly where she needed to be. A sense of purpose and resolve shone in her eyes.

Never had Cody been more drawn to her.

When Andi reached him, she took him by the hand to a spot behind a grove of trees. So they'd be completely alone. "Cody . . ." Her tone was compassionate, but clearly she was confused. "Why are you here?"

He had so many things he wanted to tell her. How he was sorry for letting her walk away and how he should have told her about the PTSD, how all he'd done since then was think about her and miss her and want her back.

But none of that came out.

Instead — with the greatest care — he took her into his arms and kissed her. Not a kiss of sudden passion or self-gratification. But a kiss that he hoped might tell her more than an hour of words ever could.

She drew back first, breathless, her eyes a mix of sorrow and shock. "What in the world . . ." Her hand moved across her lips.

Cody took a step back. Instant regret. "I'm . . . I'm sorry, I just . . . I couldn't reach you and you wouldn't take my calls or text me back. I saw you on the news and . . ." A soft rain started falling around them. "I missed you, Andi."

Her eyes welled up and for a while she stood there, watching him, like she was fighting herself for even staying around this long. Then as if she had no way to stop herself, she slumped a little. And finally she came to him and melted into his arms. For a few seconds she looked like she might kiss him. Instead, she kept her arms around his neck and rested her head on his chest. "I missed you, too."

The feeling of her in his arms was all that mattered. He could've left now and the whole trip would've been worth it. But he had so much more to say. He drew back and studied her face, her eyes. "I have to talk to you, Andi. What happened between us before, it was my fault. But there are things you don't know." He wiped the rain from his face and eyelashes. "Could we go somewhere, please? So we can talk?"

"Everything is fine?" A guy's voice came from a few feet away.

Cody and Andi turned toward the sound. It was the dark-haired guy from a few minutes ago. Before Cody could say anything, Andi jerked away from him and crossed her arms in front of herself. She seemed guilty, like whatever was going on she didn't want the guy seeing her with Cody. "It's okay. I'll be back in a few minutes." She looked at Cody and back at the guy. "This is Cody. My friend." She glanced at Cody. "This is Caleb."

Caleb nodded, his expression stone-like. "Pleasure." The guy had an accent. Something European, maybe.

"Same." Cody shoved his hands in his pockets. He felt the gift he'd brought Andi.

The guy must not have been completely satisfied that Andi was okay, because he hesitated. Then after a few seconds, he turned and walked back toward the building. When he was gone, Cody looked at Andi once more. "Co-worker?" He didn't have to ask whether the guy was more than that to Andi. Her tone said it all.

She took several heartbeats before she answered. "Yes. Caleb and I . . . We're . . . we're friends." She didn't blink. "At least for now."

The rain was still falling, still making this time with her feel like something from a dream. "Okay." He hadn't for a minute thought she might be involved with another guy. His mind was reeling. "I guess."

"Cody, I can't do this . . . You can't just . . ." She looked down at the muddy ground and shook her head.

Cody couldn't tell if she was crying. Drops were running off her cheeks and nose, but they could've been the rain. When she looked up he knew the answer. Some of the drops had been tears. He took a step closer. "I'm sorry, Andi. Please . . . can we talk? Go somewhere? Just the two of us?"

Again her expression eased and she came closer. "Why do you always do this, Cody? Draw me in again?" She put her arms around his neck and looked into his eyes. "So that all I want is you."

They couldn't stop themselves from coming together again if their lives depended on it. They held on to each other for several minutes, swaying to the sound of the rain and wind in the tree branches overhead. Cody loved this, but he wanted to talk. He couldn't wait to tell her the truth about everything.

Finally he leaned back some and framed her face with his fingertips. The sight of her took his breath. He searched her eyes. It was all he could do not to kiss her again. "Where can we go?"

"We can't." She shook her head, but this time her eyes remained soft. "I have meetings tonight. And I'm taking care of a rescue puppy. He's just six weeks old." She nodded back toward the shed. "The puppy stays here during the day, but I take care of him after work."

Cody was about to ask if he could go to the place where she was staying, wherever that was. They could talk in the lobby . . . or in the parking lot.

But she came up with a different plan, first. "Let's meet tomorrow. At that park." She pointed across the street at a small playground. "Seven in the morning." Her soft voice and the look in her eyes said she wanted to stay, wanted to make this moment last as long as they could. But she was listening to a different voice. The one in her head.

Cody's heart raced. "Okay." He hesitated. "I can do that." At least she wasn't refusing to talk to him at all. "What about dinner?"

"I can't." She looked back toward the shed once more. "I have plans." She released a tortured breath. "I have to think, Cody. Me and God. This . . . I wasn't expecting you."

Cody felt the blow of her words to his core. This was a different Andi, for sure. One who had options. That much was clear. This Andi had spent enough time helping people that she had no trouble now helping herself. Keeping her heart out of harm's way when it came to Cody. Clearly right now she knew better than to stay with him another minute.

She gave him a sad smile and took three

steps back. "I have to go. We need to clean every cage before we leave."

He nodded. "Tomorrow then." There was nothing else he could say. He didn't want to leave her side while he was here, but she said she needed time. He pulled the gift from his pocket and handed it to her. "Here."

She took it and new tears pooled in her eyes. "Thank you."

It was the least Cody could do, proof that he understood her passion for working here and helping people. Proof that he was paying attention to her now, the way he hadn't paid attention when they were engaged last time. Cody hoped the gift would tell her all of that and more, since they wouldn't see each other until tomorrow. The gift was just what she wanted, after all.

A simple pair of clean white socks.

16

The memory of his beginning with Elizabeth wouldn't leave him alone, just the way John had feared. He could only thank God that Elaine was understanding. She didn't have to tell him how distant he'd been or how he'd barely engaged in their few conversations.

Yesterday evening he'd found her out front in one of their two rocking chairs. She was reading the Bible, and as he approached she looked up and smiled. Actually smiled at him. "Hello, John."

"Elaine." He took the chair beside her. "I'm interrupting."

"Never." Her tone was soft, and he could sense her spirit was, too. "I was reading Hebrews. About faith."

John nodded. "One of my favorite passages."

She looked more intently at him. "What's on your heart?"

Elaine always said that. *What's on your heart?* She didn't want to know only the thoughts of someone she loved. She wanted to know what was going on at a deeper level. One of the reasons John cared about her so much.

"I'm sorry. I know . . . I've said it a few times these last weeks, but I really mean it. This whole interview thing . . . it's taken me back, and it's like . . ." He stared at the sky for a moment, then at her. "Like I'm living again in that faraway time and I can't quite come home yet."

Compassion colored Elaine's expression. "Can I tell you a story?"

Her question caught John off guard. "Of course." He settled back in his rocking chair. And Elaine proceeded to tell him about a high school friend of hers. Mary Ellen. Someone she'd just reconnected with through Facebook. The woman's husband was killed in a train accident on a business trip to Europe when their kids were in middle school.

"The accident devastated her." Elaine didn't have to draw the comparison. It was obvious.

Elaine went on to explain that a few years later Mary Ellen fell in love with a single man from church. The two of them were very happy, but every year around the time of the accident, Mary Ellen took a week and deeply remembered her first husband.

"Mary Ellen goes to a quiet hotel up in the mountains. She reads letters from him and looks at photos. She writes in her journal the things she would like to say to him if she could. She prays for their children, that they'll continue to grow strong in their faith and in their dad's image."

John sucked in a quick breath. What was Elaine saying? He shook his head without really knowing it. "How does . . . her current husband feel about that?"

Elaine's face relaxed, filled with a beautiful understanding. "It was his idea."

What? Sending his wife off to think about her first husband was the man's idea? John hesitated for a few seconds and then he leaned forward, elbows on his knees. "What does he do while she's gone?"

"On the last day he meets her there. She tells him the story of her first husband and some of the happier moments." Elaine paused. Like even she couldn't believe how beautiful and unusual her friend's story was. "They talk for hours and they pray for their family, and then — together — they come back home."

John couldn't think of a single thing to

say. The idea of going back every year to the beginning with Elizabeth — the way he had these last weeks — was more than he could fathom. "I'm not sure I'd want to spend so much time in the past. Every year like that."

The air was brisk between them, the moon a sliver in the sky. Elaine reached for his hand. "That's what I thought you'd say." She smiled, and even in the dim light, love shone in her eyes. "But whenever you *do* want to go back, whenever you need to go back, you have my blessing, John. Whenever."

John's heart felt suddenly light inside him. She was giving him a very great gift, something he had never expected.

Permission to remember.

"Elaine, I . . . I . . ." His throat was too tight to speak. He waited, looking into her eyes. "Thank you. This isn't about my feelings for you." He stood and eased her to her feet. "You know that, right?"

"I do." She pressed the side of her face to his. "Take your time, John. And when you're done, I'll be here." Her eyes met his again. "Always."

And now it was Thursday again and Cole and Ashley were settling in with him in the living room. For the most part, John had been summarizing when it came to telling

Cole what happened. He spared the teenager the specifics other than to say, "Your grandmother and I were passionately in love. We couldn't stay away from each other. We saw each other as often as we could."

That sort of thing.

John picked up a letter from the table beside him. "This letter" — he looked at Cole — "is what turned everything around."

As he spoke, the story came to life in living color for John. Every touch and sound and smell and feeling.

The way it most certainly would today.

Once they'd crossed the line, once John and Elizabeth had gone places they never intended to go, there was nothing they could do to leave. It was fall, and the Wesley family spent every weekend at their lake house. John would normally have gone, too. But he was taking a heavy course load. Too much homework, he told them.

Which was true.

What he didn't tell them was that those weekends gave him time with Elizabeth. And even though they'd gone too far, every Friday night when they went out, John promised himself nothing would happen this time. Nothing more than kissing. A few beers and a little kissing. He was determined.

And every time he was wrong.

John wasn't the only one to blame. Some nights — when her parents thought she was at Betsy's house studying — Elizabeth would ask to stay longer. Just another hour more. By the fifth weekend, they both knew what was going to happen. And though they promised each other it wouldn't, they were simply unable to do anything else.

What God might think of what they were doing never occurred to John. His knowledge of God never intersected with his behavior. He was a good guy. He'd barely dated until Elizabeth. He felt bad about what was happening but only because Elizabeth was lying to her parents.

Things were a little different for Elizabeth. She also felt guilty for lying. But not nearly guilty enough to stop. This was her first ever experience with freedom. Her parents' faith was the reason she hadn't been allowed to dance or sing pop songs or attend school social functions. Spending time with John was the most exciting thing she'd done in her life. It didn't matter if they went to the lake or on a drive into the country, wasn't any difference whether they swam in the river or made a bonfire on the beach.

As long as they were together.

In their sixth week, when the semester was getting hectic, Elizabeth began feeling sick. Every morning she woke with nausea and dizziness. She'd rarely been sick in all her life, but she couldn't seem to get out of bed without running to the bathroom. When the nausea turned to vomiting, Elizabeth knew she needed to see a doctor. And there was another problem.

Her period was late.

John was a premed student, of course, so when Elizabeth told him her symptoms, he didn't need a pregnancy test to know what was wrong. Elizabeth was expecting. They confirmed it with a blood test, which John performed clandestinely at the University of Michigan laboratory.

"I'm not pregnant." She had insisted as much from the moment he suggested it. "It's probably allergies. Milk, maybe."

The day John read the test results was one he would never forget. He found Elizabeth outside her next class and brought her to a picnic table on a quiet part of campus. They held hands across the splintered wood. What he was about to say would change their lives forever.

"Elizabeth, I'm sorry." If only he could turn back the clock. If he could change things so he never would have taken her back to his house that first night. He closed his eyes for a brief moment and then looked straight at her. "You're pregnant."

"No." She was in shock. She had to be. No other way to explain how her eyes grew wide and her face a chalky sort of pale. Elizabeth stood, her body clearly trembling. "I'm not, John. I can't be." She looked over her right shoulder and then her left. As if she were terrified someone might have heard him. Including herself. Then her eyes found his again. "I can't be. No."

"Elizabeth." He stood and moved around the table. "We can do this. We'll find a way."

But as he came closer, she moved a few steps back. She shook her head, tears flooding her eyes. "No, John. It won't be okay. This will never be okay."

A rough few days followed. Elizabeth refused to see him or talk to him. He'd wait for her near her classroom, but she'd turn the other direction on her way out. Then on the fourth day, he was sitting at a table on the lawn of the medical building when she came up behind him.

She sat down and turned to him. "I'm sorry." Again she seemed to be shaking.

They were in deep trouble, but the joy he felt that day was something he would carry with him forever. She had come back to him. His heart beat hard against his chest. "Why in the world are you sorry?"

Elizabeth could've answered a dozen ways but she didn't. Instead she wrapped her arms around his neck and held on to him. Only then did her tears come in earnest. She began to cry and that led to a series of sobs.

The autumn sun shone down on their shoulders, and a breeze played in the red and yellow leaves nearby. Finally Elizabeth gained enough control to speak. "I couldn't believe it was true." She shook her head. "I felt like my world was falling apart."

Her face was gripped with fear. He slid his fingers between hers. And in that moment he was home. No matter what came next, they would be together. "Elizabeth. I thought I'd lost you."

"No."

"And I'm the one who's sorry." He ran his thumb lightly along her cheekbone. "You're just a freshman. I should've never taken you home, Elizabeth."

Her cheeks grew red, but she didn't look away. "I wanted to be with you. We're both to blame."

She was right, but John was the guy and he was older. He couldn't let her feel this was her fault. "It's me, Elizabeth. I knew better." He could hear the other med students heading into the building. The break was over, but John wasn't leaving. He blinked a few times. "Where do we go from here?"

"I need to tell my parents."

"No." This time he was sure what they had to do next. He would never let her face them alone. "*We* need to tell them."

Which is exactly what they did. That night Elizabeth was home working on an essay for English 101 when John knocked on the door. Her father answered it. From where John stood he could see Elizabeth at the kitchen table, her books spread out. She turned toward him just as her father's face twisted into a scowl.

"Can I help you?" His brow lowered down around the bridge of his nose.

For a second, John met Elizabeth's eyes. She looked more certain than scared. She stood and took slow, silent steps in his direction. John looked at the man and cleared his throat. "Yes, sir. My name's John Baxter." He dug his hands deep into his jeans. "I'd like to talk to you and your wife. About your daughter, Elizabeth."

"My daughter?" He shook his head. "We're not interested. She's not interested."

He stepped back to shut the door. "Besides, she's too young to date."

Elizabeth had reached the place where she was almost standing next to her father. "Daddy . . . he needs to talk to you." She put her hand on his arm, but he jerked away. They'd come too far for either of them to turn back now.

"Sir, if you'd let me in." John waited. He didn't want to have the conversation on the porch.

"Please, Daddy." Elizabeth sounded stronger than John had ever heard her before. "We need to talk to you and Mama. Both of us."

Her father's scowl worsened. "I have no interest in speaking to this boy, whatever he has to say." He hesitated. "Leave this house now, you hear me? Leave or I'll —"

Elizabeth's mother had come up behind her husband. She must've caught the gist of the conversation, because she put her hand on his shoulder. "Let's hear the young man out."

The woman didn't look any happier than Elizabeth's father. But at least she was willing to listen to what John had to say. What they both had to say. An awkward few minutes later they were seated in the family living room. John and Elizabeth together on one sofa. Her parents beside each other on the other.

Another person could've sat between them for the space John was careful to leave. He started the conversation. "I realize you don't know me. But I've been dating your daughter for the past several weeks."

It was a bad beginning to the conversation, and things went downhill from there. John explained that the two of them had fallen in love and then John said something he hadn't planned to say. Not yet anyway.

"I want to marry your daughter, sir." His eyes found those of his nemesis across from him. "I'd like your permission for her hand."

The yelling began then. "You're out of your mind, boy." Her dad was on his feet. "Get out of my house." He pointed toward the front door. "Now!"

At that point Elizabeth was on her feet, too. "Daddy! Sit down! Please! John's not going anywhere." She looked at John, and despite the anger and tension of the moment, her eyes told him yes. Yes, she wanted to marry him. As much as he wanted to marry her.

"What's this all about?" Her mother slid to the edge of the sofa. *Uptight* didn't begin to describe her expression. "Elizabeth, you sit down. And don't ever take that tone with your father."

All of them sat once more, and John had no choice. He swallowed hard. "Sir, this is complicated."

Elizabeth reached over and took John's hand. He had never loved her more. "Daddy, I'm pregnant." She took a quick breath. Again, John could see her heart beating at the hollow of her throat. "John and I are going to have a baby."

No matter how hard John tried he couldn't remember everything that happened next. For nearly an hour, everyone took turns yelling and crying and making sweeping statements about what the plan of action should be. But the bottom line was simply this:

John couldn't take care of Elizabeth. He was a medical student, not a doctor. No matter how he might be able to support her in the years to come, he wasn't there now. And her parents made it very clear that the two weren't welcome to live with them.

Then Elizabeth's father produced an ultimatum. She would withdraw from school and leave for a home for unwed teens. Perhaps in Minnesota. Or maybe Wisconsin or Illinois. Somewhere far enough so John couldn't find her, couldn't see her.

Elizabeth would go away and have the

baby, and then she would give the infant up for adoption. At that point, she would return to Ann Arbor and start school again.

As if nothing had ever happened.

Elizabeth told John later that she had wanted to scream or throw something, gather her belongings and run out the door all the way to his house. But what were her options? John certainly understood why Elizabeth felt trapped.

She explained everything to him the next day before class. Her parents were making the call to withdraw her later that afternoon. John figured the two of them had just one last chance. He went home that day and told the Wesleys. They weren't angry or demeaning. They admitted these things happen.

But even if John and Elizabeth married that week, there was no way the two of them could move in with them. Not enough room. "It was one thing to take *you* in." Mr. Wesley was kind as he gave his answer. "We cannot take in you and your wife and a baby. I'm sorry."

And that was that.

John could do nothing to stop the chain of events that followed. He felt like a statue, his heart more stone than flesh. He was powerless to change things, unable to be with Elizabeth or even talk to her. The day after the Wesleys told him no, John went to her English class and waited for her.

But she never came out.

Like her dad had promised, she'd been pulled from school. So he drove to her house the next night at two in the morning. Her parents wouldn't be awake then, he figured. He was right. John tapped on Elizabeth's window, and she slipped out. She was wearing a long flannel nightgown, and she began crying as soon as she saw him.

"You came!" Her voice was a tortured cry.

"Shh . . ." She was in his arms now and he whispered into her hair. "We can't let them hear us."

"Right." She stifled the sound of her sobs and clung to him. "I'm so scared, John. I leave in a week. I don't even know where I'm going. Somewhere in Illinois. That's what I heard my father say."

For a long while they held each other. Time was short, so John got to the point. "We need a plan. They can't keep us apart forever."

Elizabeth nodded. Her beautiful eyes were so afraid. "Like what?"

John's mind raced, desperate for a solution. "Try to find out where you're going. You can tell Betsy and she can tell me. Then

I'll come to you, Elizabeth."

Her tears came harder. "What about the baby?" She put her hand on her stomach. "I don't want to lose our child, John. It's not fair."

John had wrestled with this, too. Her father was right about one thing. Elizabeth was young. She deserved the chance to finish her education. Until now John hadn't known whether she wanted to raise the baby or not. "So . . . you're saying you do want to get married? Keep our child?"

"Of course. School can come later. Or not at all." She used the palms of her hands to wipe her tears. "I want us to be a family."

John had never felt more helpless. "We have nowhere to live, no money." He clenched his jaw, his mind racing. "I'll find a way to make it work, Elizabeth. I'll do whatever I can."

They kissed goodbye, both of them desperate to see a light at the end of their tunnel. John almost wished he had a faith in God. Because he needed help now more than ever. Instead, as they were kissing a light came on at the back of the house. Elizabeth jerked away. "I have to go."

"I love you." John helped her up and through her window.

"I love you, too. Come tomorrow, John. Please."

He was moving away now, heading for the street. He'd parked several houses down. "I will. I promise."

His feet pounded a rhythm keeping time with his heart as he made his way to his car and drove off. Over the next few days he couldn't call her, didn't know how she was feeling or what she was doing or where her parents were about to send her. That night he waited up until two in the morning and again he went to her house.

But this time she wasn't there. He could see her bed through a crack in the curtains. It was empty. John took a few steps away from the window, shocked. What was he supposed to do now? Where had they taken her? Just then the front porch light flicked on.

"I knew that was you last night." Her father spat the words in his direction. "She's gone, John Baxter. We moved her to a place where you can't find her." He took a couple menacing steps in John's direction. "Don't come here. Not ever again."

There was nothing John could say. Nothing he could do.

The next day he talked to Betsy. "Find her for me. Please." He must've sounded desperate because she looked almost alarmed. His voice broke. "I have to see her before she leaves."

By then Betsy knew about the pregnancy. "I'll try, John . . . Her dad would kill me if he knew I was talking to you."

He thanked her but after a few days Betsy got back to him. Elizabeth was gone. Betsy had no idea where her parents had moved her. There was nothing more she could do to help.

And then John had no choice but to live his life. Wake up each morning and go to class, study for exams, write papers, then come home and fall asleep, only to do it all over again the next day.

All while he felt like he was dying.

Nights were the worst. John would lie in bed, eyes open, trying to imagine where she was or how she was feeling. He missed her so much most days he felt like he was suffocating. He'd dream at night about falling into a raging river and never having the strength to get to the bank. Just tossing and turning helplessly through the churning water.

Waking up from the nightmare didn't help.

As the days turned to weeks, and the weeks to months he did research on the progress of her pregnancy. What she must've been feeling, what her body was going through, how the baby was growing.

When the semester ended, he got a call from Betsy. She met him at a park halfway between their houses.

"I have the address. Here." She handed him a folded few pieces of paper. "She wrote you a letter, too."

He thanked her, and long after Betsy was gone, John sat at the park in the freezing cold and stared at the letter. Her words kept him warm. Over and over again he let his eyes wander the length of the page. Then he'd start over again at the beginning.

Dear John,

I'm so sorry I didn't get to say good-bye. They moved me to my aunt's house at first, and then a few days later my father drove me to Illinois. I live in a house with five other girls. Pregnant, like me. All of them sent away. Most of us want to keep our babies, but none of us know how to make that happen.

John, I ache for you every day, every hour. I want you to know that. But I couldn't write until now. My father left strict instructions with the houseparents that I wasn't supposed to write letters to anyone.

Yesterday, he called me to tell me the final adoption plan and I begged him to let me write to Betsy. I still can't believe he agreed. I guess he thinks you're out of the picture. Out of my life — just because we haven't seen each other.

Anyway, I'm sending you the address. You can't write to me, unless you give the letter to Betsy and have her send it. That would work, I think. For now, anyway. Until my father figures out what we're doing.

I still don't want to give our baby up, John. But I don't see any other way. It's harder every day without you, every day watching my belly get bigger and knowing that I'll never see this child grow up. If only there were something we could do.

> I love you always,
> Elizabeth

John couldn't get enough of the precious few pages. And by the next day — despite everything working against them — he had something he hadn't had since they'd gotten news of the baby.

He had a plan.

17

Not all their date nights were spent wandering the streets of downtown Bloomington. Ashley was spending this one helping Landon go through old boxes in the garage — something he'd wanted to do for a very long time. The boxes stood floor to ceiling taking up a large area of the garage — things her dad had left behind when he married Elaine and moved out. The year Ashley, Landon and the kids moved in.

"Look at this." Landon chuckled and gazed at the stacks of boxes that made up one end of the oversized garage. "It's a firetrap, for sure."

Ashley winced, hands on her hips. There had to be thirty boxes along with some broken furniture. "I can see what you mean." She bent down and read the writing on the nearest one. "Old Dishes." She allowed a soft laugh. "My sweet mom. She didn't throw away a single thing."

"That's what your dad said." Landon found a folding table from the other side of the garage and set it up. "We can use this to go through everything." He pointed to a large trash bin near the open garage door. "And that . . ."

"That . . ." She couldn't agree more. "We'll use that to throw away anything we don't —"

"Absolutely need!"

They finished the last part together. Then Landon grabbed the first box and set it on the table.

This one was full of Erin's schoolwork, hundreds of pages of math, spelling, science and English, along with art projects from kindergarten through high school. Ashley knew this task would be emotional at times. But she didn't expect the first items to belong to Erin. She spread stacks of the documents across the table. A's decorated the tops of many of them. "She and Brooke were always the best at school."

Landon smiled at her. "Except for art. You had to be the best at that." He always knew how to make her feel good. Even in these recent days when she so badly doubted herself.

"Possibly." She smiled at him. "Thank you." A colored page caught Ashley's attention and she picked it up. It was an art project Erin had done when she was in second grade. Ashley could tell because of the teacher's name at the top. Mrs. Isaacson. All the Baxter kids had gone through second grade with Mrs. Isaacson.

"What is it?" Landon came up beside her.

The picture showed a color drawing of the entire Baxter family — everyone except Dayne, of course. Their parents, and the five siblings who had grown up together. At the bottom of the piece, Erin had written: "My family is the best in the whole wide world."

"She sure loved being a Baxter." Landon eased Ashley closer to him. "I can't see throwing that away."

"No." Ashley blinked back her tears. "I'll save these for Amy. My dad has a box of Erin's journals he's going to give her when she graduates from high school. Otherwise . . . Dad said to get rid of it. There's only so much you can save."

"Mmm." Landon took the drawing from Ashley and set it on the table. Then he pulled her to himself. "You don't know how attractive that is, Ash. A woman who wants to get rid of stuff that's been sitting here gathering dust for years." He kissed her and grinned at her with flirty eyes. "Let's get this thing done!"

Progress on the first few boxes was slow. But then they found an assortment of old towels — all of which had gotten moldy over the years. And suddenly they were making a dent in the pile. While they worked, Ashley gave Landon a rundown on the rest of the family.

Dayne and Katy and their family were planning to spend the summer in Bloomington. "They're between films, so this is perfect." Ashley opened the lid of the next box and peered inside. Tablecloths, maybe. Or moving blankets from who knows how far back. "Goodwill."

"Nice." Landon pointed to the empty spot next to the trash bin. "Start a fresh stack."

The conversation continued. Brooke and Peter were celebrating their anniversary next week, and their girls were ready for summer vacation.

"Especially Maddie, right?" Landon smiled in Ashley's direction. "She and Connor Flanigan still dating?"

"They're taking a break." Ashley raised her brow. "This summer should be interesting for sure. Brooke thinks Maddie and Connor will get back together. If she's right, how amazing would that be if they got married someday? The Baxters and Flanigans, forever connected." She brushed her hair from her eyes. "I love it."

Ashley remembered how the two families came together so long ago. It was through Bloomington's Christian Kids Theater. Ashley had volunteered to paint sets and in doing so she became friends with Katy Hart — a young teacher at the theater. Katy lived with the Flanigans and was like part of their family.

And of course, now Katy was married to their brother Dayne. So in some ways the Baxters and Flanigans would always be connected.

Over the next hour, Ashley talked about her sisters and brothers and all of their kids. Everyone would be busy this summer. Especially Kari and Ryan's son, RJ, who had been chosen to play baseball for a competitive team from Indianapolis. The drive wouldn't be fun, but RJ's coach believed he had potential to one day play in the big leagues.

"What about Luke? He's coming to the Memorial Day barbecue, right?" Landon lifted another box up onto the table and dusted off his hands.

"Their whole family's coming." Ashley couldn't wait for the celebration. Times when they were all together were less often these days, now that the nieces and nephews were so busy. But they were more special than ever. "Luke's been handling some interesting religious freedom cases in the city. It's becoming a crime to pray in public."

Landon shook his head. "Our founding fathers would be furious."

"Exactly." She opened another box. "You'll have to ask Luke about it when he's here." She peered into the container and hesitated. What was this? Broken dishes? "Landon, look."

He helped her lift several dishes and glass pitchers from the wrapping. All of them had — at one time — been very beautiful. But now they all had one thing in common. They were broken. Broken and patched up.

Ashley took a pitcher from the box and ran her hand over it. There was something very familiar about it. She studied it, the beautiful white-gray porcelain and the designs woven into it. Where had she seen it before?

A large chip had fallen from the mouth of the vessel and at one point the handle had broken off. Somewhere along the journey of raising their family, Ashley's mother must've bought glue and put the thing back together again.

"Your mom was the most amazing woman." Landon admired the restored pitcher. "Anything to save a dollar for the family."

A memory was coming back to Ashley. Luke had thrown the football across the room and hit the pitcher, knocking it to the floor and breaking it. "She was careful with money, but that wasn't what it was." She stared at the pitcher, seeing the moment again in her mind. "My mom was going to throw it away, but she stopped herself. I can still see her holding up the pieces."

The scene was becoming clearer still. "She didn't get mad or anything. She just set it on the counter and asked Luke to find some superglue."

Landon was quiet, a slight smile on his lips. "I can imagine that."

Ashley held up the pitcher once more. "As soon as it was put together and dry, she called us over. All five of us." Ashley ran her finger over the repaired cracks. "She told us she was going to keep it forever."

"Forever?" Landon stood beside her, looking at the pitcher. "I guess she kept her promise."

A smile tugged at Ashley's lips. "She always did." Ashley could see her mother again, young and healthy and full of life lessons. "She told us the repaired pitcher was an illustration of God's grace. The way he saw us. We would have broken times in life. Times when we threw a ball where we shouldn't and next thing you knew something very precious was lying on the ground in pieces."

She remembered more from that day. "My mom set it on the table in the living room, where it stayed for the longest time. She told us God would always put the pieces back together if we were willing. The end result might not look exactly as it did before, but it would be beautiful all the same."

Her mother's voice came to her. "Beautifully broken. That's what she called it." Ashley smiled at Landon, her eyes damp. "Beautifully broken."

"I like that." He looked at the pitcher. "Might be time to get it out of the garage."

"I was thinking the same thing." She carried the pitcher to the door. "I'll run it inside."

She had some pottery sealant in her art room. Tomorrow she could give the cracks a quick once-over. She might even use it for their Sunday morning brunches. Her kids would love the story. Something special, something to remind them of their grandma.

They were halfway through the boxes, but Ashley had grown quieter than before. Thinking about her mom and the pitcher, and the story her father had been telling them every Thursday. No wonder she wanted to save the broken vessel.

It probably reminded her of herself.

"You okay?" Landon knew her. He always knew.

"Just thinking about my parents. The broken pieces of their story, I guess." She gave Landon a wistful look. "I always knew the broad strokes of what happened back then. But I guess I didn't imagine the details."

"They were human. Like all of us."

"Yes. Very true." She paused for a moment. "When I came back from Paris I thought I was the worst person in the world. And I was finished with God and my family. You know why?"

"You were angry and afraid." He came to her and took hold of her hands. They were both covered in dust and dirt from their work date, but it didn't matter.

"Yes. But more than that. I thought God and my family were through with me. I couldn't imagine any of them ever doing something like I'd done." She shrugged, her

286

smile soft. "How wrong was I?"

Landon ran his thumbs along the tops of her hands. "Your parents had a rough start. That's for sure."

She'd been keeping him apprised each week as her dad told another part of his story. But somehow here, finding the pitcher brought the cycle of things all together. "Somehow they survived it. I can't wait to hear the next piece of the story."

"Yes." Landon searched her eyes. "What about Cole? Anything more from him?"

"Not since last time." She sighed and turned to the unopened box on the table. "I wish I knew how to begin *that* conversation."

Landon removed the lid and together they peered inside. Dozens of VHS tapes — all of them from a National Geographic series on world wars. Something her father had been interested in for a few years way back. "Goodwill?"

"Definitely." She laughed. "My dad. Such a passionate guy. No matter what he cares about, he's all in."

They made their way through a few more boxes, broken toys and old bedding. Newspapers from decades ago. An easy quiet fell over them, and after a while Landon took a deep breath. "Hey, Ash, I have an idea." He smiled. "Why don't you practice on me?"

"Practice?" She grinned at him.

"Hey, hey . . . come on. That kind can wait." He laughed, and then his face grew more serious. "I mean tell me what you're going to tell Cole. You can practice on me. Go ahead."

Ashley hadn't thought about that before. She liked the idea. "Okay." She stood a little straighter. "Where do I begin?"

"Where do you want to begin?"

True. It was up to her where she began the story. She sat on the edge of the worktable. "Well . . . I guess I'd begin with you, of course. Our middle school days. When you wouldn't stop liking me no matter how mean I was."

"There was always only you for me, Ashley." He leaned against the garage refrigerator a few feet away. "Then what?"

"I was stubborn and rebellious so I went to Paris. But the whole time you were back here in Bloomington praying for me. Thinking about me. Loving me."

"Right."

Ashley liked the story so far. "I made some terrible choices, things I can't bring myself to think about, and next thing I knew I was pregnant."

"Okay." Landon's expression was kind,

encouraging her to continue. "You're doing great."

This wasn't as hard as she thought. "God saved me and my unborn baby and we came back home, back to Indiana. And from the beginning I kept running into you." She managed a smile. "Every time I did, I felt myself falling for you a little more. Then you were almost killed in that house fire. Saving the life of a little boy."

"I still hear from him every now and then. He sends me emails at the station to let me know how he's doing in school." Landon looked all the way through to the depths of her heart. "What else, Ash?"

"I came to the hospital to see you but you were in a coma. So I sat at the edge of your bed and talked to you. I begged you not to die because you had never been too safe, the way I thought. You were a hero and there you were dying in that bed. That's when I told you I loved you." She smiled at him. "I didn't think you heard me, but you did. When you woke up you told me."

"Your words in that hospital room are always with me." He came to her and took hold of her hands again. "See? The story's not that hard."

"It isn't." She kept her eyes locked on his. "I loved you way before I was willing to really admit it. And then 9/11 happened. Your friend Jalen was missing, so you went to New York City. You didn't stop digging there at Ground Zero until you found him. And all that time . . . all that time I missed you with everything in me. I thought it was too late, that I'd messed things up forever by letting you go."

"But I came back."

"I was standing in the field outside this very house, painting." She angled her face and let herself get lost in his eyes. "Remember?"

"Of course." He released one hand and worked his fingers through her hair.

"You came up to me and asked me the same thing Irvel always asked me." Ashley felt tears in her eyes again. Irvel had been her favorite patient when Ashley worked at the Sunset Hills Adult Care Home.

"You have the most beautiful hair." Landon ran his hand over the back of her head. "Has anyone ever told you that?"

"Yes. Exactly." Ashley made a sound that was part laugh, part cry. She loved the way this was playing out. "That's what you said. And just like that we had a chance." She looked deep into his eyes again. "You loved Cole from the first time you saw him, and once I let you into our lives you were amazing with him. Taking him to the park and reading him *Mike Mulligan and His Steam Shovel.* Wrestling with him and including him in our adventures every Saturday."

Landon took a step back and dropped his hands to his sides. "And . . . ?"

"And we got married months before my mom died of cancer. With Cole there to witness the whole thing." Suddenly Ashley realized something. She felt her eyes grow wide. "Wait a minute . . ."

"I know, right?" He chuckled, clearly enjoying the way the reality was landing on her.

"That's it! That's my story." She laughed, too. Standing still was no longer an option. She paced to the Goodwill pile and back, amazed. "My story isn't about some married painter in Paris." She ran to him, took his face in her hands and kissed him. "It's about you! The story is about you, Landon."

"Exactly." His lips found hers and he grinned at her. "It's about time you figured that out."

They both laughed and kissed again. The work could wait. This was the revelation Ashley had been waiting for, the answer she'd been praying about since Cole first asked about his story. It was never about his biological father. Not at all. Cole's story was rooted in the love between her and Landon. A love that wasn't only breathtakingly beautiful. It was like so many precious things in life, just the way her mother had described the pitcher all those years ago.

Beautifully broken.

Wilson Gage was restless. He hadn't been out of the house in two days and he needed a night out. But the Bingo Parlor was closed and he didn't want to play pool at the bar. Easier to drink at home.

He grabbed another two beers from the fridge and flopped into his recliner. Where was the remote? He looked beneath a stack of newspapers and found it. A few clicks and the news came on. Wilson stared at it. The world had gotten crazy lately. Applauding people who desecrated the flag. Wilson was a liberal like the best of them. But ain't no one got the right to shun the American flag.

Wilson drew the line there.

He popped the top on the beer and drank half of it. This was his fourth tonight. Fourth or fifth. Wilson wasn't sure.

He leaned his head back and stared at the screen. A pretty blond anchor was talking about religious freedom. Something about the cases adding up. People were rising up against the church, looking to eliminate God from the landscape of America. A witch hunt, the lady called it. One that was overdue.

Wilson sat up straighter in his chair. What was wrong with people? He blinked his blurry eyes. Didn't matter if he believed in God or not. The Constitution guaranteed Americans certain rights. Religion was one of them. The woman was saying something about some government officials wanting a state church. Something politically correct that everyone could agree on.

"Ridiculous!" Wilson shook his head and turned off the TV. He couldn't watch the news tonight. Too many outrageous stories. He finished the rest of his beer and his eyes fell on the cross again. The one his wife had bought so long ago.

"I asked You for a sign, God. Remember?" Wilson heard the sneer in his voice. He didn't care. God hadn't delivered. Wilson had a right to be angry.

But, angry or not, the whole religious rights thing troubled him. How long before he would wake up to an America he didn't recognize? The one he had fought for had already changed more than he could put into words.

Especially after five beers.

He stood and stretched. There had to be some way to pass the hours. He looked at the desk in the corner. His computer. That was an option. He could search what was happening with the Constitution lately. Wilson's steps were far from straight, but he made his way to the desk and sat down.

As soon as he did, he had an idea. Facebook. He could check Facebook and find out what his friends were doing. Maybe one of them lived in the area. Someone he could take to dinner or to the bar. He opened his page and immediately saw the notification on the message icon at the top.

"Someone sent me a message." Wilson grinned. "Well, look at that."

He opened his private messages and furrowed his brow. Cole Blake? Who in the world was Cole Blake? Probably advertising. Wilson rolled his eyes, but just in case he opened the message. Right away he could see it wasn't spam or an ad.

It was a letter.

His eyes worked their way down from the opening line.

Dear Mr. Gage,
My name is Cole Blake and I'm working on a heritage project for my school. I'm doing my report on my grand-

father's story. It happened a long time ago and I'm learning all about it. He said a Vietnam vet from Indiana was an important part of the story.

Are you the Wilson Gage who lived in Indiana and helped a man named John Baxter in the 1970s? If so I'd like to interview you.

I'm not completely sure what happened, my grandfather hasn't gotten to that part yet. But I wanted to write now, so we could make a connection. I get extra credit if I interview another person who was part of the story.

So please could you write back and let me know if it is you? And if you want to do an interview, I can get some questions to you. Thank you, and God bless you.

Sincerely, Cole Blake

"Well, I'll be . . ." Wilson leaned back hard in his chair and read the letter again. John Baxter. Chill bumps ran down Wilson's spine. Of course he remembered the young man. Every now and then Wilson even wondered what happened to him. Did he and the girl find each other? Did he marry her the way he wanted to?

Back then Wilson had given the guy better

advice than he'd have now. If the kid wanted to interview him, he was okay with that. He rattled off a quick message in response.

Dear Cole,
You found the right man. I can talk to you whenever you want. My number's at the bottom of this note. Tell your grandpa I hope everything worked out.
                                        Wilson Gage

Then he read the boy's letter a third time. How was that even possible? John Baxter remembered him? From that night a lifetime ago? And now the man's grandson wanted to talk. None of it added up. Why him? He was just an old forgotten Vietnam vet living in a little old house in Michigan. What could Wilson possibly add to John Baxter's story? And suddenly the truth fell on him like the first summer rain.

This was the sign.

The one he'd asked for. Wilson sat there for the better part of an hour, trying to grasp the possibility of John Baxter remembering him, and how he must've helped John. A lot, even. Otherwise the man's grandkid wouldn't have tried to find him.

Yes, this had to be the sign.

The God he had once loved, the One

whose reality Wilson had shared with a lost young man one early summer night decades ago, had not abandoned him. "I'm sorry, God . . . I never should've . . . never should've turned my back on You."

God *was* real. Of course He was.

And if that was true, then there was something he needed to do. Wilson felt tears sting at his eyes. How could he have chucked the faith he'd enjoyed for most of his life? The one Scarlett had shared with him. What was Wilson thinking? Had he really thought he could ride out his days without God?

Death came to call on everyone eventually. The way it had come to call on his Scarlett. The way it would come to call on him one day soon.

Wilson shouldn't have been angry at God for taking Scarlett. He should've been thankful he ever had her in the first place.

Hope and light flooded Wilson's dark heart. His head didn't hurt so bad. Then in a voice that was hardly a whisper, he made his declaration. "I get it, God. If You're real, then You're real." He smiled so he wouldn't break down and cry. These past few years the way he'd ignored God was almost too much for him to think about.

Instead he anchored on the here and now.

The boy's message. The miracle of this single night. "You kept Your part of the bargain." Wilson sniffed. "Now it's my turn."

He stood and walked with trembling legs to the table near his chair. His next beer was still sweaty and cold. Wilson didn't care. He took it to the kitchen, popped the top, and poured it down the sink. Whatever God saw in him, whatever reason He had for giving Wilson a sign, this much was sure: God had more for Wilson to do than sit around the house getting drunk every night. "You're there, God. I'm sorry I ever doubted You."

Wilson made his way to the cross that hung in the TV room. He touched the wood and studied the place where the pieces intersected. Maybe the Lord would tell Scarlett how much he missed her. "You died for me. And tonight . . . tonight You gave me a sign." He felt the beginning of a smile. "You know what that means."

No more beer. Not ever again. He'd had his last drink.

After all, a deal was a deal.

18

The Army had taught Cody to be early. It was a habit that stayed with him. But the habit had nothing to do with why he was at the park across from the animal shelter half an hour early that Friday morning.

He had no choice but to be here early. He'd been thinking about Andi all night, praying for her, begging God that somehow she would listen to what he had to say. Sometime around seven o'clock, he saw her step off the shuttle bus. She turned and faced him and Cody had to force himself to breathe.

There were two swings in the small park. Cody was already sitting in one of them. He watched her come closer. She was so pretty. Black jeans and a white T-shirt with the name of her relief organization. The attire of the volunteers in the flood zone. But even then she was the most beautiful girl he'd ever seen. *Andi . . . please don't turn me away.*

God, please guide our words this morning.

But as she drew closer, Cody felt his heart sink. Her eyes looked distant, closed off. She stopped when she reached him, her eyes locked on his. "Hi."

"Hi." He nodded to the swing beside him. "I saved you a seat."

She smiled, but it didn't come from her heart. The way her smile usually did. "Thanks."

"How's your puppy?"

"Perfect." Her eyes softened a little. "He's still at the hotel. I'll bring him to the shelter later. I can't leave him in a cage all day."

"Although I'm sure he likes having friends."

"True." Andi seemed like she was starting to enjoy herself. She must've noticed it, too, because her smile faded and she took a seat in the swing.

They held on to the chains and moved a little, swaying lightly, their feet never leaving the ground. She broke the silence first. "I prayed about it, Cody. About us." She paused. "I'm sorry."

She was sorry? This wasn't how he wanted the conversation to go. "I . . . There's more to tell you."

Her phone began to ring. She glanced at it and her eyes filled with alarm. "Oh, no!"

She looked up at him. "I have to go." She started walking toward the street.

Cody kept up with her. "Wait. What is it?" Was this really how things were going to end today? "I just got here."

"It's an emergency. A resident just found a single mom and her kids. They've been stranded all this time." Andi kept walking toward the shuttle stop. "I'm sorry, Cody. I have to go. I'm closest to the woman's house and my agency needs someone to help her. Now."

"Wait." He put his hand on her shoulder. "I have a car. I'll take you."

His idea must've shocked her because she stopped and looked right at him. "You'd do that?"

"Of course." He took her hand and led her in the opposite direction, to the spot where his rental car was parked. Whatever was ahead, his training as a soldier would help. "I handled a few rescues back in the day."

They hurried to his car and set out toward the address her supervisor had texted her. This was exactly what Cody had wanted to do when he first arrived in Louisiana. Work with her and talk to her. Show her kindness and consideration, the way he hadn't in far too long.

Whatever it took to remind her why she had loved him in the first place.

For that reason, as Cody navigated the debris and damaged streets, he didn't think about the emergency situation or the work ahead. That would come. For now he could only think about one thing.

Andi was in the seat beside him.

Andi couldn't get past the feel of her hand in his. In fact, she couldn't believe what was happening. Cody Coleman was driving her to the site of an emergency? She took it all in. The familiar way his hands looked on the wheel and the faint smell of his cologne. The whole thing felt like something from a dream.

Focus on your job, she told herself. *You have to focus.* She stared straight ahead and willed herself to concentrate. "I guess . . . the victims' house was nearly destroyed. The woman and her kids are stranded and the ambulance is still half an hour away." Andi could feel herself switching gears, getting into work mode. "Her family couldn't get through to her and they reported her missing." She pressed her back against the passenger door so she could see him better. And so she wouldn't be tempted to take his hand again.

The way she'd done a thousand times before.

"I don't know how they survived." Cody sounded concerned. He kept his eyes on the battered road. "Things could be bad."

"Exactly." Andi texted her supervisor, explaining that Cody had joined her and that he would help in the first phase of the rescue. At the same time she gave Cody directions through the flooded neighborhood until they weren't able to drive any further. Cody parked and they met up with a volunteer from another agency, a man waiting with a rowboat. He would take them the remaining few blocks to the house.

"The water's still so high." Cody looked around and shook his head. "The flood in this part of town was days ago, right?"

"Yes. This was part of the second flood." Her eyes met his as they climbed into the small boat. "It's always like this. People think floodwaters just dissipate." As the volunteer began rowing, Andi had no choice but to sit next to Cody. Their knees touched, and Andi shivered a little.

"You cold?" Cody wore a sweatshirt and as he spoke he peeled it off his body and handed it to her. "Here. Wear this."

"No . . . it's fine." But even as she said the words she took the hoodie from him. It was warm from the heat of his body.

"Wear it. Please, Andi." He looked at her. "You're cold. I can tell."

He was right. Whether it was the early morning chill or the closeness of Cody Coleman, Andi wasn't sure. But her shivering was worse. She slipped his sweatshirt on and immediately she felt relief.

"Better?" He put his arm around her and eased her against him. "Stay by me till the chill's gone."

It's a dream. It has to be a dream. Andi couldn't believe any of it.

Cody's sweatshirt. His arm around her. The boat and the flooded street. The emergency at hand. How could this be real? She tried to think about the rescue ahead but all she could imagine was her own. It wasn't safe for her heart, being this near to Cody. If she let herself get caught up in him again, what would become of her? She was about to slide over, put distance between them. Then she changed her mind.

It felt so good being this close to him. Maybe she could pretend they were still together. Just this one day. Because in this moment it seemed like they'd never broken up, never moved on from each other.

They reached the house and once more Cody took her hand. They didn't have waders, so as soon as they stepped out of the boat their jeans were immediately soaked. He took Andi's bag from her. In it was an emergency kit full of water bottles, medications, and first-aid supplies. Cody set the bag on a ledge as they made their way into the house.

"Wait . . . we need that." Andi looked back.

"I'll get it later." Cody still had hold of her fingers. "Right now I want my hands free. We don't know what we're going to find."

Inside, the two of them slogged through waist-deep water. A few feet from the door, a bookcase blocked their path. Cody easily moved it out of the way, and then together they navigated the other broken furniture in their path.

"They must be upstairs." Cody started up, taking the lead and testing the stair rail. It gave way and fell to the ground.

"After a flood everything can crumble." Andi was glad Cody was being careful. "Walls can collapse without warning."

"I bet." Cody took his time. "Stay on the edge of the stairs. That's where the support is."

"Okay." They reached the top. "Hello?" Andi called out. If the people were here, they weren't making a sound.

Noise came from one of the rooms. A woman's voice, weak and definitely afraid. "We're in here."

"This way." Cody led her to a door at the far end of the hallway. The carpet was drenched and the drywall that lined the hall was crumbling. Clearly the upstairs had been flooded, too.

No training could prepare Andi for the scene in front of her as Cody opened the door. A woman was huddled on a soaked couch, her two little girls and one boy beside her. The upper ridge of the sofa was the only dry thing in the entire room.

All three kids were very still, their faces blank. Like they were in shock.

"It's okay." Andi released Cody's hand and approached the woman as they came near. "An ambulance is on the way. What's your name?"

"Cara Grace." The woman's hair was matted to her head and her wet sweatshirt clung to her body. "Thank you. For finding us."

"Of course." Andi put her arm around the woman. "What happened?"

Dark circles under Cara Grace's eyes showed how exhausted she was. "It was the second flood that got us. We've been here four days." Tears filled her eyes. "I wasn't sure anyone would ever come."

Cody gave Andi a quick look. He motioned to the stairs. "I'll get your bag." Then he hurried out of the room.

Andi was trying to listen to the woman, but she kept thinking about Cody, the way he had been willing to jump in and help. Again she forced herself to focus. Cara Grace was explaining how neither of her girls knew how to swim. Tears filled the woman's eyes. "When the flood came it swept away our car before we had time to evacuate."

"So you all came up here?" Andi was in the moment now. She needed to help Cara Grace and her little ones. "But the water kept rising, right? At least it looks that way."

"The water rose so fast." The woman's tears spilled onto her cheeks. "We . . . we stayed upstairs on my bed. But then the floodwater soaked the mattress." As Cara Grace spoke, she began to shake, as if the horror of what she'd just survived was finally becoming real to her. "The water came up all around us and then . . . then it stopped."

"We almost drowned." One of the kids, a blond little boy, spoke up. He looked to be the oldest and he seemed more frightened than the others. Probably because he was

307

able to understand the danger they had been in.

"I'm so glad you didn't." Andi still had her arm around the woman. "Help is coming. It's going to be okay."

"No, it's not." The woman whispered the words. Then she began to shake harder. She mouthed her next words. "We lost everything."

"We can help you with that. Really."

"Okay." Cara Grace took a shaky breath and finished the story. She told how her cell phone had been broken, and she had no landline, so when the waters started to rise she wasn't sure what else to do but head upstairs. She had grabbed two loaves of bread, a package of sliced cheese, and a case of water bottles.

They had survived on that.

The drinking water was gone now and so was the food. Her story finished, the woman fell quiet once more. Andi was about to ask the children how they were feeling when Cody came back. He carried the bag with the emergency kit and handed it to Andi.

Then he moved to the littlest child, a girl who looked to be three or four. "I'm Cody." He sat beside her. "I'm going to help you, okay?"

Andi couldn't take her eyes off him, the

compassion in his voice and kindness in his gentle smile. Like he'd been helping with rescues all his life.

"I'm hungry." The little girl looked at Cody. "Can I have toast?"

"Soon." Cody smiled at her. He pressed the back of his fingers to her forehead and then took her small hand. He felt the pulse at her wrist. "You're a very brave girl. What's your name?"

"Emma." Her eyes were bright with admiration. Cody was her hero, no doubt.

Cody glanced at Andi. "Her heartbeat's steady. No fever." He moved to the next little girl. Like her siblings, the child wore several layers of damp shirts and sweaters. Andi watched as Cody felt this girl's forehead. "And what's your name?"

"Esther." This girl seemed to be five or six. Her eyes looked glassy, and she seemed weaker than her sister. "I don't feel good."

"I'm sorry. We're going to take care of you." Cody took the child's pulse. Clearly she wasn't well, though Cody seemed to do his best to hide the fact. "Tell me about school. What grade are you?"

"First." She managed the hint of a weary smile. "I'm the best reader in my class."

"I'll bet you are." This time when Cody looked at Andi, he silently mouthed, "Fever.

She needs a doctor."

Quiet tears filled Cara Grace's eyes again. "I've been so scared. I knew Esther was sick."

"It's going to be all right." Andi released her hold on Cara Grace and took her hand instead. She pulled a thermometer from the bag and took the woman's temperature. It was elevated, but not badly. "You're all going to get through this." She focused on Cara Grace's eyes.

She looked at Andi. "Please stay. Until we can get out of here."

"We will. We're not going anywhere." Andi continued to hold the woman's hand as the two of them watched Cody.

He had moved on to the boy, who was maybe nine years old. "How you feeling, buddy?"

"Tired." He leaned his head against his mother's arm and studied Cody. "Are you a fireman?"

Cody put his hand on the boy's forehead. "I trained as a firefighter when I was in the Army. So kind of." Cody smiled, but there was no hiding the alarm in his eyes. "We're going to get you something to drink, okay?"

"I'm not thirsty." The boy's words were slightly slurred.

With a gentleness that belied his soldierly

strength, Cody checked the boy's wrist. Then he checked it again and Andi could see the muscles in his jaw clench. "Dehydrated," Cody mouthed his assessment to Andi. Then he looked at the emergency kit. "Is there anything rehydrating in there?"

Andi let go of Cara's hand and reached for the bag. "I think so." She sifted through the items and found a few packets of mineral replenishment. They needed to work quickly. With steady fingers, Andi opened one.

"Here. Let me." Cody gently took both from her. He poured the packet into a water bottle from the kit and shook it up.

Andi felt dizzy as she moved to the boy and took his temperature. This was why she had fallen in love with Cody in the first place. He was calm and completely focused, stronger than any guy she knew and completely in control. No wonder she felt protected around him.

She read the thermometer. The boy's fever was high. Nearly 103 degrees. A quick look at Cody. "He's hot."

Cody knelt down in front of the child and handed him the mixed water. "Here, buddy. Drink this."

"I'm still not thirsty." The boy remained with his head against his mother.

"You know what this is, right?" Cody held the bottle out to the child. "This is a superhero drink. It'll make you really strong, okay?"

Andi watched, mesmerized. Cody was brilliant with the boy. The superhero bit seemed to make the difference. The boy took the bottle and drank a few sips. "It's salty."

"Superheroes need salt." Cody sat beside the child. "What's your name?"

"Edward." The boy took another few sips.

In the distance, Andi heard sirens. The ambulance would be here soon. Then the family would be taken to the hospital and examined more thoroughly. Andi stayed next to Cara Grace while Cody continued talking to the kids.

Emma was the chattiest. "I wanna be a superhero, too."

"You are a superhero, Emma." Cody smiled at her. "I can tell."

Minutes later two paramedics hurried through the bedroom door and began working with the family. Once they could see the situation was stable, they directed Andi and Cody to help move the family to the ambulance down the street.

"We'll have to take two trips." One of the paramedics took Edward in his arms and the other carried Esther.

Cody lifted Emma, then he turned to Andi. "You got Cara Grace?"

"Yes." Andi helped the woman to her feet and the two followed the others. "We'll be right behind you."

One of the paramedics took Cara Grace and the kids, and then the rowboat returned for Cody and Andi and the second paramedic. After they were all safely in the boat, Cody sat beside Andi on the quick trip to dry ground. Their bodies were so close Andi could hear him breathing. They arrived just as little Emma was being helped into the waiting ambulance.

Cody gave the young girl a thumbs-up as the child was loaded into the back. "Superhero, okay? Don't forget?"

An innocent smile lit up her eyes. "Okay."

Andi stood beside Cody and they watched as Cara Grace and her other children were placed in the ambulance, and the vehicle pulled away. After several seconds Andi turned to him. "You were amazing back there. With the children." She searched his eyes. "Thank you."

"Of course." He watched her for a long moment and then he pulled her into his arms. "And you . . . you were beautiful with that woman, Andi. You have this . . . peace.

A strength. You helped her be brave."

"You, too." Andi pressed against Cody. Wrapped in his arms and still wearing his sweatshirt, she didn't want the moment to end. If this was a dream, she would have to wake up sometime. Just not yet. She closed her eyes and rested her head on Cody's chest.

Once, a long time ago, Cody's mother had shown Andi a few photos from his time at war. Pictures of Cody with several Middle Eastern children. They clambered around him, hanging on to his neck and grinning at him.

Was that how he would be with his own children one day? He would make an amazing father. He had proven that much over the past hour.

Andi took a quick breath and stepped back. What was she doing? Standing here with Cody and dreaming about his ability to be a father? Andi blinked. She needed to get out of here, had to find her way back to reality. She crossed her arms and looked at the ruins around them. "Cara Grace and her kids will be okay."

"They will." Cody looked bewildered. Like he wasn't sure why she had pulled away.

Andi studied the street. The neighborhood

was destroyed. Several houses had floated away. It was a miracle Cara Grace and her family had survived at all. Everyone had been evacuated from the area except the mother and her three children.

Somehow they had been forgotten.

Andi and Cody were both wet, and now that she no longer had Cody to keep her warm, Andi began to shiver again. "Those kids could've drowned."

"Definitely." Cody reached for her hand once more. "Let's get you back to your room. You need dry clothes."

Neither of them said a word as they walked back to his car and Cody climbed behind the wheel. The quiet between them remained the entire drive back to Andi's hotel. As long as his hand held hers, there were no words needed.

Cody waited in the lobby as she headed up to her room. Once there, Andi checked on her puppy. He was sleepy, and he barely moved as she patted his silky ear. The events of the last few hours hit her all over again and she moved slowly to the window. *What's happening, God? Why is he here?*

She loved everything about this morning. Working beside Cody, watching his tender strength, pretending they were a couple. Just for today. The moments with him were everything she had dreamed.

He was everything she had dreamed.

As if in response, scenes from their past filled her mind. The times Cody had grown distant and silent. Nights when he seemed a million miles away. She stood a little straighter. She couldn't do this again. Couldn't let herself be swept away. No matter how wonderful this morning had been.

They still needed to talk.

With new determination, Andi changed into fresh jeans and her own sweatshirt, and then she returned to him. He watched her as she approached and as she handed him his hoodie. "Thanks for this." Her smile felt slightly awkward. "I needed it."

"Hey . . ." He looked more deeply into her eyes. "Andi? Something's wrong."

She took a slow breath. "Do you have a few minutes?"

Panic fell over his face. He must've changed into a fresh pair of jeans from his car because he was dry now, too. He slid his hands into his pockets. "Sure. Where do you wanna go?"

"Back to the park." She didn't want to break down here. All of her co-workers were staying at this hotel. She met his eyes again. "If that's okay."

"Of course."

As they drove to the park Andi thought about the animal shelter and how she would need to go back to the hotel and get her puppy. Then she would meet up with Caleb and they could pick up where they'd left off with the frightened cats and dogs.

Anything to keep from thinking of Cody and the way it had felt being with him today, working with him, wrapped in his arms. No, she couldn't think about any of that. Because the talk they were about to have would be one they'd both remember forever. Andi was sure of it. And after today Cody wouldn't be there to help her.

He wouldn't be there at all.

19

Cody took his time driving to the park.

Something had changed with Andi. He could feel it. The drive took only a few minutes, and Cody had no idea what to say, no idea what had gone wrong in such a short time. Back at the rescue site, Andi had warmed up to him. The two seemed to have found the love they'd lost. But after she changed clothes, she returned to the lobby closed off. Like the morning had never happened.

They walked in silence to a bench near the swings. This time Cody didn't take her hand. He could tell she didn't want that.

They sat down. He broke the tension first. "Did I do something wrong?"

"No . . ." Andi seemed to steel herself to whatever pain she must've been feeling. "It's not you." She stared at her hands, folded in her lap. "It's me."

"Don't do this, Andi." He could read her

tone. She was giving up on them. She already had.

"Cody."

"Please . . ." He tried to talk above the sound of his pounding heart. "I still love you . . . I never stopped." This couldn't end badly. Not after the morning they'd just shared.

"I know." Andi seemed to dismiss the importance of that. "It's just . . . Cody." She turned to face him. "I can't love you again." Her eyes welled up. "The possibility of . . ."

Cody knew what she was going to say. "The possibility of me hurting you one more time? Is that what this is about?" He slid closer to her. "Andi, I'll never hurt you. Never again. I never meant to in the first place."

"Don't, Cody." She stood and walked to the nearest tree. She leaned against the trunk and hung her head. "Please. Don't."

Cody could do nothing but go to her. With every fiber of his being he wanted to hold her. But he couldn't. The walls she'd placed between them were too great. "I won't hurt you again, Andi." His voice was little more than a whisper. "You have to believe me."

When she lifted her face, when her eyes met his, the pain there was so great it sliced all the way to his soul. "For a while this morning . . . I let myself go there."

Of course she had. They both had.

She had to finish her thought. "I let myself believe things were different. That we were . . . *us* again."

"Andi . . ."

"No." She couldn't bear to hear his explanation now. "I can't take the chance, Cody. You always hurt me. Every time."

"I'm sorry. I know what went wrong and now . . . now I'd do better. We can make it work." Frustration took a swing at him. He fought back. Steady, Cody. Stay calm. This was no time to let his emotions get in the way. *Give me the words. Please, God.* He shook his head. "The thing is, Andi, it was never your fault. There's things you don't know about me. About how things were after our second engagement."

Andi looked at him for a long time and she shook her head. She made a sound that was more cry than laugh. "This can't happen." She grabbed a quick breath. "Don't you see, Cody? Can't you hear yourself? Things fell apart after our *second* engagement. If that isn't a sign that it's never going to work, I don't know what is."

He tried to think of the right words, the best way to explain the past. The PTSD, the dreams, the obsessive feelings that plagued him in crowds. The sporadic episodes. She needed to know how the terror had come back after their second engagement. The way it could always come back as long as he lived.

Then Cody thought of something. There had been no episode this morning, no flashbacks. Usually stressful situations acted as triggers. But not today. That was at least an improvement.

But when he looked at her face, he knew. Her heart was clearly too far gone. And only here and now did Cody understand how very hurt Andi was. When she said she couldn't go through another round of losing him, she meant it. "So . . . you won't give me a chance to . . . to fix this?"

A single tear rolled down her cheek. "Haven't we tried, Cody?"

Haven't we tried? Her words lodged in his heart and stopped him from wanting to tell her anything more. He couldn't fight for something she was so afraid of. Not if she was still this hurt. Cody took his place on the bench again. "You want to be my friend, is that what you're saying?"

It took her a minute, but finally Andi shook her head. "No." She returned to the bench and reached for his hand, closing the distance between them. "I'm saying I can't be your friend. We can't be anything, Cody." Her tears came harder now. "We need to move on. Have our own lives."

Cody worked the muscles in his jaw. There had to be a way to ease her heartache, a way to tell her that he'd never be closed off to her again. But he couldn't think of the words. "I get it." He studied her eyes. "You want a fresh start, right? Someone new who . . . who hasn't broken your heart." He paused. "Someone like that . . . that Caleb you work with."

For the first time since he'd gotten there, uncertainty clouded her eyes. "No . . . Maybe . . . I don't know what I want."

"Just not me."

"You don't get it." She slid a few inches away as she stared at him. "I love you, Cody. I always have." A tear rolled down her cheek. "But you have a pattern. A pattern of breaking my heart, and I can't stay here and let it happen again."

He touched her cheek and then let his hand fall back to his side. "So what now?" His tone was softer than before. Kinder. "You spend the rest of your life wondering what if? Is that what you want?"

"I know what I want. I've made up my mind." The anger had faded from her voice, too. She stood and took a few steps back. "Not everyone gets the happily ever after, Cody. You and I, we weren't meant to be. Can't you see that?"

"No." He was on his feet now, walking to her, erasing the distance between them. "I love you, Andi. The way I've never loved anyone in all my life."

She looked down and for a moment she covered her face with her hands. "Don't say that, Cody. Please."

"Andi, look at me." He took a step closer. So close he could smell her sweet breath, see the way her eyelashes curled on their own. "I need to see you."

Clearly she didn't want to do as he said. But after a minute she lifted her face and looked at him.

He wanted to take hold of her hands. But he didn't dare. Not the way she was feeling now. Their eyes connected, almost like they used to when they were together. "When I tell you I love you still, I mean it. I've been praying for you . . . for us . . . for the chance at this. I've been praying ever since you left." He put his hand on her shoulder and removed it almost as quickly. "I'll always love you, Andi. What happened before . . . that was my fault, it was —"

"Don't." She pulled back from him. "I

don't want excuses, Cody. I've written a thousand of them for you. The reasons you might have forgotten I existed after our second engagement. The bottom line is this . . . it doesn't matter what you were going through. You didn't tell me." She turned away for a moment and then faced him again. "Don't you see? If you were having some real issue, you should've told me. I was your fiancée, Cody." She took a quick breath. "And if it wasn't big enough to tell me, then it shouldn't have been big enough to come between us."

Every word she said made sense. Sure, he could explain himself. He could tell her now about the PTSD and the horror of the dreams. But she was right. It was too late. He should've told her back then.

"I need to go, Cody." Her eyes brimmed with tears again. "I heard that Adele song the other day. The one from a few years ago. 'All I Ask.' Do you know it?"

Everyone knew it. He nodded. "Yes." His heart was already racing, the panic already setting in. Andi was standing right here, but he was about to lose her. The way he had lost her every time they were together, and there was nothing he could do to stop it. In a few minutes she would be gone.

Forever.

Andi took a step closer. "That's how I want you to leave this time. Like the Adele song." Her eyes had never looked more sad. "It matters how this ends. Just in case . . . I never love this way again."

No! The word screamed through Cody's mind. This was crazy! He had to stop her. But there was nothing more he could say, no argument that remained. She was still coming to him, still drawing nearer. "Hold me, Cody . . . like we're more than just friends." Her voice broke and the tears ran down her face. "One more time."

The song played in Cody's heart while he took Andi into his arms. This was their last goodbye. He could feel it. She was sobbing now. Not loud or uncontrollably, but with quiet tears. She pressed her hands into his back, as if she never wanted to let go. Same as him.

When she stepped away, her eyes were puffy. "I love you, Cody. Please . . . let me have my life."

He had thought for weeks about what he would say if he was given this moment, how they would work through his issues together, and if she still struggled to trust him, they would work through hers.

But now, she had made it clear she didn't want his excuses. However valid they might be. His eyes filled with tears, too. His sorrow made it hard to talk. But there was still one thing he had to say. "I'll wait for you, Andi. If you can ever find it in your heart to trust me again, I'll be there. One call and I'll be on the next plane."

After all she'd told him that morning, Cody expected her to reiterate the impossibility of that ever happening. But she didn't. She stood there and watched him. Just looked deep into his eyes as if she were memorizing him.

One last time.

He walked with her toward the street then, and hugged her a final time. Cody hated that this was happening. He hadn't come here to tell her goodbye. "I love you." He wanted to kiss her, but he didn't. There was no point. "I always will."

"Me, too." Again she looked at him for a long moment, and then she crossed the street toward the animal shelter.

His only choice now was to leave. Get in his car and drive away. But he wouldn't do it, he couldn't. Not as long as he could still see her. She glanced over her shoulder. Then, with a last look she turned away and disappeared into the tent.

Only then did Cody walk to his car and drive back to his hotel. He packed his things and headed to the airport. His heart was still beating, but he had died the minute she left. If he had nightmares on the flight home, they wouldn't be about Afghanistan. They would be about something else. A blond, blue-eyed girl he would always love, walking out of his life.

For the last time.

Andi didn't remember to breathe until she was inside the animal shelter and Cody Coleman was completely out of sight. The ache in her heart was so great she physically hurt.

Only then did she remember she still had to return to the hotel and pick up her puppy. She was grateful for the distraction. She cried the whole way. On the shuttle to the hotel and on the way back to the shelter. It took that long to stop her tears. All last night she had wrestled with God, asking Him whether she should get back with Cody or cut things off for good.

In the end, she felt the Lord leading her to say good-bye. But as the day played out, as she worked in the shelter and kept her distance from Caleb — who was more chatty than usual — Andi wasn't so sure.

Telling herself that she was fine alone, that all she needed was her faith in God, sounded good. Altruistic, even. She was better off like this, living life where no one could break her heart.

But was it true?

She thought about Cody's last words. If her heart ached for him before, this was a new gut-wrenching level, one she wasn't familiar with. If he loved her . . . if he wouldn't move on until she stopped being afraid of him . . . then what was she afraid of?

It was a question that haunted her the rest of the day. Was she wrong to let him go? After watching him help those children? Andi wrestled with her thoughts. Were her fears the only thing keeping her from a happily ever after with Cody Coleman? That night when Andi and her puppy reached their hotel, she wasn't sure what to do. By now Cody had no doubt flown back to California. After all, she had made it clear she didn't want to be with him.

Doubts collected in her heart like bits of debris on the local roadside. She read her Bible — 1 Timothy this time. It was full of warning. But there near the end was a verse that gave Andi the most beautiful hope. Especially tonight.

But godliness with contentment is great gain. For we brought nothing into the world, and we can take nothing out of it . . . if we have food and clothing, we will be content with that.

Yes, Andi would be content with just that. Food and clothing and a life of serving the Lord. That would be enough. Andi remembered how it felt to be in Cody's arms. She'd never feel that way again. Which would be okay, because God's Word promised it would be. Food and clothing. She needed nothing else.

Or did she?

Andi looked at another verse, in Song of Solomon. One part stuck out to her: *I found the one my heart loves.* She read the words again. *The one my heart loves.* Yes, she had already found him. But no matter what he said, no matter how many times he promised her otherwise, the truth was he had always ended up hurting her. If he wasn't leaving her, he was leaving her alone.

Either way was more than Andi could take.

She'd never been more confused. Alone in the hotel room with her puppy, Andi wondered if she was crazy. Cody loved her still. She believed that. So why was she too afraid to take him back again? Then she remembered the single mom and her children and suddenly the answer was clear once more.

She didn't want to be that woman. Didn't

want to someday be alone and desperate in a house that was falling apart with three children and floodwaters rising. No, she couldn't take the chance that Cody would leave her again. Better to be alone.

Even if she missed him as long as she lived.

20

Bailey was at lunch with her husband, Brandon, about to go shopping for a few last-minute baby items. Three weeks till her due date, and Bailey could hardly wait to meet their little girl. They hadn't settled on a name for sure, but they had narrowed it down to a few.

That's what today was for. A chance to shop and talk and share their feelings for all that lay ahead. They were eating lunch at a quiet café a few blocks from the university. Bailey felt full after only a few bites.

"How are you?" Across the table from her, Brandon wore a baseball cap, the way he often did so he wouldn't be recognized. At home in Bloomington, they were rarely stopped by people. But both of them wanted this time without being interrupted.

"So many feelings." Bailey smiled. Not just the baby. *The Chance* movie had exceeded everyone's expectations. The national media was talking about people finding forgiveness and hope after seeing the film. Just like she had felt at the premiere, God had done something very special with the project.

Bailey felt dizzy over all the happy times past and ahead. Especially the infant girl about to enter their lives. "I can't wait to hold her."

"Me, too." Brandon grinned. "She's going to be so little."

"I know." Bailey might be the oldest of six kids, but the only one she could remember as a baby was Ricky. And even then she'd never changed his diapers. "It'll be a lot of learning."

They both laughed. Brandon rubbed his palms together and then reached for Bailey's hand. "I'm a little nervous."

"A little?" Bailey's laugh tapered off. "I have to give birth to her."

"True." Brandon smiled.

They talked about the nursery, the things they still needed. They had bought the crib a few months ago and last week her parents had bought them a stroller. One of the theater teachers had thrown her a shower a few weeks ago, so there was very little they didn't have. A few odds and ends, mostly. Monday, when Brandon had meetings in

Indianapolis, her mom was planning to come over and help her wash the baby's clothes and bedding.

So everything would be ready.

"Are you scared of the delivery?" Brandon seemed glad for the chance to ask. "I mean, I know we're both praying. God's over it all. But still . . ."

"Most of the time I'm fine." Bailey narrowed her eyes. "But then I think about all that could go wrong. I really don't want an epidural or a C-section. No Pitocin. Nothing like that."

They had agreed that even though Bailey wanted to have the baby as naturally as possible, they were open to the possibility that if needed, they would resort to medical intervention. That's why they were having the baby at the hospital instead of at home. Just in case.

Brandon smiled at her. "It'll be okay. God will be with us, whatever happens."

"Exactly." Bailey loved this, being with Brandon on a quiet Saturday afternoon, just the two of them. The way they wouldn't get to do again for a very long time. "Can I tell you something a little sad? Just between you and me?"

"Of course." He looked deep into her eyes. Brandon adored her. He had since the first day they'd met.

Bailey wasn't sure she wanted to voice her thoughts. But they were there and they were real. She had no choice but to be honest with him. "I'm a little sad about losing this. You know, losing us. Just the two of us."

An understanding smile lifted Brandon's lips ever so slightly and his eyes filled with tenderness. "I thought I was the only one. I didn't want to say anything in case you thought I was terrible."

"It must be normal, right?"

"Definitely." Brandon squeezed her hands. "It's a big change." He leaned closer, his eyes locked on hers. "But no matter what happens, Bailey, you'll always have me. We'll always have us."

His words were exactly what she needed to hear. "We will, won't we?"

"Always." He grinned at her. "*Us* might include a few more seats at the table over the years, but that won't change this. The two of us. Not ever."

A relief came over her and she felt herself relax. "I'm so excited. I can't believe we're going to have a little girl. I can't wait. It's just . . ."

"I know." He brought her hand to his lips and kissed it. "We'll never lose this, Bailey. I promise."

The conversation kept things intimate through the rest of lunch and into the shopping trip. They held hands and laughed as they looked for baby fingernail clippers and an ear thermometer. Things they'd never heard of or used. And they talked about how Bailey's brothers were doing.

Connor would be home in a few days, and no doubt he would at least call Maddie West. The two were on a break, but if things went well, they would probably spend a lot of time together this summer. "I think he loves her. For real." Bailey raised her brow at her husband. "He just doesn't know it."

"Time will tell." Brandon's eyes held hers, as if she were the only person in the store. "We don't all end up with our first love."

"True." Bailey loved how this felt, wandering through the store with him beside her. "I told him we'd both pray about it."

Her parents were better than ever, her dad still coaching football and her mom writing a regular column for the *Indianapolis Star.* Her other brothers were all working out this summer, getting ready for fall football in a few months.

By the time they got home, Bailey could easily say it was one of their best Saturdays. They were taking things out of the bag when Bailey's phone rang. She looked down and saw it was Andi. "I'm going to take it, okay?"

"Of course." Brandon smiled. "I'll finish unpacking."

Bailey took her phone to their back porch. From here the view of Lake Monroe was like something from heaven. "Hello? Andi?"

"Ah . . . I'm so glad you answered." Andi sounded like she'd been crying. "I need your help. I don't know what to do."

"Hey, I'm here." Bailey sat on the outdoor rocker and put her hand on her belly. Her baby was kicking again. "What happened?"

She heard Andi take a deep breath. "Cody came to Louisiana to see me."

"He did?" Bailey sat up a little. "What for?"

"Well . . . it's a long story." Andi launched into the details. How Cody had come to ask her one question: Would she give him one more chance? "He said he could explain how he'd acted after our second engagement." Her single laugh sounded like a mix of sadness and frustration. "*Second engagement.* Every time I say that I can't believe I'm still even *talking* about Cody Coleman."

Bailey tried to sort through the details of her friend's story. "You said something about Cody explaining himself?"

"Right. That's what he said." Andi sighed.

"But I got this emergency call and then Cody helped me with this single mom and her kids who were stranded in the flood. The whole day was crazy. And later when we talked, I told him I couldn't do this again. That I was finished."

"Wait." Bailey was still missing something. "What was Cody's explanation? For the way he treated you after your last engagement?"

Silence. Andi didn't talk for several seconds. "He never told me."

"What?" Bailey wished they were in person having this conversation. The details didn't add up. "He came with an explanation and he never told you?"

"No, because . . . well, I told him I didn't want to hear it. If he couldn't tell me back then, there was no point telling me now. Plus . . . there's this other guy. The one I told you about. Caleb." She paused. "I don't know, I just needed Cody to leave. Before I fell for him again."

Bailey's heart sank. With all her heart she believed Cody and Andi belonged together. She'd been praying about that very thing for years. And now, Cody had gone after Andi, chased her to Louisiana to tell her how much he loved her, and Andi hadn't let him explain himself? She kept her tone level. "Andi . . . I think maybe you should've let him tell his story."

Again Andi was silent. "You might be right."

"I mean, he flew across the country to tell you."

They talked awhile longer. Andi explained that it wasn't a question of whether she loved Cody. Rather, she didn't trust him. And she didn't want to wind up a single mother someday. "I seriously don't know if I can believe in him again. And what about Caleb?" Andi sighed. "That's why I had to call you."

Bailey took her time responding. This was a strange situation, giving her best friend advice about the boy she, herself, had once loved. It had been many years since she'd thought about Cody that way. He hadn't been the one for her, she knew that, of course. But that didn't mean she couldn't remember the way she had cared for him back then.

She pictured Cody, the sincerity in his eyes, the honesty in his smile. The way he would lay down his life for someone he cared about. Or even for a nation full of strangers, like he'd been willing to do in Afghanistan.

There were very few guys with the character and strength of Cody Coleman. Bailey needed to share that with Andi. "I think a lot of this is your fear talking." Bailey didn't want to offend her friend. But this had to be said. "If there's one thing I know about Cody Coleman it's this: He's trustworthy. You could trust him with your life, Andi. If you two ever married, he would never dream of leaving you. Not ever."

"He left me before." Andi's answer was quick.

Bailey considered that. "He broke up with you, yes. But he didn't leave you. Not in the normal sense, like because he didn't care about you or love you."

"I guess." Andi was softening. "So . . . you think I should have let him explain?"

"Andi . . . Do you still love him?"

There was a sniffling sound on the other end of the line. "With everything in me."

"Then what are you doing talking to me?" Bailey allowed a soft laugh. "You can trust him. You have to find out what he came to tell you. Maybe that will clear all this up."

They talked another few minutes about the baby and how Bailey was feeling. At the end of the call Andi thanked her. "No one knows me like you do, Bailey. You can talk me off a cliff. You always could . . . ever since college."

Bailey smiled. "Call Cody. Ask him what

he wanted to talk about. Please, Andi."

"Okay. Eventually." Andi exhaled. Her doubt was easy to hear. "Oh, and hey . . . that donation you and Brandon made. Wow . . ." Deep gratitude filled her voice. "None of us can believe it. That was just what we needed."

Bailey smiled. "Good. It's the least we can do." She didn't want to annoy Andi, but she wanted to finish the call on Cody. "Don't forget . . . reach out to him. Okay?"

"I will."

That would have to do. The call ended and Bailey returned to the kitchen. Brandon had made them each a glass of lemon water. As Bailey reached for it, her stomach tightened. "Ooooh." She winced. "They're getting stronger. These false contractions."

"One of these days you'll have one that won't be false." Brandon looked nervous. "I hope you know the difference."

Bailey waited while her abdomen slowly relaxed. She thought about Brandon's words. She could've said the same thing to Andi. Cody was not like other guys. He was a catch, a true and genuine guy who would never intentionally hurt anyone — least of all the girl he loved.

Now if only Andi could see that.

Aaron Baylor found Cody as soon as practice ended. The kid could barely talk he was so happy. "She said yes, Coach! Macy Withers! She's going with me to the prom!"

Cody was collecting the bags of gear alongside his assistant coaches. No matter how terribly his visit had gone, he was happy for his player. "Atta boy, Baylor. I told you. Show a girl a glimpse of your heart, and she'll be yours forever." He patted the kid's shoulder. "How does it feel?"

"Amazing." Baylor grabbed one of the gear bags and walked with Cody toward the locker room. "Every guy on campus wants to be me." He hesitated and then cast a sideways glance at Cody. "Whatever happened with . . . Andi, right?"

Cody couldn't tell the kid that he'd gone after her, but he hadn't done the very thing he'd taught Baylor to do. Cody hadn't shared his heart. He'd come home with the truth untold, the facts about his PTSD still hidden deep inside him. Cody forced a smile. "Hasn't worked out yet, Baylor. You'll be the first to know."

The irony of it stayed with Cody long after he was home and after he took Riley for his run. The scrawny kid had done the difficult thing and taken a chance. So what about Cody? How could he have gone all the way to Louisiana and not told Andi the truth? Never mind she didn't want to hear him.

If he would've pushed she would've listened. And that might've changed everything. Yes, he should've told her sooner, but that was all part of the learning curve in a relationship, right?

Cody piled Riley into his truck and headed for his mom's house. Every Monday he mowed her lawn. Today he welcomed the task. Anything to take his mind off the hurting. He missed Andi so much he couldn't eat. Couldn't see straight into tomorrow.

A few times he had even played the news segment again, the part where Andi was interviewed. He had kept it on his DVR. For times when he couldn't go another minute without seeing her.

His mom met him at the front door and called Riley into the house. "Come on, boy, come to Grandma."

Cody found the mower and set about the job. Later tonight he would tell his mom what happened with Andi, how she never wanted to see him again. Then he would tell her the other news. He was seriously considering moving to Montana. The headmaster had offered him a job. Now it was up to him. He had a week to decide.

The conversation with his mother went better than he expected. She didn't want him to move, of course, but she recognized it would only be for a time. So Cody could get Andi out of his head.

"Actually, I'm thinking of moving to Solvang. For a year, anyway." She grinned at him. "One of my friends is moving there to work at this great church. It's been around forever, but they're hiring. I'd be working with this great couple — Larry and Evelyn Foster. My friend said she could get me the job if I was willing to move there."

Cody smiled, despite his breaking heart. Nothing stayed the same. Not even the two of them living in the same city. "Good for you, Mom."

"Everything happens in seasons, Cody." She patted Riley, who was sitting beside her. "You're a football coach. You should know that more than anyone."

She was right. Everything in its season. Just like Ecclesiastes in the Bible. He thought about that after he was home and in bed. He reached for his phone on his bedside table and opened his Bible app. He found his way to the third chapter in Ecclesiastes.

There it was.

. . . a time to weep and a time to laugh, a time to mourn and a time to dance . . .

A time for everything. And right now it was Cody's time to grieve, time to figure out what the rest of his life held. Never mind the day he'd shared with Andi in Louisiana, or the progress he'd thought they had made in those few hours. That was behind him. The future held something unknown, a challenge Cody was almost certainly going to take. Working with a team of troubled kids in the open plains of Montana.

Where just maybe, Cody's heart might finally heal.

21

John had just one more week to talk with Cole before the interviews would wrap up. He had organized his thoughts and a few more photos in anticipation of today's meeting.

But he didn't need them to remember what had happened next. It was a miracle he and Elizabeth had ever found each other again. And when they did, the heartache was so great it was a wonder they survived at all.

Cole and Ashley were on time, and both of them looked anxious for the final piece of the story. "So much I didn't know," Ashley told John as they settled into the living room again. "Where did you leave off?"

"I know!" Cole held up his notes. "And I don't need these to tell you. Grandma was gone to that house, the place where she lived with other pregnant girls. And Papa was trying to figure out how to find her."

Cole looked at John. "You had just come up with a plan, right?"

His plan. Yes, that was the next part. John appreciated the way Cole cared so much. He took a deep breath and let the rest of the story fill his soul. And like every other week, the memories came to life. They consumed him, taking over his senses until he was no longer sitting in his living room, talking to his grandson about the past.

He was reliving it.

The plan was simple.

John thought about it constantly. In class and in the library when he was studying and at home every night. Not because the strategy required so much work. But because John couldn't wait to see Elizabeth. His arms ached for how badly he wanted to hold her.

He told no one about his intentions. He would wait until a week before Elizabeth's due date, and then drive to Illinois, straight to the house where she was staying. No one could keep him away from her. By then her father would've been convinced he'd kept them apart. Everyone would think John Baxter had given up on Elizabeth.

Everyone, that was, except Elizabeth herself.

Whatever she was going through, whatever lonely nights she faced without him, she had to know he was coming for her. And not just her. He was coming for her and the baby. He had promised he would do what he could. Now he knew how.

School got out the end of May. The next day John would set off for Illinois. Once he arrived at the house, he'd wait until nightfall. Then while everyone was sleeping, John would find a way into the place. He'd wake up Elizabeth, and take her back to Ann Arbor.

At first they'd stay at the Wesleys' house. Sure, the family had already told him no, but once they saw Elizabeth nine months pregnant and without any options, they were bound to change their minds. At least for a short while.

His plan didn't stop there.

Their first day back in Ann Arbor, John and Elizabeth would go to the justice of the peace and get married. They could do a more formal wedding later. Then John would figure out where to take his wife and baby next. He would have to increase his hours at the pharmacy, of course. Which would make med school more difficult. But not impossible. John had straight A's. His professors would work with him. They believed John would run a hospital one day.

Yes, certainly they would work with him.

John found a piece of cardboard and taped it to his wall. At the top he used a marker and wrote "154 days." That's how long he still had to wait before he could see her, before he could hold Elizabeth in his arms again.

Every day he crossed out the number and wrote one day less. He relished the times when 100 days became 99, and when 50 became 49. Every sunrise took him one day closer to seeing her. This time Elizabeth's father wouldn't be waiting for him. He would rescue Elizabeth and their child and they would start a life of their own.

Forty-five days. Twenty-two. Eleven.

Finally it was time to leave. Time for John to go get his family.

He packed a few blankets and pillows in case Elizabeth needed them for the ride home. And since she wouldn't be expecting him that particular night, he brought food, too. Peanut butter sandwiches and a thermos of water. They could get more food on the road.

He tried to think of everything as he set out that afternoon. The house where she was staying was in Marion, Illinois — an eight-hour drive from Ann Arbor. If he drove fast he could shave maybe thirty minutes off that, but not much more. He couldn't afford a speeding ticket.

John didn't want to arrive until after midnight, so he waited until four that afternoon to leave. At first the drive was smooth. John played his eight-track in the car's deck. *Billboard's Top Hits* with "Never My Love" on it. In honor of Elizabeth. He couldn't believe he was about to see her again. After all this time.

But he was nearly five hours out of Ann Arbor when his engine began to smoke. *This can't be happening.* John pulled to the side of the road. His gas and temperature gauges were fine. So why was the engine smoking? He found a flashlight in his glove box, climbed out, and lifted the hood. It was already after nine o'clock. He'd be lucky to find an open gas station.

A quick look and he saw the problem. His oil pan was leaking. Which was maybe why the oil gauge wasn't working. He looked more intently. There was barely an inch of oil left, if the dipstick was right. "Great." He couldn't drive far with so little oil. He could blow his engine, and then he'd be finished. Without a car, he'd not only miss his chance at rescuing Elizabeth and the baby . . .

He'd miss his chance at ever seeing her again.

As soon as the baby was born, if her father had things his way, the baby would be adopted out to another family and Elizabeth would be brought back home. Probably to some undisclosed location with some other friend or relative. If it meant keeping Elizabeth from John, her father would probably enroll her in some other school. Somewhere far from Michigan. Then Elizabeth's parents could go on as if John had never existed.

Whatever it took to keep John and Elizabeth apart.

John turned off his flashlight. The highway wasn't busy, and the few cars that passed him while he checked his engine hadn't even slowed down. John slammed the hood shut, climbed back behind the wheel and drove on the shoulder to the next off-ramp. The sign above the exit said:

WELCOME TO BLOOMINGTON

John had never heard of the place. He drove his car another few miles along a country road, but he didn't make it far. The smoke coming from under the hood grew worse and his temperature gauge showed that the engine was overheating. He couldn't afford to blow a gasket.

Finally he killed the engine again. His heart beat erratically inside him. What was he going to do? He'd come this far and now if he didn't get help he wouldn't make it to Elizabeth. John thought about his financial situation. He had twenty-four dollars in ones, cash he'd made helping his classmates study for their medical exams.

Not nearly enough for any major repairs.

He was about to get out of his car and start walking when a light flicked on at a house thirty yards away. John stepped out. *Let them be nice, whoever they are.* He felt sweat gather on his forehead. A man stepped out onto the porch as John walked slowly up the driveway.

"Can I help you?" The man had a shotgun in his hand. "Or should I call the police?"

John froze and put his hands in the air. "I . . . my car broke down, sir. I'm not sure what to do."

The man lowered the gun and chuckled. "Must be your lucky day." He set the gun on a chair and walked down to meet John. "I was a mechanic in the war. Vietnam. Fixed everything." He held out his hand. "Name's Wilson Gage."

"John Baxter." The two men shook. "I'm

trying to meet up with my girlfriend. We're . . . she's . . . she's going to have a baby. I need to be there tonight."

Wilson Gage raised his eyebrow. "You don't have much time."

"No, sir. Not much."

A slow nod from Wilson. "What's wrong with your car?"

"Oil pan's got a leak. It's too bad to drive." John felt the weight of the situation. "I need a repair and new oil." He glanced back at the road. "This time of night not sure where I'll find either."

"Well, John. I told you." Wilson talked like the two of them were old friends. "You broke down at the right place."

Over the next thirty minutes, Wilson found something to plug up the hole in the oil pan. Then he refilled it with an entire quart of oil. The exact type John needed. "How do you happen to have this stuff lying around?" John couldn't believe his luck.

"I keep lots of oil around." Wilson grinned. "Never know when you'll need it."

John almost wondered if he'd fallen asleep in his broken down car and he was dreaming. "I don't have much money, sir. I'm not sure . . . how I can repay you."

"Nah, don't worry about it. Christians are supposed to help people." Wilson eyed him again, a one-eyebrow-up sort of look. "Tell you what." The man motioned for John to follow him. "Come inside and talk for a spell. Have a cup of coffee with me and Scarlett. Then you can be on your way and we'll call it even."

With a desperate urgency, John wanted to get on the road. But after all the man had done, John could hardly just leave. Better to get it over with. He followed Wilson Gage into the house and sat across from him in the living room.

"Scarlett, love," Wilson called into the next room. "We got us a guest." He stood and pointed to a chair. "Sit there. My wife will fix something to warm you up."

John tapped his fingers on the arm of the chair. He didn't want to be warmed by anyone but Elizabeth. But Wilson had been kind enough to help. He could at least stay and visit. After a few minutes Wilson returned with a pretty brunette. She carried two mugs and a pitcher of what looked like coffee. Wilson had a plate of cookies in one hand, the other one around Scarlett.

John stood out of respect. "Ma'am."

"This is Scarlett." Wilson stood a little straighter, his eyes warm as he looked at her. No question the man was proud of his wife. "The love of my life, right here."

She blushed a bit and set the coffee down on an end table between the two chairs. She reached out her hand. "Nice to meet you."

"And you." John nodded.

Scarlett waved her hand in the air. "I'll leave you two to talk." She smiled at Wilson. "Let me know if you need anything, my love."

"Nothing the Good Lord hasn't already given me." Wilson watched her until she was out of sight. Then he turned to John. "So what's your story, young man? Your girlfriend's pregnant, living in another state. Has to be a story there."

John felt the chains of anxiety tighten around his chest. He needed to get out of here. But since there seemed no other way, they both sat back down and John took a sip of his coffee. Then he told Wilson Gage the story. How he'd met Elizabeth at a dance he wasn't supposed to be at and how they'd quickly fallen in love. Every detail right up to the drinking and losing control.

"Her father sent her away." John gave Wilson a wary look. "He's a Christian. Like you."

Wilson leaned forward in his chair and pointed a finger at John. "Now wait a minute. That man's not a Christian like me." He shook his head. "No, no."

"He says he's a Christian."

"That's it." Wilson's eyes lit up. "See, not all people who say they're a Christian actually are." He grabbed a Bible sitting on the same end table with the coffee. "The Good Book tells us that. Not everyone who says 'Lord, Lord,' will enter the kingdom of Heaven. Only those who do what the Lord asks." He tapped the Bible again. "That's the truth. Right here, John. It's all right here."

If the man was trying to sell him on Christianity, it wasn't going to work. John took another sip. "Doesn't seem very Christian for him to send his daughter away."

"No." Wilson paused for a moment. "No, it doesn't." He took a cookie from the plate and offered one to John.

John took two. Even though he wanted to get on the road, he was hungry. He bit into one and raised his brow. "These are amazing."

Wilson smiled. "Scarlett can bake. She's heaven-sent, for sure." The man finished his cookie and then leveled his gaze at John. "Look, John Baxter. Here's the way it is." Wilson sat back in his chair, never breaking eye contact. "This girl you're going after, the one pregnant with your child . . . do you love her?"

"Very much." The conversation was getting interesting. "I'd do anything for her."

"And right now? You're going there against her father's wishes." Wilson seemed beyond perceptive. "That right?"

"Yes, sir." John waited.

Wilson took another cookie and ate half of it in a single bite. "Pay attention, son. This is something you're gonna want to remember." He paused. "God gave you that young woman. And He'll see you through together. But it's gonna be hard. So hard you're gonna wish you could die some days." He leaned forward. "I mean it. That's how it was for me in Nam. Wished I could die."

John could imagine.

"But the whole time I knew I had the Good Lord on my side. Not just with me." He gave his chest a few hearty pats. "But right here. Inside me. For believers, God's Spirit is always there, inside us. Talking to us. Working things out for us." He squinted. "Know what I mean?"

John had no idea. "Sure. Yes, sir."

Wilson looked unconvinced. Then, so that John would have no doubt, the man went into a monologue about Jesus being fully God, fully man. How he'd come to earth and lived a sinless life, teaching people how to love and live the way God wanted. Wilson went into great detail about Jesus being betrayed and arrested, beaten and crucified.

"Now hear me." Wilson leaned forward again. "Jesus did nothing to deserve any of that." He hesitated, staring deep into John's eyes. "Know why he did it?"

John had gone to church with the Wesleys when he was younger. He knew about Jesus on the cross. But he had no idea how any of that related to him. "No, sir."

"For *you,* John Baxter." Wilson pointed straight at him. "He did it for you. So you could get through times like the one you're smack in the middle of right now. And so when this wild ride is over, you and that girl of yours can go to heaven."

John was twenty-four years old. Heaven felt like it was a million years away. Right now he had to find a way to get through the next few days.

But they'd come this far, so John listened. He had no other choice.

After all, Elizabeth was waiting.

22

Cole and Ashley were gripped by the story, that much was clear. John took a breath and looked at them. "I always hoped I might find Wilson Gage someday, tell him how things worked out and thank him for that night."

"I can't believe God led you right to his house." Cole's notebook looked full, like he'd taken more notes this afternoon than all the other days combined. "So Wilson Gage told you about Jesus. Even though he didn't know you." Cole positioned his pen over the paper again. "You can't stop there, Papa. What happened next?"

"Yes, please, Dad." Ashley had tears in her eyes. "I never knew any of this. We have time."

John couldn't stop the story if he'd wanted to. "I can still see Wilson, sitting across from me, telling me information he thought I wanted to hear." He shook his head. "I was so stubborn back then."

He took a drink of water and once more the years melted away.

Wilson kept talking.

Whatever compelled the man to think the young stranger in his house needed his words of wisdom, John didn't know. But now that he'd told John about Jesus, he had more to say.

"You think you've got trouble now." Wilson picked up the Bible and stared at it a moment. "This whole life here, it's just earth, John. Just earth. The great adventure begins the day you take your last breath." He pointed at John again. "That's when all the suffering here will make sense."

"Yes, sir." John finished his coffee and took another cookie. The man was looking at him like he was waiting for John to say something. Or maybe hoping John would make a promise to believe in God. John swallowed a bite of the cookie. "Thank you. For telling me."

Wilson cocked his head and scrutinized John for a long few seconds. "You don't believe me, do you?"

"It's just . . . No, sir. I'm sorry. I never could believe in a God who took away my parents when I was so young." John didn't want to get into a debate, but he had to be honest. "Not just that. Forgive me, but . . . people do a lot of terrible things in the name of religion. That's what I've seen, anyway."

Wilson leaned back in his chair and rocked for a while. The whole time he kept his eyes on John. Finally he drew a slow breath. "I'm going to ask God to show you just how much you need Him. Because hear me on this . . ."

John listened.

"You're right." Wilson set his half-eaten cookie on the plate and narrowed his eyes. "Parents die, yes. And people do a lot of terrible things. But God's bigger than religion. He's bigger than even our greatest losses." He nodded once. "Don't forget that."

"Yes, sir." John needed to get going. At this point, he'd say anything for the chance to leave.

Wilson set the Bible in his lap. "All right. I'm gonna pray for you, John. That you and that scared pregnant girl of yours will get married and find faith in Jesus. Faith that will see you through every hard thing ahead right on into eternity." He grinned. "And in return that God will give you a marriage and family so beautiful all the world will

360

want to know your secret."

That sounded pretty good, John had to admit. He still didn't believe. Never would. But at this point he wasn't sure what else to do but agree. "Uh . . . yes, sir. Thank you."

Wilson folded his hands on the Bible, bowed his head and prayed. John couldn't remember every word Wilson said to God that day, but the part that stood out was that last line. That God would give Elizabeth and him a marriage and family so beautiful all the world would want to know their secret.

They were about to stand when Wilson jabbed his pointer finger in the air. "One last thing."

John lowered himself back to his seat. "Yes, sir?"

"You don't believe me. I can see that, no use telling me different." Wilson didn't look upset by the fact. "But every time you think about this day, I want you to remember something." His voice dropped a notch. Like he was speaking straight to John's conscience. "Only God could've worked it out so you'd break down in front of *my* house. Someone who knows how to fix an oil pan and has your kind of oil sittin' around."

The slightest chill ran down John's arms.

"Someone who could tell you about the one thing you need a whole lot more than oil." Wilson leaned closer and patted John's knee. "Oil will take you down the road, John. But Jesus will take you all the way home. Know what I mean?"

John still had no intention of changing his mind about God. Right here in some stranger's living room. But he nodded, anyway. "Yes, sir." If he didn't get on the highway, he would miss his chance to see Elizabeth tonight.

Before he left, John thanked Scarlett and Wilson for the snack and the conversation, and especially for fixing his car. Wilson said one more thing to John before he pulled away — his car good as new.

"Don't forget me now!" Wilson smiled. "You hear?"

"I won't." This time John was serious. The man couldn't convince him to be a Christian, but John would definitely remember this night. It was too strange and fortuitous not to remember.

But once he hit the road, John turned on the music and thought only about Elizabeth. The unusual encounter with Wilson Gage grew more distant with every mile. And sometime around two o'clock that morning John pulled up across the street from the house where Elizabeth was staying. He flipped off the lights and killed his engine.

It looked like any other house on the quiet street. Two stories, gabled windows, shutters and a front porch. No one would know that behind those walls was a houseful of girls who had no choice but to give up their babies. Girls sent away by parents too concerned about appearances to love their daughters through the most difficult time of their lives.

John gritted his teeth and looked for the best way in. Like Wilson, the man of the house might have a gun. In which case John had to be very quiet. If the man woke up and mistook him for a burglar, things could take a terrible turn.

Take your time, he told himself. *You've come this far. No need to rush.* He stepped out of his car and padded silently across the lawn. Every light was off. They were all sleeping. The timing couldn't be more perfect.

John studied the situation. The front door would be too obvious. He crept along the side of the house and made his way to the back. A cement porch ran across it. Another good sign. No creaking boards with cement. John walked up the steps and with the slightest movement, he tried the door.

In the silence of the night, the squeaking handle sounded like clanging pans. John could do nothing but continue. He'd come too far to stop now. Besides, he'd rather face a shotgun than miss the chance to see Elizabeth. The door wasn't locked, so John made his way into the house and — without making a sound — he shut the door behind him.

Now to find Elizabeth.

His heart pounded so loud he was sure it would wake up everyone. *Be calm. You can do this,* he told himself. *One step at a time.* He waited a few minutes while his eyes adjusted to the dark. All the girls in the house were pregnant. Asleep in their beds they were bound to look much the same.

Which was why it was a crazy stroke of luck when John peered into the first room and saw her. The space was small, with only one bed. But he knew the sleeping figure under the sheets was her for one reason. His photo was in a frame on the dresser.

She was here! His Elizabeth was right here in front of him. John couldn't draw a breath until he closed her bedroom door behind him. Then he waited. One minute, two. Until he was sure no one had woken up. When he was convinced, he moved to the side of her bed.

Beneath the sheets, lying on her side, Elizabeth didn't look pregnant. Her face was soft and young, like that of a girl still in high school. John stared at her for a moment. She was so beautiful. He would never love anyone the way he loved her. He bent close and put his hand on her thin shoulder. Her flannel nightgown and long dark hair made her look like a porcelain doll.

"Elizabeth," he whispered as quietly as he could. "Elizabeth . . . it's me, John."

It took a minute, but gradually her eyes opened. They fluttered a few times and then they grew suddenly wide. She started to cry out, but he gently put his hand over her mouth. "Shhhh." He brought his face close to hers. "I snuck in. No one knows I'm here."

She was still waking up, still trying to make sense of his presence. "How . . . how did you know where to . . ." Her voice was a whisper now. She was awake enough to understand what was happening. "John . . ." Her eyes filled with tears and she squeezed them shut. She shook her head and buried her face in the pillow.

At first John thought she was merely overwhelmed with seeing him. But after a minute, alarm coursed through him. "Elizabeth, what is it? What's wrong?"

A series of sobs racked her body and she kept her face turned away from him. Only after several minutes did she look at him. The pain in her eyes scared him more than anything ever had. "I . . . I already had the baby."

"What?" John felt the floor fall away. The room seemed to start spinning and he couldn't draw a breath. What had she said? She'd already had the baby? He looked around the room, desperate to see a crib or a bassinet, some sign of their child. "Elizabeth, what do you mean? You're not due for another week, I don't . . . I can't . . ." He looked around once more. "Where's the baby?"

Elizabeth shook her head. They were still talking in whispers, still trying to control their emotions. The tears came harder until it looked like she would pass out from the grief that consumed her. "They . . . they took him. We had . . . a boy, John. He was perfect."

She'd had a boy. A son. They had a son. Their firstborn child was a boy. But John was too late, and now the baby was gone. He was gone forever.

John's heart raced so fast, he could barely think. He felt sick to his stomach, all the room blurred, the walls collapsing in on them. They had a little boy. So where was he? John helped Elizabeth sit up and he searched her eyes. "Who took him?"

"The couple. They were from overseas, John. Missionaries." She covered her face as another run of sobs shook her small frame. "I couldn't stop them. My father made . . . he made the arrangements."

Arrangements.

John stood and walked silently to the window. Arrangements? Like a funeral? And that's what this was. A funeral for their little boy. John couldn't exhale, couldn't think, but it didn't matter. He had to know where the child was now. He returned to Elizabeth and sat on the edge of her bed. "We can get him back. We have to."

"No," she whispered. She shook her head. "I had him two weeks ago, John. The couple is back overseas by now." Her face twisted into a sort of grief John had never seen before. "He was so beautiful. His face and eyes. John . . . I got to hold him for an entire hour." She squeezed her eyes shut and worked to catch her breath. "He looked . . . like you, John."

His son had looked like him. The baby boy he would never know, never hold. Never teach to read or ride a bike. His son had

367

looked like him, but now he was gone. The tears began to come for John, too. How could this have happened? How could her father have been so wicked?

The shock was wearing off, the reality strangling the life from them both. He pulled Elizabeth to his chest and held her, just held her and rocked her while they both quietly wept. "I'm sorry, Elizabeth. Sorry I wasn't here sooner. If I had only known." He clung to her. "I'm so sorry."

They stayed that way for an hour, grieving over the futility of what had happened. When they were finally able to see through their tears, John asked her about the delivery. Other than the fact that the baby had come early, everything had gone the way she expected.

"I wish I could've been here with you." His anger was only beginning to grow inside him. Her father had done this to them, and one day he would pay. "I should've been beside you."

She nodded. "Every time I closed my eyes, whenever the pain was too strong, I thought of you. I knew . . . you would've been here. You wanted to be here."

And if he'd been here, they would still have their son.

Elizabeth explained that she had been

weak after the baby was born, so her father made plans with her houseparents to pick her up a few days from now. John shuddered at the news. If he'd waited even a little longer . . . or if Wilson Gage hadn't been there to fix his car, he could've missed her.

The fact stirred an urgency in John. "We need to leave. Now, Elizabeth. Before your houseparents wake up. Otherwise they'll call your father, and he'll stop us."

Fear darkened her eyes. "Okay."

A thought hit him. "You still want to come with me, right?" He kept his voice lower than a whisper. With tender care, he put his hands on either side of her face and tried to see the answer for himself. "You still love me?"

"Of course." She leaned her forehead against his. "It's just . . . Where will we live, John? What's going to happen to us?"

"I have a plan. You can trust me, okay?" John moved his face back a bit so he could see into her eyes. "I love you, Elizabeth. I want to marry you. As soon as possible."

With every word he spoke, her fear seemed to lift. Her voice was barely audible. "I wasn't sure . . . I didn't know when you'd come back or if you still wanted to . . ." She blinked away new tears. "I wasn't sure, John."

"I'll never leave you. Never again." He told her how he had counted down the days and how he had barely made it because of his car. "I broke down in front of this guy's house. He fixed my oil pan, otherwise I wouldn't be here." The other details of his encounter with Wilson Gage could wait.

They weren't important now.

"Marry me, Elizabeth. Let me take you back to Ann Arbor, and then as soon as you're feeling well enough, we can go to a justice of the peace. We'll have lots of children, and I'll take care of you for the rest of your life." He ran his thumb over her velvety cheek. "Will you marry me?"

For the first time since he'd crept through her bedroom door, the hint of a smile played on her lips. She whispered her answer. "I will. As soon as we can, yes."

John felt his world right itself, just a little. "And one day . . . one day we'll find our baby boy."

It was four in the morning when they packed her things and quietly set out. John took her to the Wesleys and the next evening the couple met with them and agreed to a plan. John and Elizabeth would get married and live there in John's room, on one condition.

They had to tell Elizabeth's parents where

they were.

Neither of them wanted to make that call, but the next day John took the lead. He called her parents and told them what he'd done, that Elizabeth was safe with him. Then he advised them that the following Monday the two of them were getting married. On their own. No parents allowed.

The first time he'd spoken with Elizabeth's father, John had been nervous, embarrassed, and certain the man hated him. This time, John didn't care. He couldn't change the past, couldn't go back and protect Elizabeth's innocence. But he could take care of her from this point on.

It was no surprise that Elizabeth's parents didn't protest not being invited to the wedding. Elizabeth's father shouted at John when he heard the news. "You have no right to take my daughter without my permission!"

"She's an adult, sir. This is what she wants." John managed to keep his tone calm. His mind was made up and so was Elizabeth's. There was nothing her parents could do to keep them apart.

Her father yelled and screamed and said lots of things John didn't really focus on. Bottom line was this: Elizabeth was disowned. Neither she nor John were allowed back to the house where she grew up ever again.

They got married that Monday in a ceremony that was short and sweet. Elizabeth wore an outfit she'd been given by the houseparents while she was pregnant. A flowing white gauzy dress with long sleeves that flared at the ends. John wore a suit, and the justice of the peace took their picture.

A photograph John would keep forever.

It wasn't until three weeks later that the Wesleys sat them down for another meeting. Space was tight. Money tighter. They gave John and Elizabeth a week to find somewhere else to live.

That afternoon John drove Elizabeth to Independence Lake Park. The irony hit John hard as they pulled in. *Independence.* They were hardly independent, now that they were about to be homeless. And it was there — in a parking spot overlooking the lake — that John remembered everything Wilson Gage had told him.

He shared the story with Elizabeth, and the whole time she never looked away, never did anything but nod and wipe an occasional tear. At the end of the story Elizabeth said only this: "I think he's right, John. We can't do this without God's help."

And suddenly, John could feel his heart open up for the very first time. Yes, they needed God. They would never survive the coming week, let alone a lifetime together, unless they had the help of God Almighty. A God that John believed in now, because without His help John's car would've broken down somewhere else.

It was as if God Himself cared enough about John Baxter to let the oil leak out of his car at exactly the right time. And to place him right in the living room of a man whose story would change the course of John's life forever.

There in the car that day at the park, John and Elizabeth asked Jesus to forgive them for what they'd done, for going against His ways and for making such a mess of things. They gave their lives to the Lord and asked Him that one day they might find the son they'd lost.

Then John prayed one more thing.

That God would give Elizabeth and him a marriage and family so beautiful all the world would want to know their secret.

23

Ashley stood at the edge of the kitchen table and studied the finished project. Cole had gotten an A on it. As she looked over the letters and photos she realized even now, with the interviews over, the story stayed with her. And when she was alone — the way she was this morning — it made her cry.

So much of their lives had been shaped by that summer. The choices that led to heartbreak and the fact that after that season, her father had made a commitment. He would never drink alcohol again. He and her mother both.

The Bible made it clear that getting drunk was wrong, and so was making someone else stumble. "Doesn't leave a lot of reasons to have a drink," her father liked to say. So none of the Baxter family drank. They didn't want to.

Besides, they'd seen firsthand how much

fun a family could have without alcohol, how much laughter and happy times. All of it around a glass of iced tea or a mug of coffee or hot chocolate.

A lifestyle that began because of that long ago summer.

That wasn't all, of course. In the days before she died of cancer, Ashley's mother begged God for the chance to see her baby boy. Hold him and kiss his cheek. Let him know that she'd never stopped loving him.

And in what could only be a miracle, that grown-up boy came to her. There in the hospital he found her and told her who he was. He had hired a private investigator to find his birth parents, since his adoptive parents had been killed in a single-engine plane crash over an isolated jungle.

Later that day, Ashley's mother and father talked about the meeting. Her mother explained that she'd met their firstborn son. Ashley's dad at first thought she was delusional, that she'd had a dream perhaps. He didn't believe their firstborn son had actually found her and made peace with her. But eventually the boy found Ashley's father, too, and confirmed the story. The meeting had happened.

Their firstborn was Dayne Matthews. A Hollywood movie star known by the whole world. He was a Christian now, too. Long gone were his days of wild living and partying. Now he was part of them, at every holiday and summer barbecue. Married with three children and still celebrating the miracle of their reconnection.

Thankful to finally be part of his family. The Baxter family.

And of course the most dramatic thing to come from that summer was the way her parents turned their lives to God. How they grabbed on to His Word and never let go, never again let religion or mean people stand in the way of their faith.

Just like Wilson Gage had prayed that long ago night.

Ashley wiped at a few tears on her cheeks. She ran her fingers lightly over the copy of the photo at the center of the project board. The one the justice of the peace took of her parents the day they were married. "Mom, you were so beautiful." Ashley smiled through her tears. "I wish I'd known you back then."

Ashley had always known that her parents had made mistakes. Learning about Dayne's existence made it clear that no one was without fault. Not even her parents. But not until Cole's project did Ashley truly understand the details of what had happened.

She only wished she'd known about all this when her mother was still alive. So they could've sat across from each other and talked about it. How her mother must've felt much the way Ashley did when she came home from Paris.

They had so much more in common than Ashley ever knew.

She grabbed a tissue from the counter and dabbed at her eyes. The Memorial Day barbecue was tomorrow. She had lots to do today to get ready. The younger kids were working with Landon this afternoon cleaning up the backyard. Landon's way of giving her time with Cole.

Today was the day she was going to tell him what he wanted to hear. The details of his story. Ashley took a deep breath and tried to pull herself from the display in front of her.

She was still at the table a few minutes later when Cole came bounding into the room. "You ready, Mom?"

"Yes." Ashley turned to face him. She smiled and tried to still the anxiety building within her. The next few hours would be critical to her relationship with Cole. "The car's out front."

They drove to Lake Monroe, the place the Baxters often came when they wanted fresh air and space to think. Together they hiked partway down the main path, and at the first bench they stopped. "How's this?" Ashley smiled at him. *Please, God, don't let him see how nervous I am.*

"Great." Cole sat down beside her.

For a while they looked out at the lake and didn't talk. Warm temperatures had hit Indiana that weekend, and combined with the sun on the water the day was beautiful. Ashley broke the serenity between them first. "You did a beautiful job on your project."

"Thanks." Cole smiled at her. "I'm glad you were part of it." He turned so he could see her better. "I'll always remember going through that with you."

Ashley looked into his face, her handsome older son. "At the end there, all I could think was how they lost their baby. And how their pain made them so much more understanding when I came home from Paris."

Cole nodded. "You got to keep me." His eyes reflected the light off the water. "Like, the saddest part of Grandma and Papa's story — giving up their son — made it easier for you to keep me. Because Grandma understood what you were going through." He paused. "That's so cool." Then he reached over and took hold of her fingers

378

for a brief moment. "You've been the best mother ever."

The best mother ever? The last thing Ashley wanted to do was cry. This talk was for Cole and about Cole. She needed to keep herself together. But the words Cole had just spoken would stay in her heart as long as she lived. She could always look back and think herself a terrible person, an accidental mother without a clue how to raise her son.

But because of *her* mother, Ashley had learned from the best. Cole's kind words were proof. What better endorsement could she ever have than that?

He got to grow up with her . . . and she was the best mom ever.

Ashley sniffed a few times and closed her eyes. She could do this, she could get through the story and not break down. Her son was counting on her. Her eyes opened. She took a sharp breath and lifted her face. "I'm sorry for making you wait."

"It's okay." Cole rested his elbows on his knees and looked deep into her eyes. "So . . . I guess my first question is easy. How did you meet him? My dad?"

The breeze off the lake could do nothing to take the edge off her sick stomach. She could picture him, Jean Claude. The handsome well-known artist who welcomed her into his studio and raved about her paintings. The man who filled her head with dreams of becoming his protégée. Yes, she could still see him. After all, his face still looked back at her every morning over breakfast.

Ashley blinked a few times. "His name was Jean Claude. He was a famous artist with a studio in the heart of Paris."

"Wait." Cole looked confused. "Mom? What are you talking about?"

The confusion became hers. She shifted so she could see Cole better. "Your father. Isn't that what you want to know?"

"No." A slight laugh. "Mom . . . not him." Cole shook his head. "I want to know about my *dad.*" He raised his brow. "You know, the one you married?"

Her mind raced ahead of her heart and an understanding began to dawn in her soul. Could it possibly be? All this time? "You . . . want to know about Landon?"

"Of course. He's my dad." This time Cole's laugh came more quickly. As if he were truly astonished at the turn of events. "You're so funny, Mom."

"I am?" Ashley felt light-headed. She pressed her back against the wooden bench so she wouldn't feel as dizzy.

"Yes." Cole took her hand again. "Is that

why you've been so worried?" His laughter died and compassion filled his expression. "You thought I wanted to know about some painter in Paris?" He shook his head. "That man wasn't my father. Never." He released his grip on her and sat up, his tone light. "Now that we have that out of the way, will you please tell me about my dad?"

It was Ashley's turn to laugh, and she did so without reservation. Head tipped back, rejoicing for the turn things had taken. *Thank You, God . . . How wonderful is this?* When she could breathe again she looked at Cole and felt her joy double. She was going to talk about Landon. The way she had practiced. The way she had wanted to from the beginning.

And for the next hour that's just what she did.

On the way home, Ashley's spirit felt lighter than it had in a month. She had given Cole what he had asked for. The details of his parents' love story. When they were still a few minutes from home it occurred to Ashley again the importance of that single meeting, decades ago, between her father and Wilson Gage.

The man had written to Cole and the two had shared a conversation. The details made it into Cole's project and Cole earned his extra credit. But more than that, the man told Cole that whatever good he'd done for John Baxter had now come around to do good for him. He didn't elaborate, but he did tell Cole this: *I needed a good dose of my own advice. Run to Jesus. I'll never stray from Him again.*

That very quote was in Cole's project.

Cole was singing along to a Colton Dixon song from his phone's playlist. Ashley smiled to herself, her eyes on the road. Wilson Gage had taught Ashley something very important. She could never underestimate the power of a single conversation with a stranger. The importance of sharing God's love with someone who needed it, the way Wilson Gage had shared with Ashley's father that night.

The man could never have known — without Cole's project — the impact of his words. How her father would go on to find faith in Christ. How when given the choice between four cities where he could finish his internship as a doctor, her father had chosen Bloomington.

Because it was there on that single night that his life had changed forever.

Her dad had tried to look up Wilson Gage through the years, but eventually he figured the man and his Scarlett must've moved on.

It took Facebook and the determination of Cole to find him.

Ashley let the wonder of it all stir her heart and stay with her.

The most incredible detail of the whole story was the prayer Wilson Gage had prayed before her father left the man's house that night. Everything he had asked God for had happened. Especially the last part. Because the Baxters were absolutely that family everyone looked to and everyone wanted for their own.

And now Ashley knew the reason why.

There was only one place John wanted to be, one place where he could finish the rest of the story. The love story he shared with Elizabeth. He pulled into the cemetery and took his time walking to the plot where her body lay.

John had been here more times than he could count. On special occasions, in the early morning hours before a birthday or anniversary. The anniversary of her home-going. But this Memorial Day morning was different. He was still in the story, still caught up in the details, still listening for her voice. He could feel her in his arms, even now.

The bench where John always sat was

there, waiting for him. But somehow he expected her to be there, too. His Elizabeth. Looking for him, smiling in his direction. *Where have you been?* she would ask. *I've been waiting for you.*

John breathed deep the sweet summer air and took his seat. He looked at the stone, engraved with her name. "Elizabeth, my darling, I'm here."

There was no response, of course. No word from God or whisper in the wind. Elizabeth was gone. She was not here beside him. This side of heaven, she never would be again. John leaned back on the bench and lifted his eyes to the blue sky. She wasn't here, but she was there.

He smiled, in case she could see him.

Then he let the rest of the story come. Not in great detail like before, because there were too many moments, too many beautiful years and decades to relive. He would have to spend the rest of his life trying. And that wouldn't be fair to anyone — not his family and certainly not Elaine.

He thought back to those long ago days once again. He married Elizabeth in a civil ceremony with only the Wesley family in attendance. She wore a simple white dress and he, a plain dark suit. It didn't matter. Even now John could see the hope in Elizabeth's eyes that day.

John sighed and leaned forward, his eyes on her tombstone. After the wedding, the two of them begged God for a solution to their housing situation.

The next day one of John's professors offered them a garage apartment.

It was a beginning, and John completing his medical degree was another. Years later after Erin was born, John was offered positions at two different hospitals. One of them was in Bloomington. The city where John's car broke down, where he met Wilson Gage.

The place where his life was changed forever.

The decision was easy. Their family moved to Indiana and found a beautiful house in the country, along with a church where they could watch their family grow.

A week later Elizabeth received a letter from her mother seeking reconciliation. It was an answer to years of prayers, and finally . . . finally they had healing over the heartache of the past.

All except the loss of their firstborn son.

At the time of his birth, the social worker had told Elizabeth not to think about her baby boy. Don't talk about the adoption or tell anyone about it. She was to act like she'd never given birth. Like none of the terrible, painful ordeal had ever happened.

"Try to forget," the woman had told Elizabeth.

Here, still, John's eyes stung at the pain of that time. Forgetting about that little boy was as impossible as forgetting how to breathe. For both him and Elizabeth. But the years played out anyway, in the most beautiful way. Brooke was born, then Kari, and a few years later, Ashley and Erin. The Baxters' own little women.

And with every girl that joined their family, John rejoiced. But he still thought every day about his firstborn. His son. The years passed and John and Elizabeth were in love with their family of girls. They were chatty and tenderhearted, helpful with their mother and silly. They danced and sang around the house and they loved their daddy more than words could say.

And then God gave them Luke. Their youngest . . . their second son.

The fact that Elizabeth overcame her first bout with cancer when Luke was in elementary school was a miracle John would always be thankful for. It allowed them seasons of learning and growing in their love for God and each other. A dozen Christmases they would have otherwise not had.

But then the cancer came back.

His eyes shifted to her tombstone again. "How good is our God, to let you meet Dayne before you died."

The wind picked up around him and played in the trees that lined the cemetery. All his life there had been one thing John wanted to give his precious Elizabeth, one thing that was completely out of his control. The chance for her to hold that baby boy one more time. To hold him and love him and whisper in his ear the precious truth: That she had never — not one day since he was born — ever stopped loving him.

And that week before she died, God again did what only He could do. He brought Dayne to Elizabeth. She died knowing the goodness of a God who answers prayers.

John lowered himself to his knees and pulled a handkerchief from his pocket. The letters on the gravestone needed polishing, so he ran the cloth over each one. As if he were etching her name on his heart once more. When he was finished, he stood and breathed in deep. "I miss you, darling Elizabeth. I always will." He looked to the heavens again. For a single moment he could see her once more, dancing in his arms that first night.

You have to teach me how to swing!

John smiled. Oh, how he still missed her.

Before she died, Elizabeth said something to the entire family, something John remembered now. She would always be with them. In Ashley's paintings and Cole's laugh . . . in Kari's kindness and Luke's gentle spirit. She would always be with them.

And so she was.

John brushed off his knees and walked back to the car. He would go home and meet up with Elaine and he would take her in his arms. The story had played itself out. He belonged to Elaine now, and he would tell her so. Something else hit him. Maybe Elaine might need time, too. Time to remember her first husband, the man who had died long before Elizabeth did. They would have to talk about that. Then later today the two of them would go to Ashley and Landon's for the big barbecue.

They were going to be okay.

Still, as he climbed in his car, as he took a last look in the direction of her tombstone, John couldn't help but think one thing. Someday he would take his last breath here, and the next he would be there, with her again. Not like it was on earth. But he fully believed the first thing he would see when he got there was a bench, much like the one on the U of M campus.

And there she'd be, his Elizabeth. Smiling

at him, looking for him. Her pretty hair pulled back in a ponytail. *There you are, Elizabeth. You get more beautiful every time I see you.*

He could almost hear her words.

Come sit with me, John. I've been waiting for you.

Wilson Gage pulled into the driveway of the pretty farmhouse just outside Bloomington and for a minute he stared at the place. Just took it in. If he understood Cole Blake, this was the house where it had all happened.

The place where John and Elizabeth Baxter raised their family.

Now the house belonged to Cole's parents. And today was the family's annual Memorial Day barbecue. Far as Wilson knew, Cole hadn't told anyone he was coming.

"Let's surprise my papa." Wilson had given Cole his phone number and the boy had called him last week. "I've been looking for a way to thank him. For taking time to tell me his story."

Wilson liked the idea then, and he liked it now. The driveway was filled with cars, and as he inched closer to the house, he rolled down his window. He could hear laughter coming from somewhere inside. Tears stung his eyes.

He had a feeling Scarlett would've loved the Baxters.

His steps weren't as fast as they once were. Old war injuries got worse with every sunrise. But that wasn't going to stop him from being here today. From seeing if what Cole had said was true.

That somehow on a single evening his actions had affected this family forever.

He straightened his Vietnam veteran pin, the one he wore on the lapel of his sweater whenever he went anywhere special. Then he knocked on the door and waited. Footsteps and then the door opened and a man answered. A man not a whole lot younger than him.

"Hello." The man looked kind and happy. He smiled. "Can I help you?"

Just then a teenage boy ran up. "Papa . . . this is your surprise." The boy stepped forward. "I'm Cole Blake. And you're . . . ?"

"Wilson." His eyes moved from the boy's to the man's. "Wilson Gage." He grinned. "You must be John Baxter."

"Yes!" John's eyes filled with recognition. He laughed a few times, like he was completely caught off guard. "Come in, Wilson. I can't believe you're here."

Cole stepped up and shook Wilson's hand. "I know it was a long drive. But thanks for coming." He grinned at his papa. "You and my papa have a lot to catch up on."

Which is just what they did. John welcomed Wilson into the house and introduced him to all the family. Like he was a hero.

And maybe that was part of the miracle, after all. Wilson smiled to himself.

As John bid Wilson goodbye a few hours later, they hugged and John looked at him, real deep like. "Do you remember that prayer? The one you said before I left your house that night?"

"Yes . . . Yes, I remember praying." Wilson fiddled absently with his veteran's pin.

"You said something I've never forgotten." John hesitated, his eyes shining. "You prayed that faith would see me through every hard thing ahead . . . and that God would give me a marriage and a family so beautiful all the world will want to know the secret."

Wilson blinked back tears. "I guess that was my prayer."

"Yes." John laughed. "It happened just like that, Wilson." John smiled. "It's not every time that a man gets to thank his hero." He hesitated and an early summer breeze drifted through the front door to the place where they stood. "Thank you, Wilson. That night changed my life."

Wilson couldn't find his voice. He nodded and gave John the slightest salute. Then he waved and walked to his car. The tears didn't come until he was behind the wheel. God had a purpose for him after all.

Him. Wilson Gage.

An old vet he figured no one would ever care about again. But God cared. He cared so much He brought him here to John Baxter and his beautiful family and He reminded him that a single prayer can change a life. Amazing grace, indeed. Wilson's tears came for all that, but they came for another reason, too. He looked at the rearview mirror and the pin on his lapel, and a smile stretched across his face.

For the first time since the war, someone had called him a hero.

24

Andi hadn't lived in California for a year, but she knew exactly where she was going. Knew it like she knew her own name. She gripped the steering wheel of the rental car and took the next exit.

Cody's townhouse was two blocks away.

She'd taken the trip as soon as she could. Her mind was made up that this was the thing to do. Especially after her last conversation with Bailey. Since then she'd come to understand the truth. God hadn't told her to stay away from Cody.

Fear had done that.

A fear that was understandable given their history, but one she had to stand up to all the same. Every day after talking to Bailey she thought about picking up the phone and calling Cody. Telling him she was sorry for making him leave . . . sorry for not hearing him out. But always she came to the same conclusion.

This conversation would be better in person.

She would've come sooner, but she had to wait for the floodwaters to finally dry up. Had to wait until she was sure Caleb wasn't the guy for her. He was nice. But he wasn't Cody Coleman. He never could be.

It took time, but in the last few weeks the people in the temporary tent housing found places to live, apartments or homes. Some moved in with friends or relatives, others found situations arranged by the city.

Only then could Andi take her month off for a job well done. Not once did Andi have to wonder where she was going to spend her time, or who she would spend it with.

As soon as she was released from her duties she caught the first flight out. She and her puppy, Max. The owners never came to claim him. Her supervisor was pretty sure the mama dog and puppy belonged to an old man killed in the flood. Andi glanced at the seat beside her. Max was in his travel crate sleeping. She smiled at him. "You're going to like Cody's dog, little guy. He'll be your friend."

Max yawned and settled into a deeper sleep.

Two more turns and Andi pulled up in front of Cody's house. It was late afternoon.

Cody had to be out of school for the summer by now, which meant he was probably home. Unless he was out running errands or hiking with Riley.

Andi stepped out of the car and headed up the walk. How many times had she come here? Nights when he made her dinner or the two of them watched a movie. Always he was sure to get her home before it got too late.

Not once had Cody put them in an uncompromising situation. Even when both of them were tempted, they never gave in. *We're going to do this God's way,* he would tell her. And so it was. Cody was strong like that.

She reached his front door and knocked. After a few seconds she heard footsteps. For days she'd been thinking about what she would say when this moment came, and now Andi wasn't nervous. She simply couldn't wait to be in his arms.

The door opened, but before Andi could run to him she took a step back.

The man at the door wasn't Cody.

"Can I help you?" He waited.

Andi shook her head. "I'm . . . I'm sorry. I'm looking for Cody Coleman."

"Oh." The guy was in his thirties, maybe. Balding with glasses. "I worked with him at

Oaks Christian. I'm staying here through the end of his lease."

Knots began to form in Andi's stomach. "The . . . end of his lease?" She tried to make sense of what was happening. If Cody wasn't here, then . . . "Where is he?"

"He moved." The man's expression grew more serious, like he was just understanding the situation. "You're a friend of his . . . I thought you must know."

"I didn't hear." Andi felt like she was floating above herself. This was a nightmare, that's what it was. It had to be. She forced herself to focus. "Where did he go?"

"He took a job in Montana. Left last week." The man shrugged. "Sorry I don't have more details." He hesitated and then seemed to get an idea. "His mother still lives in town. She might know."

His mother! Yes, that was it! Andi knew exactly where Cody's mother lived. She smiled at the stranger in Cody's doorway as she backed away from the porch. "Good idea. Thank you." She waved and like that she was down the path and back in her car.

She was at Cody's mother's doorstep five minutes later. As soon as the woman opened the door, Andi didn't hesitate. "Mrs. Coleman!"

"Andi." Cami Coleman looked shocked

to see her. "What in the world . . . ?"

They shared a quick hug. Andi didn't have time to wait. She needed answers. Now. She searched the woman's face. "I made a terrible mistake. Cody came to find me in Louisiana and I sent him away."

A knowing look came over his mother's face. "I heard about it." There was no accusation in her tone, no finger-pointing. Just a sadness that reflected the way Andi felt. "Cody told me. You didn't get to hear his story, his explanation."

"No." Andi felt terrible. What had she been thinking, not to at least hear him out? Especially when she still loved him so much?

"Come in, Andi." Mrs. Coleman stepped to the side. "I'll pour us some coffee."

"I'd love to, but . . ." She looked back at her rental car. "My puppy's sleeping, and I need to get to Cody. As fast as I can."

The woman nodded. "Let me get the address. For the school in Montana. It's a ranch for boys with severe emotional issues."

Andi wasn't surprised. It sounded like exactly the type of place Cody would be drawn to work. Her heart surged with hope. She was about to have an address! A quick drive back to the airport and she'd be on the next open flight to Montana. Even if it cost her half a month's salary to get there.

Mrs. Coleman returned and handed her a slip of paper. "Here you go."

Every minute counted, but suddenly Andi hesitated. She looked into the woman's eyes. "Cody will tell me the details later, but . . . what was the reason? Why did he act so distant after we got engaged last time?"

For a moment it looked like Mrs. Coleman wasn't going to say anything. She started to shake her head, and then she caught herself. "He can tell you more. But I'll tell you this." She hesitated. "It was his PTSD, Andi. He had terrible episodes after your second engagement."

Andi felt her heart fall to the ground. Cody was suffering from PTSD that badly and he never said anything. "Why?" Tears welled in her eyes and her voice fell to a whisper. "Why didn't he tell me?"

Cody's mother had tears in her eyes, too. She smiled through them. "He didn't want to burden you."

In a single instant the entire situation made sense. Andi hugged the woman once more. "Pray for us. That I get to him as soon as possible." She drew back and looked into the woman's eyes. "And that he'll forgive me for taking so long to figure it out."

"I'll pray." Mrs. Coleman hugged her again. "Go. Cody's waiting for you."

All the way to the airport Andi thought about what his mother had said. Cody hadn't wanted to burden her. Of course that was it. Just like Bailey had told her, Cody would lay down his life for someone he loved.

Especially Andi.

She knew enough about PTSD to know it would be part of Cody's life forever. If he took her back, then she had to know that there could always be times when the nightmares would return, when something would trigger his memories of Afghanistan and he'd start looking for snipers in every corner of a room.

If only he would let her help him through those times, everything would be okay. They would pray for God's mercy and rely on His strength and they would get through any episode.

Together.

After a night at Los Angeles International Airport, Andi flew to Montana and drove to the boys ranch. She arrived just after ten the next morning, and parked in a lot overlooking a football field.

Immediately she spotted him.

399

Cody Coleman, standing in the midst of a group of football players, instructing them on the game. Andi climbed out of her car and watched him. The air around her was cool, much more so than in Louisiana or Los Angeles. Mountains ringed the area where the school was situated, and everywhere she looked the view was breathtaking.

This was where Cody belonged, here with kids who needed him most. She watched him, his strong muscled arms and the handsome shape of his face. He couldn't see her, didn't know she was there.

Andi slipped back in her car and took her journal from her purse. Then she wrote Cody what might be her last letter ever. Because there was no guarantee he'd forgive her. He may have moved on and decided he needed to be single.

Or he might have decided he didn't want her, after all. Since she hadn't been willing to hear his side of the story. Andi's heart hurt at the reminder of what she'd done, how she had sent him away. But now there was no time to waste, so she started at the top of the page.

Dear Cody,

I'm here in Montana. It doesn't matter how I found you, just that I did.

Cody, I'm so sorry for how I treated you. I should've listened to your explanation, taken your words to heart. I know now that this is about your PTSD. I'm so sorry about that. Sorry about what you went through in Afghanistan and what you are still going through now.

My heart hurts for you.

I'm including the address of my hotel. It's a few miles away on the edge of a lake. My flight doesn't leave until tomorrow afternoon. So if you're willing to forgive me, if you're willing to tell me everything that happened, I'll be there. Helping you through your healing would be a privilege, Cody. Never a burden.

Anyway, I'll be there. Come find me if you still want to talk. If not, I understand. After how I treated you I would understand if you let me leave tomorrow without coming by. I'm more sorry than you'll ever know.

I love you . . . I'll be waiting.

Love, Andi

The campus was sprawled out, so Andi drove to the front and took the letter to the main office. She asked for an envelope and slipped the note inside. Then she sealed it and wrote Cody's name across it.

"Could you see that Cody Coleman gets this, please?" She handed it to the office manager. "It's very important."

The woman seemed to recognize that this was something out of the ordinary. She smiled at Andi. "I'll make sure."

Andi drove to her hotel and took Max outside on his leash. The woods were thick around the edge of the water — very different from any lake she'd ever seen. And so very beautiful. Andi sat with Max on a fallen tree not far from her hotel room patio. She took a deep breath and tried not to worry. Whatever happened next, it had to be Cody's choice.

Once and for all.

Cody read the letter three times before he left the parking lot. Each time he felt his heart flood with a sort of joy he'd never known. She had found him. She'd come back to him! Andi Ellison was only a few miles away!

He could hardly wait to see her, to hold her in his arms and know that the impossible had happened. Andi was ready to give him another chance.

The only one they would ever need.

He wanted to drive straight to her hotel, but he had to do something first. He had to stop off at a different hotel, the one where he was staying until his apartment would be ready next week. He moved as quickly as he could.

Andi was waiting for him

At his hotel, Cody ran in. Riley met him at the door and Cody gave him a quick break outside. Once he was back in the hotel room, Cody stopped to pet him. "I'll be back soon, boy. Wait till you hear what happened!"

Then he rushed to his suitcase to get something very important. Something he kept with him as a reminder. A reason to pray for Andi and their future. Proof that he meant what he'd told her: He'd wait as long as it took for her to work through her fears.

Cody slipped the small velvet box into his jeans pocket.

Ten minutes later he parked his car in the lot behind her hotel. The place was situated on the edge of the lake, just like she'd said. The place was beautiful and the view was even better. Cody was about to get out of his car when he noticed someone sitting on a fallen tree near the water.

She had a puppy with her.

Like all his life had led to this moment, Cody stepped out of the car and walked toward her. He had called Andi's parents on the way here. He had their permission. Like her father told him a few minutes ago, he would always have their permission.

Cody took in the sight of Andi, the way her hair fell over her shoulders. The lyrical sound of her voice as she talked to her puppy. He didn't want to rush this, and he definitely didn't want to frighten her. But as he reached her, she still hadn't heard him approaching. Cody stopped a few feet away and called her name. Like it was the most beautiful word in all the world.

"Andi . . ."

She turned and as soon as their eyes met, she stood. "Cody . . . I'm sorry."

"I know." He came to her and took her in his arms while her puppy frolicked around at their feet. Cody blinked back tears. "I knew you'd come. I've prayed every day since I left."

"Me, too." Tears filled her eyes and mixed with her laughter. "I can't believe you're here. That you actually . . . you're not mad at me."

"Of course not." He looked into her blue eyes, all the way to her kind, sincere, brave soul. He felt his smile fade a little. "And Caleb?"

"He's not for me." She shook her head and more tears shone in her eyes. "There will never be anyone for me, but you."

Cody figured that much, after reading her letter. But he had to hear it from her. Like this, face to face. He smiled again. "I have so much to tell you."

"I'll listen, Cody. Forever." She wiped the tears from her cheeks and as she did, he closed the distance between them and kissed her. The puppy was still playing nearby and Andi laughed. "Max, you're okay, buddy."

"Max." Cody chuckled. "I like it." Then he hugged her again and kissed her one more time. The puppy moved to a spot at the end of the log, bored with the two of them. Cody had longed for this every day for as long as he could remember. "Andi Ellison . . ." He whispered her name, his cheek against hers. Then he drew back and slowly — so he'd know he wasn't dreaming — he dropped to one knee.

Andi gasped and covered her face with her hands. "What?" She squealed. "Cody . . . I never thought . . ."

From his jeans pocket he pulled out the ring. Not the same one he'd given her two times before. But a new one. The ring he'd bought before he moved to Montana.

Just in case she changed her mind.

"Andi . . ." Cody opened the velvet box and took the ring from inside. He slipped the box back into his pocket and held the diamond solitaire up to her. This time there were no parties, no photographers. Nothing but the two of them. "I meant these words before, but they're different now. I understand them better. What they mean for the two of us, together." He paused. "Andi . . . will you marry me?"

She nodded. "I will. And I'll stay here with you in Montana. I'll go wherever you go, Cody. And this time it will be different. I know it will."

He stood and wrapped her into his embrace one more time. Then he slid the ring onto her finger. "Look at that." He grinned at her. "A perfect fit."

And so it was.

"I have an idea." A plan was unfolding in his heart even as the words came to life. "Here, sit beside me."

They sat together and Cody took a deep breath. "What if we . . ."

It took little time to convince her. They held hands and prayed and made their decision. Surely they could have a wedding party later, but after all they'd been through this seemed the only right thing to do.

An hour later they stood at the county clerk's office. Cody glanced at Andi, the love of his life. He squeezed her hand so he'd know this was real, and she was here in front of him. He had never been happier in all his life.

They filled out paperwork, paid the fee, and there — before a court justice — they promised to take each other as husband and wife, for better or worse, in sickness and health. Now and forever more.

Until their final breath.

Hannah Jennifer Paul came into the world right at sunset, after eight hours of labor. The doctor and nurse worked together to clean her off, and then they laid her on Bailey's chest. Both she and Brandon wrapped their arms around her.

Their little girl's very first minutes on earth.

"She's perfect." Brandon's tears slid down his cheeks, the same way Bailey's did. "She looks just like you."

"God is so good." Bailey lifted her tiny baby and kissed her cheek. "She has your eyes. See . . ." She looked at her husband. "The deepest, most beautiful eyes."

Across the room, Bailey's mother stood smiling and wiping her tears, too. "She does look like you, Bailey. When you were first born." Her mom's voice was full of emotion. "I can't believe I'm a grandma!"

"Come look, Mom. Hannah's so pretty." Bailey was grateful her mother was here. She'd been there all day, she and Brandon helping Bailey through every contraction.

Her mom came and stood on the other side of the bed. "Hannah, sweetie . . . My little grandgirl. You're a precious miracle." Her mother reached out and touched the infant's small hand. Then she smiled at Bailey and Brandon. "I'll let you three have some time. Your dad and brothers are down the hall waiting for the news."

"Okay." Bailey locked eyes with her mother. "Thank you, Mom. We've always shared everything. And now we have this."

Brandon smiled. "Besides, I couldn't have done this without you."

Her mom kissed Bailey's forehead. "That's what family is for." She looked at Bailey again. "I love you, honey. And your precious little family."

When she was gone, when it was just the three of them, Bailey leaned back on her pillow. She had never been so happy, so sure that God was right here with them. He had given them their very own baby girl.

A week late, but none of that mattered anymore. Hannah was here — that's all Bailey cared about. They were a family, like her mother said. The three of them. Brandon leaned in and kissed her. "See?"

"See what?" She let herself get lost in his eyes. Her favorite place to be.

Brandon kissed her again and then he looked at her for the longest time. "We're still us."

It was exactly what Bailey wanted to hear, the greatest gift Brandon could've given her. Other than the baby girl in their arms. Yes, life would be different and busier and even crazy at times. There would hopefully be more children in the years to come. But with God at the center of their family, what Bailey had found with Brandon would always be like this.

Long after their last child left home.

A chiming sound came from Bailey's phone, sitting on the table a few feet away. "Probably Connor." Bailey laughed. "Wondering when they can all pile in here."

Brandon smiled. "Maybe give Hannah a few minutes to catch her breath."

"Exactly." Bailey snuggled their little girl. "Because this 'us' is important, too."

"Right." Brandon reached for her phone

and glanced at the text message that had just come in. He looked at it for a few seconds and then he grinned at Bailey. "It's from Andi."

"Oh . . . she doesn't know I went into labor!"

Brandon looked at the phone again and then back at Bailey. "That's not why she texted." He paused, and a smile filled his face. "Andi and Cody are married."

The happiness in Bailey came out as the easiest laughter. "That's amazing." Joyful tears flooded Bailey's eyes. Here, on the day her first child was born, the most wonderful thing had happened.

Andi and Cody had finally figured it out.

"I'm so happy for them." Bailey reached for Brandon's hand. Who could have seen this coming? Bailey having her first baby on the day Andi and Cody got married. "It all worked out, didn't it?"

"It did, baby." Brandon kissed her and then he kissed the top of Hannah's little head. "It definitely did."

The long road all of them had walked, the road of friendship and finding their way, had led to this one special day for all of them. Just like they had dreamed and prayed about all those years ago.

Once upon an adolescence.

And one day, Bailey couldn't wait to introduce their little girl to her friends. Cody and Andi. Yes, the two of them had taken a long time to get here. Their love story had not been easy. But they ended up just where they needed to be.

Together.

ACKNOWLEDGMENTS

No book comes together without a great deal of teamwork, passion, and determination. That was definitely true for *Love Story*!

First, special thanks to my amazing publisher, Jonathan Merkh, along with Jennifer Smith and the team at Howard Books. Your continued belief in me and your desire to always raise the bar in the marketplace is unmatched. Thank you for believing in me!

A similar thanks to Carolyn Reidy and the team at Simon & Schuster. I think back to our meeting a year ago in New York and the way your creative brilliance became a game changer. Thank you for lending your influence in so many ways. It's an honor to work with you!

This book wouldn't be so very special if it weren't for the incredible talents of my editor, Becky Nesbitt. Becky, you have known me since my kids were little. Since the beginning of the Baxters. How many authors actually look forward to the editing process? With you, it is a dream. And always you find ways to make the book better. Over and over and over again. Thank you for that! I am the most blessed author to have the privilege of working with you.

Also thanks to my design team — Kyle and Kelsey Kupecky — whose talent in the industry is recognized from Los Angeles to New York. Very simply, you are the best in the business! My website, social media, and newsletter, along with so many other aspects of my touring and writing, is what it is because of you two. Thank you for working your own dreams around mine. I love you and I thank God for you every single day.

A huge thanks to my sisters Tricia and Susan, along with my mom, who give their whole hearts to helping me love my readers — Tricia as my executive assistant for the past decade, and Susan, for many years, as the head of my Facebook Online Book Club and Team KK. And Mom, thank you for being queen of the readers. Anyone who has ever sent me an email and received a response from you is blessed indeed. All three of you are so special to me. I love you and I thank God for each of you!

Thanks also to Tyler for your help in writing screenplays and other projects. You are such a gifted writer, Ty. I can't wait to see your work on the shelves. Maybe one day soon! Love you so much!

Thank you to my office assistant, Aurora Galvin. You make my life so much easier! Writing as much as I do would not be possible without you.

I'm also grateful to my Team KK, who covers social media with news of my upcoming releases and hangs out on my Facebook page answering questions from all of my readers! I appreciate you so much. May God bless you for your service to the work of Life-Changing Fiction™.

There is a final stage in writing a book. The galley pages come to me, and I send them to a team of five of my closest, most special reader friends. My niece Shannon Fairley, Hope Painter, Donna Keene, Renette Steele, and Zac Weikal, you are wonderful! It always amazes me the things you catch at the final hour. Thank you for your love of my work, and thanks for your availability to read my books first and fast.

My books only happen with the help of my family, especially my amazing husband, Donald. Honey, thank you for your spiritual wisdom and leadership in our home, and thanks for the countless ways you help me when I'm on deadline. I love you, honey!

And over all this, there is a man who has believed in my career for two decades: my amazing agent, Rick Christian of Alive Literary Agency. From the beginning, Rick, you've told me to dream big, set my sights high. Movies, TV series, worldwide reach. You imagined it all, you prayed for it all. You believed. While I write, you work behind the scenes on film projects and my work with Liberty University, along with every book I've ever written. You are brilliant and driven, compassionate and dedicated. I used to dream of having you as my agent. Now I'm the only author who does. God is amazing. Thank you, Rick, and thank you for praying for me and my family. That most of all.

Finally, my greatest thank-you to God Almighty, who is First and Last and all things in between. I write for You, through You, and because of You. Thank You with my whole being.

Dear Reader Friend,

Ever since I first introduced John and Elizabeth Baxter many years ago, I knew that one day I'd write about their love story. Through the journey of more than twenty books about the Baxters, I've waited until just the right time to tell that story.

That time was now.

As I wrote *Love Story* I felt like I was pulled back in time. I was there at the dance watching them meet for the first time, a bystander at a nearby picnic table as the spark of their relationship turned into a flame.

A flame so bright all the world might see it.

That's the way it is with love stories. Even fictional love stories. It's the reason I included not just the love story of John and Elizabeth, but also of Cody and Andi, Brandon and Bailey, Landon and Ashley, and others.

I pray that as you read *Love Story,* you took a minute to think of your own. Or if not yours, then your parents' story or the story of someone you care about. Real-life love stories teach us much about loyalty and dedication, passion and devotion. And when the story is so beautiful it takes your breath, love stories teach us about faith.

After writing the love story of John and Elizabeth, I felt like I learned something about loving my own husband. Maybe just a realization that it never lasts long enough.

I hope you feel that way, too. That's the point of Life-Changing Fiction™. That you not only be entertained, but that you also walk away closer to God and the people you love.

And now that you've finished *Love Story,* pass it on. Share it with a friend or give it to your mother. Leave it on a table in a restaurant or in the waiting room of your next doctor or dentist appointment. Give it to a cashier or your child's teacher . . . or your teacher.

That one random act of kindness could change a life.

As always, you can find me on Facebook, Twitter, and Instagram. And join my free newsletter! I send out a monthly blog, and once a month I'll choose one of you to win a free autographed book.

Until next time, remember God loves you most of all!

Love and blessings,

www.KarenKingsbury.com

ONE CHANCE FOUNDATION

The Kingsbury Family is passionate about seeing orphans all over the world brought home to their forever families. As a result, they created the One Chance Foundation!

This foundation was inspired by the memory of Karen's father, Ted C. Kingsbury. Ted always said, "Life is not a dress rehearsal. We have one chance to love, one chance to truly live!" Karen often tells her reader friends that they have "one chance to write the story of their lives!"

Now with Karen's One Chance Foundation, readers can join her in the belief that all of us have one chance to make a difference in the lives of orphans.

In the Bible, James 1:27 says that true Christians ought to care for orphans. The One Chance Foundation was created with that truth in mind.

If you are interested in giving to Karen's One Chance Foundation and having your dedication printed in one of Karen's up-coming novels, visit www.KarenKingsbury. com and click on the Foundation tab. The following dedications were made by some of Karen's readers, who forever are making a difference in the lives of orphans around the world.

- Kelsey, you are the melody in my music . . . and you are my love story. Happy 5-year Anniversary! — Love, Kyle
- Praying for Good Health, Love & Happiness for all of You! Love, Mom
- In honor of Beth Montgomery, a woman who loves well. Love, Kevin, Megan & Michael
- My dear friend, Betty O'Neil. Your struggle with cancer is over & you are at peace. I miss you. Love, Mary Jo Srgo
- Best wishes, Sue, on your retirement! Love, Deb, Fran, Cynthia, Sandra & Kim
- Dixie Roof, thank you for always being there for us. Love, Joseph
- To my mom, Sharon, for always showing me unconditional love. All my love, Brenda Lacey
- Celebrating our four precious grand-

blessings + more joy on the way! K&S Holman

- In memory of my husband, Ted Kingsbury. Our Love Story began in 1961 and though he is in heaven now, he lives in my heart forever.
- Thanking God for our love story: Bo and Peggy, 55 years, August 12, 2016!
- Forever in our hearts mom/grandma (Norma Pedersen). We love you! — Bass family
- Julia & Stephanie, you're so precious and unique to God! Love you, Ouma Wouda xx
- In memory of Dala Ann Vonderheide. A wonderful woman. Thanks for introducing Karen Kingsbury to me. Love, Danielle
- For Emilie H. and Elizabeth A., sisters from WI who love the Baxter Family!
- Mom, Carolyn Ann Sexton – you taught us how to love. Love, Tonya, Tara and Tasha
- In memory of Oleta Hardy. A loving wife, mother and mawmaw. Until we meet again.
- For Margaret Elaine Powell, now in the arms of Jesus. Beloved Wife, Mum & Grandma
- Hubba Hubba, I will cherish each mo-

ment of our love story forever. Love, your wife, Tamara

- Tim, love stories aren't perfect; they just begin and end with love. Jolena
- Thank you, Grandma & Grandpa Grim, for being such great disciples of Christ, showing all of us His love.
- To Christina Evans, an amazing wife and a wonderful mother. — Joey and Kimberly
- In loving memory of Papa & Granny, Big Will & Meme — in our hearts forever! — Melinda
- For my parents, Houston & Linda, on your 50th. Your Love Story is my favorite! — Susan
- In memory of my grandmother, "Nanny," and in honor of my mom and aunt who cared for her. Love, Christina
- To my cousin, Nancy James, who shares my love of reading about the Baxters. — Jan
- To my Tati, Ruth Fones, who cheers me on positively with laughter and love. — Jan
- With love to the One Chance Foundation, Leslie Smith
- Michelle Lynn Gee: You left this world too early. You are missed. Love, Mom

& Sisters

- To my beautiful mother, Christa Leckebusch, your love & warmth came straight from the heart. We rejoice in knowing that you're dancing with Jesus. See you in Heaven. — Your Youngest, Tanja, with Nico, Enya, Mocha, Shadow & Cookie
- In loving memory — Bob Roberts & my precious son Douglas Pruitt. Forever in my heart.
- To Duane and Hazel, who had a great love story. You were a shining example of love and commitment.
- To Isabelle and A.R. Motley, who had a 57-year "love story" marriage of their own!
- To my Mother-In-Love Arlene! Thanks for years of fun and friendship! Love, Shelly
- Helen Kay McClintock, you are our greatest blessing! With much love, Your Family
- To my lovely love sweetheart sweetie! Blessed Anniversary! Love your Hubby, Eric
- In memory of our mom Caroline, gone too soon. In our hearts always, Deby & Dianne
- Carrie, let's continue to grow old

together. I wouldn't trade a moment. — Hoke

- With love to the One Chance Foundation, Malinda Blevins
- R&J, one heart resides in heaven but your love story will live on forever. J, J&R
- To Amber Rachi, my loving wife, soul mate and best friend. Love, Benjamin Rachi.
- To Melissa, my favorite flute player & biggest Karen Kingsbury fan I know; & for our 10-year-old miracle baby — Rebekah
- Ann, it is one of my greatest honors to be called your dad. Love you both — Gregg Johnson
- Dedicated with love to Renette Steele — loving wife, mother and grandma! Love always, John
- Dearest Jessica Danielle Bartholomew, we love you so much! Your life is a testimony of God's faithfulness & love! Love, Mom & Dad
- Bob + Judy B: Your love story = Steve & I. Grateful you're our parents. Love, Connie
- Rick, Happy 32nd Anniversary! My life is beautiful because of you! Tammy
- Jan & Ray Buckingham: U instilled

faith and love & inspired us! Love B1
B2 B3 & M&J B&G B&A

- In honor of my wife, Myrtie. Love,
  Sammy
- To Peggy Sparks, a special friend shar-
  ing books and concerts for many years!
  — Jan
- Honoring Barbara McPheeters' cour-
  age & her 95th birthday!! Lovingly,
  Your Family
- To the woman who inspires us and
  loves us unconditionally. We love you.
  XOXO, Kristie, Lindsey, Alexis & Ash-
  ley
- Happy 1st anniversary to Shirley East-
  erwood & Jerrell Hightower! Love, Sha
  & Tut
- Jim, I thank God for placing us to-
  gether in our Love Story. I love you
  deeply, Donna
- Colby, you are a blessing to all who
  come in contact with you. Love, Mom
  and Dad
- In Loving Memory of our son, Mick
  Craig — Love you so much, Mom &
  Dad
- In memory of Marvin & Darline Lau-
  bach, my dear parents. — Ellen
- Wendy, you are my beloved, and I am
  always yours. Love, Brian

- In honor of my parents, Auston and LaVerna Davis. What a love story! Love, Vicki
- Kim — Thanks for loving me & allowing God to create our own Love Story! Love, Ry
- Happy 60th Anniversary to Glen and Margaret Witt. Thanks for modeling a Godly marriage!
- Happy 32nd anniversary, Don! You're the reason I believe in dreams. Love, Peggy
- Dad & Mom, Your Love Story touches many & SHINES for Jesus! Love, Jim & Schellie
- Leslie Miller, my best friend and wife, you've amazed me for 34 years! Love you, Paul
- Thank you for loving us unconditionally, Mom! Love, Rachel, Robin & Ryan
- Kaley — wishing you a life full of love. — Mom
- Happy 70th Anniversary, Ma & Pa Deardorff. You're such an inspiration to your family & our community through your service. Your daily prayers for our family have continued to surround us each day. Thank you for teaching us about Jesus, showing us

how to serve others & leaving a legacy.
Your family loves you!

READING GROUP GUIDE: LOVE STORY

KAREN KINGSBURY

The following are questions for your reading group or family. Have everyone read *Love Story,* then have a night of talking about the book, answering these questions and making a memory in the process!

1. What did you think of Cody Coleman's advice to his player, Aaron Baylor, when it came to the prom?

2. How does it sometimes help your own situation when you give advice to someone else?

3. What's the best relationship advice anyone ever gave you?

4. What mixed emotions do you imagine John Baxter might have had after Cole asked him to help with his school project?

5. What are some of your most beautiful memories?

6. What's the most beautiful real-life love story you know?

7. What did you think of Elaine's attitude toward John at the beginning of the story?

8. What's the kindest thing anyone has ever done for you?

9. Talk about your favorite part of the mixer where John and Elizabeth met.

10. How did you meet your spouse? If you're not married, share a romantic story about another couple and how they met.

11. Despite Cody's two failed engagements with Andi Ellison, how do you feel about his decision to pursue her again?

12. When John and Elizabeth were at their lowest moment, how did people around them respond?

13. Tell about a time when you were strug-

gling. How did people around you respond?

14. Do you think Elizabeth's parents were bad Christian people? Why or why not? What makes someone a true Christian, in your opinion?

15. Cody suffered from PTSD. Talk about a veteran in your life who has struggled with memories of war. (And tell them thank you for serving!)

16. Have you ever had a difficult situation turn into a blessing, the way it happened with John when his car broke down?

17. Share what you liked most about Wilson.

18. When has a stranger helped you or someone you love? Discuss that time.

19. John and Elizabeth eventually found faith in God. How has faith helped you through the difficult moments of life?

20. What do you think changed Andi's mind at the end of the story? Have you ever had to change your mind about someone you love? How did that turn out?

ABOUT THE AUTHOR

Karen Kingsbury, #1 *New York Times* bestselling novelist, is America's favorite inspirational storyteller, with more than twenty-five million copies of her award-winning books in print. Her last dozen titles have topped bestseller lists, and many of her novels are under development as TV movies and major motion pictures. Her many Baxter books will be the subject of a TV series — *The Baxter Family* — in conjunction with Roma Downey, Mark Burnett, and MGM Studios. Karen is also an adjunct professor of writing at Liberty University. She lives in Tennessee with her husband, Don, and their five sons, three of whom are adopted from Haiti. Their actress daughter, Kelsey, lives nearby and is married to Christian recording artist Kyle Kupecky. The couple recently welcomed their first child, Hudson.